KING OF SHADOWS AND SECRETS

THE SHADOW KING TRILOGY
BOOK ONE

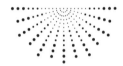

PIPER EASTON

PIERCED SOUL PUBLISHING

Editing by Comma Sutra Editorial

Cover Design by Opulent Swag and Designs

Map made with Inkarnate

To all the ladies who hate when Persephone is a shy, wide-eyed, inexperienced virgin. This one's for you.

Dear Reader,

Please be aware that *King of Shadows and Secrets* contains content that may be triggering for some. For a list of content warnings, please see the next page.

King of Shadows and Secrets contains the following content: descriptions of sexual assault, domestic abuse, child abuse, and child sexual assault

PRONUNCIATION GUIDE

Acaria (A-car-ee-ah) - Land of the Gods
Aeris (Air-iss) - Goddess of Chaos
Basal (Baz-al) - Shadow Realm ferryman
Dremen (D-rem-en) - Village of Elora's Birth
Elora (E-lore-ah)
Fontoss (Fawn-toss) - Acaria's Capital City
Hayle (Hail) - Shadow Realm Judge
Iluna (Ill-luna) - Goddess of Night
Irios (Ear-ee-aw-ss) - The Healing Fields
Kaia (K-eye-ah) - Goddess of Witchcraft
Meera (M-ear-ah) - Elora's horse
Meren (M-air-en) - Prison Realm
Nevon (Neh-vin) - Shadow Realm Judge
Orella (Or-el-ah) - Goddess of Love and Lust
Pramis (P-ram-iss) God of Music and the Arts
Railan (Rye-lan) - Shadow Realm Judge
Rhagana (Rah-gah-nah) - Capital City of Goddess of Witchcraft
River Grense (Gren-ss) - River of Memories
River Loret (Lore-et) - River of Shadows
Síra (S-ear-ah) - Mountains of Eternal Torture
Thieran (Th-ear-an) - God of Death
Yorrai (Y-or-eye) - God of Sea and Storms
Videva (Vih-day-vuh) - Village of Souls
Zanirah (Zah-near-ah) - Queen of the Gods

THE SHAD

RIVER AXAN

IRIOS

RIVER

THE PALACE

VIDEVA

CHAPTER ONE

Elora

There's something intoxicating about death. About planning the perfect kill and stalking my prey and drawing my blade through flesh. Some might call me a monster, but this puts food on the table better than any other trade I've worked. And a girl's got to eat.

The man ahead of me stops at a stall selling roasted meat, the rich, aromatic spices floating to my nose. I used to love this part of Acaria, with its pretty views of the sea and delicious foods and brightly colored clothes. But the memories are no longer fond, painted over with betrayal and heartache, and I find myself eager to finish my task and move further south.

I linger a few paces behind, feigning interest in a large red fruit I've never seen before. If I had the time, I'd buy it just to see what it tastes like, but I have other business here today.

The young girl managing the stall with her parents glances up at me and sends me a nervous smile. With my long hair hidden under a thick wool cap and my breasts bound by cloth, I can pass for a boy running errands for his master.

I flash her a wink because it's what a young boy did to me once, and since I have no intention of hurting her the way I was,

1

it seems innocent enough. Her father notices our exchange and immediately sends her inside with a warning glare in my direction.

Taking a step back, I melt into the crowd and refocus on my task. My target is happily munching on a thick cube of meat, careful not to drip any juices onto his pristine white robes. When the shopkeeper holds out his hand for payment, the other man raises a single brow.

They stare at each other in a battle of wills until the shop-keeper slowly closes his hand into a fist and drops it to his side with a tight smile. Satisfied, the man pops the rest of the meat in his mouth and steps away.

I'm still surprised he moves through the city without guards flanking him. Most high-ranking temple priests don't leave the temple walls without beefy swordsmen following their every move. This priest doesn't even have a serving boy to carry coin or packages. Perhaps an unnecessary companion when you don't intend to pay for anything.

All the better for me. It gets messy when I have to kill witnesses too. Killing a priest is bad enough.

The gold embroidery on his robes catches the light when he stops abruptly to avoid an oncoming horse and cart. A large sun with twelve long, thin triangular rays. I have no idea why the God of Music and the Arts is obsessed with the sun, but Pramis plasters his symbol anywhere it'll fit across his lands.

The traffic trundles by while we wait to cross, and my fingers twitch at my side. It wouldn't take much to step up behind the priest and shove him into the busy street. Being trampled by a horse or two would kill him just as well as the blade strapped to my waist, but for all the harm he's caused, I want to look him in the eye as he draws his last breath.

When it's finally clear enough to cross, I follow him at a distance, across the street and past rows of neat shops with stalls out front. Between the shops, I can see the rolling blue of the sea, and if I breathe deeply enough, I can smell it.

But I can't afford the distraction memories bring. I have a job to do. One I'm being paid handsomely for. So I stuff the memories of the boy with golden hair and dark brown eyes down deep where it belongs and angle myself away from the sparkling water.

The crowds thin as we move further away from the shops and wharves. People pay me no mind as the shops give way to small homes packed so tightly together there's barely a sliver of sunlight shining through the space between them. The thatched roofs look like a single mass settled over sturdy wood frames.

The longer we walk, the larger the temple becomes, and my pulse quickens. No matter how many times I inflict death, there's always a thrill to it. A challenge, a reminder that people trust me to deliver them the vengeance they deserve.

For a price. And this price is higher than most. Killing a temple priest is considered treason against the god they serve, and Pramis especially takes the ceremony of worshipping him very seriously. Just not seriously enough to keep his own priests in line.

The houses are replaced by large shade trees, and the breeze off the water whispers through the leaves. The only thing dominating the landscape in this part of the city is the temple looming behind a low wall, the white stone weathered to a soft cream.

A large, round tower emblazoned with Pramis's sun juts out of the center of the compound. In less than an hour, the bells will toll for afternoon offerings. I intend to be well on my way south by then.

There's an opening in the wall where a gate should be, and the priest steps through it, barely sparing a nod at the lower priests and worshippers alike, who stop to bow their heads out of respect. This man doesn't deserve their deference.

I slip through the opening behind him, keeping my head down but my eyes locked on his back. He turns right when he reaches the covered walkway, and I follow, careful to keep to the shadows.

I've spent several days wandering this temple to get my bearings, and there's nothing in this direction except private rooms and studies. He's most likely going back to his chambers to rest before accepting afternoon offerings. It's exactly where I want him because no one is likely to disturb him until he doesn't arrive in the receiving hall.

He pauses to speak to a young priest, and I duck behind a fat column. At the shuffle of feet, I peek out from my hiding spot and mutter a curse. They've both changed direction, heading instead for the kitchens.

I could leave him to tend to whatever matter needs his attention and wait for him in his rooms, but I can't risk missing my opportunity. If I don't kill him today, I have to wait another three days, and I've already lingered here long enough.

The scent of freshly baked bread envelops me the closer we draw to the kitchens. There are more people in this part of the temple than I'd like, and I'm forced to stop and pretend to study the sculptures set in alcoves in the wall and lit by torches.

Pramis on the back of a large steed. Pramis playing a pipe. Pramis holding a paintbrush and palette. There's an unnamable quality to his face that makes him look both innocent and worldly all at once. Or maybe it's the delicate curls framing his head like a halo at odds with the sharp cut of his jaw.

I tilt my head to study the sculpture closest to the kitchen door. This one is of Pramis holding a sword aloft. Of all the sculptures so far, it's the most amusing. Like the god is play-acting a hero.

Shouts ring out from behind the closed door of the kitchens, followed quickly by the crash and splinter of pottery shattering.

Whatever is happening in there, the high priest is not pleased about it.

He breezes out a moment later, his white robe churning behind him in a froth.

"If this happens again, Esto, the brothers will be stripped of their titles and sent to the labor house."

"Of course, your grace. I'll be sure the matter is resolved."

"See that it is," the high priest replies with a sneer. "My lord Pramis would not like to know his high priests are being treated in such a manner."

The younger man's face blanches white, and the high priest seems to preen under the fear, his shoulders straightening and his chin lifting higher.

"He would be very displeased, your grace. Please forgive me."

"I'll be in my rooms until afternoon offerings. Do not disturb me."

The young priest drops into an awkward bob, renewing his apologies as the high priest sweeps away. The hallway remains frozen until the edge of the robe disappears around the corner, then everyone scurries off to their duties.

I jog to the top of the hallway and follow the open walkway to a heavy oak door. It groans when I pull it open, and I creep left, my fingertips trailing across the cool stone. Only one other priest has rooms in this section, and he left in a gilded carriage two days ago. He's due back tomorrow.

Unsheathing the knife from my belt, I tuck it against my forearm and push open the last door on the right. The priest stands at the washbasin on the far side of the room, dabbing his face with a thick cloth. He glances up when he hears the door snick closed behind me, eyes narrowing on my face.

"What are you doing in here, boy? I said I wasn't to be disturbed."

I reach up and remove the cap from my head, my hair tumbling free to frame my face. "I'm sorry, your grace," I say, forcing a tremble into my voice. "I was told I could seek a private audience with you."

A lecherous grin stretches across his lips, and he drops the cloth next to the basin. "Of course, my child." He motions me further into the room and meets me in the center. "I'm always available for those in deepest need. How can I help you today?"

His eyes drop to my lips, and I wet them with my tongue, watching his nostrils flare. "I wish to be wed, but my father will not approve."

"And you want Lord Pramis to change your father's heart."

"Yes, your grace," I whisper as he moves closer, his robes brushing the tops of my feet.

"A father's word is law." He sighs dramatically. "It would take quite a lot to persuade me to go against a father's wishes and plead your case to Lord Pramis."

"I'll do anything to marry my love, your grace."

"Anything, you say?"

His words make my skin crawl, but I nod. I know what this man is, the way he's preyed on the women who come to him for help. He delights in humiliating them. And I want to return the favor.

He takes a step back and sinks into a chair piled with cushions. His eyes never leave mine as he slowly undoes the long line of buttons down the front of his robes and parts the fabric to reveal a pair of thin linen breeches underneath.

His cock is small, but the hard outline of it is obvious even before he rubs it lewdly, wrapping his hand around it and giving it a squeeze. I avert my eyes to the floor, and he chuckles, continuing to rub himself.

"You said anything, girl. Come here and beg on your knees with your pretty mouth."

"But, your grace, I cannot betray my love."

"I'm sure he'll appreciate you learning a thing or two before your wedding night." He pulls his cock out and gives it a rough tug. "Unless you don't really want to marry him."

The weight of my dagger is heavy against my palm as I drop to my knees in front of him. I didn't doubt the stories I heard from the women who sought me out to tell me about Pramis's favored high priest. They were why I agreed to kill him in the first place.

But hearing about it and witnessing his depravity firsthand are different things entirely. I'm going to enjoy this more than I expected.

He grins down at me as I crawl between his legs and reaches out a hand to pet my hair when I lick my lips again. They're going to find him with his pathetic cock hanging out of his pants and his throat cut, and the image bubbles a laugh from my throat.

"What's so funny?" he barks.

"The stupidity of men."

CHAPTER TWO

Elora

H is hand moves to grip my hair, but I'm faster, knocking his arm away and bringing my dagger to the tip of his cock. He squeaks in protest, his eyes glued to the blade as I collect a drop of shiny precum on the steel.

"You've been abusing your power, your grace. I've never heard of temple vows including sexual favors in exchange for seeking a favor from a god."

"Lord Pramis—"

I tsk at him. "You hardly want to add blasphemy to your charges, your grace."

"You won't get away with this."

I grin up at him, drawing the tip of my blade down the length of his shaft and welling a thin line of blood. "I already have. But don't worry. I'll leave your little cock intact. They'll want to see what you were raping the faithful with."

I stand and press the dagger against the pulse point in his throat, my own blood humming in my veins when it jumps under the contact. I so want to take my time with him. He deserves to experience every awful thing he's ever done to the women he swore to guide and protect.

But the afternoon offering hour draws closer, and I need to be outside the city walls before his body is discovered. A pity. I'm certain he's a screamer, and that would be music to my ears.

"They'll kill you when they find you. This is treason."

I position myself behind him, pressing the knife in firmly until I break skin and blood stains the collar of his robe. "Then I guess I'll see you when I cross the veil."

I drag the blade across his throat, closing my eyes and relishing the soft gagging sounds he makes as he chokes on his own blood. His stark white robe is spattered with gore, and more spews from his mouth each time he coughs.

He can't scream; I cut too deep for that, but it doesn't stop him from reaching up to grip his throat as if he might be able to hold all the blood in and keep himself alive until help arrives.

When he finally goes still and slumps over on himself, I use the edge of his robe to clean my blade and slip it back into the leather sheath circling my waist. It all feels a little anticlimactic.

Moving deeper into his chambers, I bypass a second smaller seating area and a bedroom. The bed stands on a raised dais, covered in mountains of pillows and fine silk sheets. I shudder to think how many women he abused on that bed while facing no consequences.

I've made sure his punishment is permanent. The high priest belongs to the God of Death now.

A narrow door in the rear wall of his bedroom leads to a small private garden, and I open it a crack, scanning the pretty flowering bushes and stone pathway for signs of life. Seeing none, I duck out and quickly make my way through the neatly trimmed bushes.

The wall is low enough to scale, but the clomp of a horses's hooves and squeak of cart wheels urges me to use the rear gate instead. The wrought iron is warm in my hands, and the gate swings silently open.

When the horse and its load finally pass, I dart across the street and into the grove of trees shielding the temple from the view of the sea. Sunlight dances over the soft grass as the wind teases the branches, and I finally take a deep breath when I reach the clearing.

My mare is right where I left her, tied to a tree and delicately munching grass. Her nostrils flare and her ears flatten when she hears me approach, and she paws the ground until she recognizes my scent.

"That's right," I say, stroking down her nose and giving her flank a pat. "Did you miss me?"

She nickers and bumps my shoulder for a treat. She knows this game well. We've been playing it long enough. I leave her tied up somewhere near my kill, and when I finally emerge, she gets her favorite food as a reward for waiting so patiently.

I dig an apple out of my saddlebag and cut it in half with my dagger, letting her nip it gently from my palm. Normally I would change, disguising myself as much as possible before exiting the city gates, but I don't have time to deal with a corset and gown.

Digging my long coat out of my bag, I tug it on over my tunic and breeches. It's a bit warm out for a coat, but it can pass for a gown if I tuck it just right in the saddle and no one looks too closely.

I grip the saddle horn, but before I can mount, Meera gives me a searching look. I shake my head with a soft sigh.

"You'll want to save the rest of it. We have a long ride before we can stop for the night."

She stares into my soul with her big brown eyes and gives a pathetic little whinny. Bested by a horse, I dig the other half of the apple out of my bag and hand it to her. I swear she makes a triumphant sound as she chomps away, paying me no mind as I swing up into the saddle and guide her back the way I came.

The bells remain silent, but it won't be long before they ring to announce offerings. Twice a day, the faithful are called to gather in the temple and seek assistance from the high priests. They bring offerings in return for favors from gods they think can help them with their plight.

But the gods are stingy with their favors, and help never seems to make it to the people who really need it.

Meera tosses her head when we reach the edge of the trees and draws my attention to the road. A small group of women in bright dresses carrying baskets of food stroll by, talking excitedly. On their way to offerings, no doubt.

I wait until they pass and guide Meera onto the packed dirt. The gates to the city walls hang open, guards in white and gray livery with the golden sun on their chests perched atop the stone above. They barely glance in my direction as I lead Meera through.

Houses are clustered together just beyond the city walls, and by the time they begin to thin, the distant sound of tolling bells reaches my ears. When no one shouts for me to stop, I urge Meera into a gentle canter, and once we clear the last house, I push her to a full gallop.

The bright green of the softly rolling hills flash by, and the wind from our ride blows my hair away from my face. My pulse races and a smile curves my lips.

A decade ago, I would have sworn I wasn't capable of looking a man in the eyes and taking his life, but I've yet to kill someone who didn't deserve it. Rapists, abusers, thieves, and, worst of all, people who hurt children. None of them have escaped my blade. None of them deserved to.

Most of them were nameless, faceless nobodies. People who wouldn't be missed. But a high priest's murder certainly won't go unnoticed. Which is why I intend to travel as far south as I can go and lay low there for a while.

The money I insisted on for killing the priest padded my already generous reserves. A sum I can live on for close to a year without taking another kill if I do all my own hunting and am careful with it. A year is more than enough time to let this blow over.

Something sizzles in the air as we crest a hill, and when Meera snorts, I know she feels it too. The invisible barrier separating one god's land from another's always feels like a whisper of lightning over my skin.

I can't remember whose land borders Pramis's to the west, but if we've crossed into another god's territory, I'm far enough away from the city to give Meera a rest. Slowing her to a walk, I pat her neck and sit up straighter in the saddle.

Another few hours following this road and we should hit a village. A village with a tavern and hot food and strong wine. I don't drink often, but after every kill, I raise a glass. Not to the dead but to their liberated victims who can rest easy knowing their tormentor is beyond the veil.

It's a gruesome truth, but each kill heals a small part of me. It soothes the girl I once was. The girl who had no one to protect her from monsters.

I ride until the sun dips below the trees and the sky slowly shifts from blue to pink to purple and then descends into inky black. I've always loved the darkness. Even as a child, it comforted me. The way it swallows you up and shrouds you from the world.

I begin to wonder if I've misjudged the distance to the next village until we crest a small rise and a blanket of lights fans out beneath us. It's not a large village, but hopefully there's somewhere I can buy a hot meal and find a warm place to sleep.

Meera ambles through the narrow street. There aren't many

people out at this time of night, but a door to a large square building opens ahead, and music spills out into the dark.

I aim for it, dismounting and leading Meera to a small stable that's little more than a lean-to with fresh hay and water in small bins. Tethering Meera to the post inside, I ignore her hopeful stare until she nudges my arm.

"You got greedy and ate it," I remind her, but she nudges me again. "That was the last one, I'm afraid, but I'll see if they have anything inside for you. Be good," I add, chuckling when she huffs out a sigh and takes a single blade of hay between her teeth.

I run my fingers through my windblown hair and round the side of the tavern, letting myself in to the soft sound of voices singing a gentle hymn I don't recognize. A few people glance up when I cross to the bar, but no one seems eager to ask any questions or pry into my business. Exactly the way I prefer it.

"What can I get for you?" a man with a thick gray beard and eyes so dark they're almost black asks.

"Spiced wine and whatever's hot to eat."

"Got a good goat stew."

My stomach rumbles, reminding me I haven't eaten since this morning and I won't be picky. "Sounds delicious."

The man grunts, pouring wine into a glass and disappearing through a door behind the bar. He returns with a large bowl and a plate of bread and sets both in front of me. My mouth waters, and I dig in with my spoon, closing my eyes at the first bite of perfectly cooked meat.

"You're not from around here."

"No," I agree. "Just passing through on my way south."

He takes a long look at my unbound hair and black coat but doesn't comment on either. Instead he says, "Need a room?"

I hesitate. Normally I stay close to Meera while traveling. Find a secluded spot to sleep and let her alert me to danger close by. But I slept in the woods while I watched the priest to avoid anyone at a tavern being able to recognize me. A bed sounds nice after a week on the ground, but it's not worth the risk.

"No, thank you."

He doesn't say anything, just moves down to the other end of the bar to pour another round for the two old men arguing, but he watches me, his eyes darting up to check on me every few minutes. I finish my meal quickly, draining my glass, and leave my payment next to my plate on the scarred wood.

A hint of chill in the air races down my spine and raises goosebumps over my skin when I push out of the tavern's comforting heat. I briefly consider going back inside and asking for the room again, but Meera nickers when she sees me, and I banish that thought. I feel safer in the open with her by my side than I would behind the locked door of a strange tavern.

We're a team, Meera and I, and have been since I rescued her from an abusive master five years ago. I pat her neck and push enough hay into the corner to make a nest. Almost like a bed, but not quite. It'll do for tonight.

As soon as the sky is light enough, we'll keep heading south, and once we settle somewhere safe, we'll both enjoy a much deserved rest.

CHAPTER THREE

Thieran

T hunder rumbles in the distance behind me, the wind kicking up with the storm. A bead of sweat gathers between my shoulder blades and drips down my back as I circle my opponent.

His eyes dart from my face to my hands and back again. He's hoping for a tell, a clue as to where I might attack him next, where I'm most likely to draw blood. But he won't get one from me. I've been doing this for centuries.

He feints to my left, and I let him have the small gain. He'll make more mistakes if he thinks he's winning. Scenting his fear on the air, I inhale it deeply into my lungs. It fuels me. His terror is the entire point of this exercise.

Lightning illuminates the fat, dark clouds overhead before forking to the ground again and again. The man circles closer with each lightning strike, swiping a hand over his sweat-soaked brow.

He holds a dagger at his side with trembling fingers. Twice he's tried and failed to wound me, twice I've delivered deep cuts to his flesh. The wounds weep blood, soaking through his threadbare tunic and dripping down to the parched earth.

Another strike of lightning lances a tree close by, and the splintering crack is deafening. Flames shoot up into the dark, licking the sky, and the man takes another step closer to me before thinking better of it.

Caught between me and the flames, he's not sure which is the better option. You'd think after all these years, he'd know the flames would deliver less pain and a faster death.

A gust of wind knocks him to the side, throwing him off balance, and I capitalize on it, spinning in the opposite direction and bringing my elbow down against his temple. His head snaps back and he groans, clutching the side of his face as he stumbles and falls to his knees.

He makes a weak attempt to swipe at me with his dagger, and I kick it from his hands. I could end him here and now with a single thought. A jolt of power through his body until he's dead on the ground, eyes wide and staring. But that would be too easy for him. He doesn't deserve easy.

When he moves to stand, I force him back to his knees and draw my blade across his chest, watching him thrash violently. It's a deep cut, but not enough to kill him. At least not yet. Another gash across his stomach, and he gasps from the pain, dropping to his hands, fingers curving into the dry earth.

It doesn't take much to shove him onto his back. A slight nudge from the toe of my boot and he drops to the ground like a lead weight. He's crying now, tears seeping from the corners of his eyes and carving lines through the dust and dirt on his face.

He looks up at me, mouth open to speak, but no sound escapes. He wants to beg and plead for his life, but he can't. I took his tongue. The tears come harder now, as they always do at this stage, and I wonder if he's remembering all the unimaginable horrors of his life.

In case he isn't, I wave my hand in the air in front of his face and make him watch. One scene rolls into the next and he gasps for breath, coughing up blood as he struggles to stay alive.

I leave him to suffer a few moments more, until the final scene of his death plays before him. He watches in wide-eyed horror as he's forced to kneel in front of freshly dug graves, his body twitching from the pain and anticipation of what's coming next.

The steel of a sword sings as it's drawn from a sheath, and there's a murmured plea before a wet squelching sound and a dull thump. I give him a moment to experience the pain of being beheaded all over again, and then I drive my dagger into his heart and wrench it until his mouth contorts in a silent scream.

The moment his body goes limp, it disappears in a cloud of black smoke, and the flaming tree is instantly whole again, unmarred by fire. As I rise, the clouds overhead recede until the sky lightens to its usual perpetual twilight.

Grabbing my discarded robes, I slip them on over my black tunic and breeches and adjust the collar, letting them billow out behind me as I walk. A lone figure waits for me at the edge of the clearing, arms crossed over her chest, and I'm already disinterested in whatever it is she's sought me out to discuss.

"You're not responsible for torturing them personally, you know," she says, falling into step beside me.

I raise a brow at her tone but she is undeterred, flashing me a disarming smile. She's up to something, and at the moment I don't care what it is. I want to enjoy the high from my kill a little longer before I have to deal with anything, let alone her.

"Go away, Aeris. I'm busy."

Her head swivels as she looks around us, her long blood-red curls swaying with the movement. "You don't look busy, my lord."

I shift to the palace grounds, hoping she'll take the hint, but she appears at my side with a silver shimmer, and I sigh.

Crossing the courtyard and climbing the deep stone steps, she again matches my pace, a mischievous smile on her face.

"Does he have to be tortured the same way every time?"

"That's what you wanted to talk to me about? The methods of his torture?"

"It just seemed"—she wrinkles her nose—"unnecessarily bloody."

"The Goddess of Chaos can't handle a little blood?" I ask, opening the door with a wave of my hand and stepping into the tomb-like quiet of my palace.

"There are less messy ways to torture someone, my lord. That's all."

"He deserves the pain," I inform her. "The man raped his own daughter every day for years and then killed his whole family when his wife found out."

"Oh, I could make it hurt," she assures me with a wicked gleam in her eye. "But that isn't what I wanted to talk to you about."

"I'm waiting," I prompt when she doesn't continue.

"A forest guardian escaped into Acaria."

Stopping short, I swivel to face her. "When?"

"Yesterday." She studies her nails, expression bored. As if she isn't the one who initiated this conversation. "He nearly killed a man in one of my border towns while he was tending to his goats."

"What did you do with the beast?"

Aeris rolls her eyes. "I did what you should've done. I took care of it."

My eyes narrow, and I take a menacing step forward. Aeris, to her credit, has the good sense to look somewhat cowed.

"Apologies, my lord. I—"

"I don't want your apologies. I want to know I can trust the members of my court not to withhold information from me." I motion for silence when she begins to speak. "Next time you find a forest guardian wandering that far from the veil, I want to be informed in seconds, not hours or days. Understand?"

She gives a curt nod, disappearing in a shimmer. I could summon her back, remind her of her manners and protocol, but Aeris has never been one for curtsies. And I don't care about the empty etiquette nearly as much as my brother does.

The energy of new souls arriving washes over me, drawing me to a wide staircase and down. New arrivals always seem to give the realm a boost. A momentary reprieve from the way the power seems to be leeching from the land no matter what I do.

Torches line the wall every few paces in this part of the palace, but it doesn't do much to make up for the lack of windows. Not that there's much light in my realm. We exist in the shadows.

I like the dark, the anonymity of it. It suits me.

The hum of energy and voices gets louder as I draw closer to the large chamber at the end of the hall. New souls mill about the back of the room, facing a table where three men with dark skin and long white locs tied back with leather cords are seated.

Railan, the oldest of the triplets, bangs a gavel against black marble and motions a soul forward. Souls in the Shadow Realm look like normal mortals until they catch the light just right. This one passes in front of a torch and becomes momentarily translucent before solidifying again.

The judges are responsible for determining a soul's placement in the Shadow Realm based on how they lived their mortal lives. The process is quick and painless.

Unless the soul is found to be unredeemable. Unredeemable souls belong only to me, relegated to Síra until I decide their method of torture for all eternity. It is a weighty responsibility, and one I enjoy entirely too much.

When the judgment is made, Railan bangs the gavel and the soul disappears. Off to heal or to live or to work or to suffer,

PIPER EASTON

depending. When the room is nearly empty, he notices me in the doorway and inclines his head.

The souls follow his gaze, and one by one, they all gasp and drop into deep curtsies or bows. I bid them rise with a flick of my wrist and wait until Railan and his brothers are finished with their judgments before sweeping into the room.

"Perfect timing," Hayle says, pushing away from the table. "Several unredeemables in this batch."

A slow smile tugs at my lips. That is perfect. My session with the rapist earlier wasn't enough to erase all my tension at the new breach I found this morning. Likely the same one Aeris's guardian slipped through. Assigning eternal torture might be just what I need.

"I'll go with you," Railan says, but I don't wait for him, shifting quickly to the edge of Síra's boundary.

He appears beside me on the craggy mountain face, and a moment later, so do three souls. In this light they all appear solid. I look at Railan with raised brows when I see one of Pramis's high priests among the dead. He nods, and the look on his face tells me all I need to know. I decide to save that soul for last.

"You've been judged," I say, infusing power into my voice and rousing the breeze to whip the edges of my robes.

Railan hides a grin while two of the three men cower. The priest's head remains high, his gaze unflinching, though I smell the fear on him.

"Lord Thieran," the man closest to me mutters, dropping to his knees.

"Silence," I command. "You've been judged, and your actions in life have condemned your souls to Síra. Your fate is eternal torture."

The first man moves to speak again, and I silence him with a thought. I want to add a layer of punishment simply for his disobedience. You cannot bargain your fate in my realm. I tilt my head and call up his life, sifting through his deeds, good and bad.

I've never had cause to doubt Railan's or his brothers' judgments, and they haven't failed me here either. This man has been murdering innocent people and stealing from them for years. Not because he needed what they had, but because he enjoyed it.

With a snap of my fingers, I send him off to be sealed into a cave. He'll live in total darkness, the cave steadily filling up with water until he drowns. Every single day for eternity.

The next man is an abuser of children. He delighted in breaking their bones and hearing them scream. I send him to receive the same fate. Every single bone in his body broken and then slowly knit back together with excruciating pain until it begins again.

The last soul stands before me, his bright white robes starkly contrasting the black rock he stands on. His chin lifts higher when I meet his gaze, but his mouth trembles. It's not often we get a high priest condemned to Síra. I can only recall one other. A woman who captured and sold young girls into slavery under the guise of helping them.

This one forced women to service him in exchange for favors from his master, Pramis. Favors he never bothered to take to the sun god at all.

"M-my lord, if I may."

His voice wobbles, and he swallows hard. But I'm intrigued enough to see what he has to say, so I motion for him to continue.

"My actions are deeply regrettable. But I was murdered. Surely that was punishment enough."

My lip curls back over my teeth in a snarl, and I raise my hand to banish him.

"Please," he begs, the steady look on his face faltering for the first time. "I was a loyal and faithful servant to a god for many years. I am sure my lord Pramis would speak for me."

I bark out a laugh and grip the man by the throat, lifting him off the ground until his eyes are level with mine. "Do you really think Pramis would come to my realm to bargain for your soul?"

The priest nods as much as my hand on his throat will allow, and this time Railan laughs with me.

"Then you're a fool, priest. Pramis wouldn't sully himself with shadows for the likes of you. But I'll enjoy knowing you'll spend every day of the rest of your miserable existence having your cock and balls carved from your body."

He whimpers before disappearing from my grip, and Railan claps me on the shoulder.

"Someone's in a mood."

I snort. "They always assume someone will bargain for them. When have you ever known Pramis to waste a favor bargaining for a mortal's soul?"

"Never. He wouldn't even do it for his own daughter a few decades ago."

"And she wasn't nearly as sure as the priest."

Railan stares into the cavernous valley below the steep mountain of jagged rock. "Something else happened. What is it?"

I sigh. It's a heavy sound that seems to echo in the air around us. "I found another hole. On the eastern border. A small one, but enough for a guardian to snap its tether. Aeris said one of them nearly killed a man in her territory."

"Were you able to seal it?"

I stare down at the unblemished skin of my palm. Just a few hours ago, I'd drawn a dagger across my flesh and used it to patch up yet another weak spot in the veil between my realm and Acaria. The veil meant to separate the living from the dead.

"I was. Now we just have to wait and see how long it holds."

CHAPTER FOUR

Elora

It's midday when we reach Rhagana. The village is a flurry of activity, and my suspicions as I traveled closer to it are confirmed. Today is the Goddess of Witchcraft's feast day. Every door I've passed for the last several hours has had sacred herbs twisted into the shape of a five-pointed star hung on it.

To call Rhagana a city is too generous. Southern capitals are much smaller than northern ones. I'm not sure if it's because southern lands are owned by gods who belong to the dark court or the long winters or the thick forest shrouded in mist, but most of Acaria's population is packed in the central and northern territories.

With so many people in town for the festivities, finding lodgings for the night may prove to be a challenge, let alone a permanent place to live until it's safe to head north again. I lead Meera into the heart of the village, a large circle with streets branching off it like spokes on a wheel.

In the center, an enormous bonfire has been laid but not lit, and every so often someone wandering by throws a bundle of herbs onto the wood and whispers something to themselves. A prayer, a wish, I'm not sure.

People wave and call out greetings to one another as if this is the first time they've seen each other all year. And it might well be. Feast days are as much a time for the faithful to gather and catch up as they are to celebrate their god or goddess.

Meera stops short when a pair of small children dart in front of us, and I lean over her back to whisper gentle words into her ear. We haven't been around this many people in at least two days. I'm praying for a warm bed and a nearby stream so I can wash.

There's a chill in the air, but not enough of one to keep me from washing the stench of travel off me. I desperately need to clean the dirt from my hair and find somewhere out of the elements to sleep. Even if it's just a room in a tavern for a night or two, I'll take it.

When the crowd thickens, I dismount and brush soothing fingers down Meera's side. She's as uneasy around people as I am. A woman smiles at me and hands me a bundle of dried lavender bound with twine. I take it, twirling it in my fingers before tucking it behind my ear.

"Are you here for the feast?"

"Yes," I lie. "Do you know if there are any rooms?"

"I'm not sure. Best to ask for Hellena at the Inn. She might have some left or know where you could get one."

I smile and make my way through the crowd until I see a sign for the Nightingale Inn. Looping Meera's reins around a post outside, I murmur my apologies. It's going to take a lot of apples to soothe her nerves after this.

A woman wearing a beautiful ruby-red dress exits the Inn, and I slip in behind her, giving my eyes a minute to adjust to the low light. To the left, a steep, narrow staircase leads to a second floor, and to the right is a large room with tables and chairs where people sip what I assume to be tea from pretty painted cups.

It's as busy inside as it is out, and I scan the room for

someone who looks like they might be in charge. I spot a round woman with rosy cheeks and a quick smile, and when she makes eye contact with me, she crosses the room, her gaze never leaving mine even as she waves at people who call out a greeting.

"I was told to ask for Hellena?" I say when she stops in front of me. "I'm in need of a place to sleep."

"I'm all out of rooms, I'm afraid," she says, folding her hands in front of her.

"I'll take anything with a bed," I tell her. "I'm not picky."

She tilts her head, and the intensity with which she studies me makes the hair rise on the back of my neck. It's like she's reading words written on my insides.

"I do have something else. But it's on the outskirts. Against the forest."

"Private?"

Something lights in her eyes at my question. Understanding, maybe. She nods. "My daughter used to live there with her husband, but they moved up north a few weeks ago so he could look for different work. I asked her to wait until after Lady Kaia's feast day, but she insisted they couldn't delay." Hellena sighs. "My loss is your gain, it would seem."

"The price?"

Hellena waves her hand in the air. "Let me show it to you first. I only have a few minutes, but the walk's not long."

I follow her back the way I'd come, freeing Meera from the post and trailing Hellena through the crowd in silence. The further we get from the village center, the less busy it becomes, and I feel Meera relax beside me.

"Are you from the north?" Hellena asks me when we're able to walk side by side on the road.

"No. I was born in Dremen."

"In the land of the Goddess of Nightmares."

I nod. My life has certainly been full of them. I've always

wondered if that was because of where I was born or a trick of the Fates.

The road curves to the right, and the edge of the forest comes into view. Acaria is a vast land with seas to the north and east, mountains to the west, and hills and valleys and fields in its center. The southernmost part is edged by a dense forest of blackened trees, the ground crawling with mist.

Most people avoid the forest, but I have always felt drawn to it. The thick trees with their branches like reaching fingers and the way sunlight never seems to reach the forest floor.

When my parents died, I was sent to live with my father's brother and his wife. Every spare minute I had, and I didn't have many, I wandered down to the forest's edge and basked in the quiet. The air always felt heavy, charged. It called to something inside me, no matter how many times my uncle tried to beat it out of me.

The forest is the line between Acaria and the Shadow Realm, he said. There were untold dangers in its depths. Beasts eager to pounce on little girls and eat their insides. For as much as he hated me, I would have thought he'd delight in letting me wander in too far so he could find my mangled body and be done with me. Maybe he delighted in beating me more.

"Here we are," Hellena says, pulling me from my thoughts.

We've stopped in front of a rough log cabin that looks as if it's been built from the same black trees from the forest. That only makes me love it more. It's not very big. If I had to guess from the outside, I'd say it has two rooms at most. But really, all I require is a good bed and a door that locks from the inside.

She opens the door, and it swings in silently. I release Meera to graze, and she dips her head to nip at the blades of grass. I'll have to find somewhere warm to board her before the weather turns. But I have a few weeks yet before that happens.

As I suspected, the cabin has two rooms. But it isn't empty. There's a small table with two chairs on one side of the large room and a wide bench piled with cushions and blankets on the other side. Between them is a fireplace large enough for a small child to stand in.

The room beyond has a bed in it that's bigger than I expected. The mattress looks overstuffed with feathers from here, and I sigh at the thought of a good night's rest on something that doesn't include hay or dirt.

"Your daughter didn't take any of her things?"

Hellena gives me an indulgent smile. "They wanted to travel light and fast. They took their plates and dishes and blankets, of course. You can buy all that in the village for a good price if you like."

I'm not sure I believe the story, but if it gets me this secluded cabin on the edge of the wood, I won't push it too far. Unless she demands an exorbitant sum.

"How much?"

"Five pieces a week if you can pay up front."

It's practically a gift. "I'll take it. I can pay for a month."

"Only a month?" There's that look in her eye again, the one where she's seeing into my depths.

"For now," I say.

She nods, gesturing to the back wall of the cabin. "There's a creek about twenty paces that way for washing and cooking. I have a tub for bathing I can have my husband and son bring down if it's hot baths you're after."

"I can use the creek for now, but that would be lovely."

"We take our feast days seriously here. Lady Kaia is good to us, kind and generous. But I can send them down in three days when the feasts are over."

"That's fine."

I follow her back outside and retrieve the necessary coins from my bag. She doesn't bother to count them when I hold them out, just opens a small leather sack so I can drop them in and then hands me the key.

"Enjoy your rest, my dear. You look like you need one."

I run a hand through my hair as she walks away. I must look worse than I thought. Meera watches me debate whether I should take her back to the village for the few supplies I still need or bathe first.

In the end, the idea of washing the dirt from my body and fresh clothes wins out, and I take what I need from my saddlebags and store the rest inside. Locking the door behind me, I follow Hellena's directions to the creek, and the sound of rushing water reaches my ears before I see it.

It's a few steps into the forest, and tendrils of mist lap its banks on one side. Scanning my surroundings, I quickly peel off my travel clothes and wade into the deepest part of the creek. It only comes up to my thighs, so I sink down and submerge as much of my body as I can.

Tipping my head back, I quickly wet my hair, using my fingers to scrub every bit of dirt and grime I can from my scalp. The water is cool, but it's refreshing enough that I don't mind the goosebumps.

Once my hair is as clean as I can make it, I splash water on my face and breasts, watching the dirt slough off my skin and wash away down the creek. The tub is days away, but already I'm dreaming of reclining in the steaming water. With all these herbs around here, surely I can find some to add to a bath and a pretty-smelling soap.

I look up to see Meera watching me, ever-present and disapproving of my bathing habits. She could use a good groom too, now that we've found somewhere to settle. She won't like it, but I'll give her a bath tomorrow, and then we'll both smell better.

When the tips of my fingers begin to go numb, I force myself out of the water and wrap myself in a clean cloak to dry off. Tugging on a pair of leather breeches, I tuck my tunic into them and fit my most comfortable corset over top, deftly tying up the front laces. I'm nearly finished when the snap of a tree branch draws my attention.

Meera gives a warning snort, and I keep my eyes trained on the forest as I shove my feet into my boots and slowly back away toward the safety of the cabin. Whatever's in there, I don't want to give it the idea I'm prey by running.

My hand instinctively goes to my thigh, where I'd normally strap my dagger, but it's bare. I left it in the cabin. Meera paws the ground behind me and snorts again when I hear another snap, but I'm still watching the forest for any signs of a threat, my heart beating a fast rhythm in my chest.

The woman takes my breath away when I see her. Hair black as a raven, falling in thick curls down her back, and a dark green dress sewn with thousands of tiny silver stars that sparkle when she moves. She's beautiful, with bold red lips that stand out against her pale skin, high cheekbones, and an elegant nose.

She lifts her hand in greeting when she notices me and changes direction, a serene smile on her face as she approaches. When she stops in front of me, I refuse to bow. I haven't shown deference to a god since I was eleven and they refused to save me. I don't see the need to start again now.

Her smile turns amused, and when she reaches out a hand to stroke Meera down her nose, I see the godmark on the inside of her left wrist. A five-pointed star ringed by a circle. I expect Meera to shy away and be as standoffish with the goddess as I am, but she betrays me, leaning into the contact with a contented sigh.

"I am Kaia," the goddess says, not using her title like most gods would. "And you are?"

"Elora of Dremen."

She smiles and gives Meera a pat. "Not too terribly far from home, then."

Her eyes drift to the forest, and mine follow. The woods have felt more like my home than anywhere else I've ever lived.

And I've traveled all over Acaria searching for something impossible to find.

"I hope you'll come enjoy the festivities. My people are generous and kind."

"That's exactly what they say about you," I reply, remembering Hellena's words from earlier.

"Then I am honored." She turns toward the village and then pauses, looking back at me over her shoulder. "Be wary of the forest, Elora of Dremen. Dangers lurk within its borders."

She doesn't wait for me to agree, pivoting in a rush of skirts and setting off for the village. I expect her to shift and make a grand entrance to her own celebration, but she walks until she disappears from sight.

Once she's gone, my eyes are drawn back to the trees and the mist that climbs their trunks. I feel that familiar tug in my gut, and I ache to explore it, despite the goddess's warning. She didn't tell me not to go in there, only to be careful.

But it'll have to wait until another day. Soon enough, I'll have time to wander past the creek and introduce myself.

CHAPTER FIVE

Thieran

"Síra's boundaries are holding, my lord. As are the boundaries around Meren."

"And all the souls who should be in each are accounted for?"

My sentry inclines his head in confirmation. Garrick's technically a mortal. Or a half-mortal. A demigod general killed in battle so long ago I don't remember the exact date. I do know he fought on my side during the war between the gods, and he was one of the earliest souls I governed after the truce was called.

He's been here so long he knows the Shadow Realm as well as I do. He's watched the power that created it, that holds it together, slowly fade over the last few decades. The only thing keeping it at bay has been my blood. And lately that isn't working as well as it once did.

"Did you find the forest guardian that escaped?"

His mouth thins, and his shoulders square before he answers me. His tell for bad news.

"No, my lord. Not yet. We've scoured the forest around Lady Aeris's territory and have seen no sign of the beast."

"Cast a wider net. If you need more men, you can have them.

I don't want it wandering further into Acaria and doing real damage."

Or I'll never hear the end of it from my brother.

"Of course, my lord."

"Was there something else?" I ask when he hesitates to leave.

"When was the last time you fortified the eastern border, my lord?"

"A few days ago. Why?"

"You might want to have another look."

His tone is all business, but his eyes are apologetic. I nod, dismissing him with a wave of my hand. His boots make no sound on the floor as he crosses to the door and closes it quietly behind him.

I lean back in my chair and conjure a glass of liquor. The dark amber liquid burns a trail down my throat. The new distillers have outdone themselves with this batch. It might be the best one yet.

Thunder rumbles in the distance, drawing my gaze to the wide window looking out over the dull, gray terrain of the Shadow Realm. I didn't want this place when my brother offered it as part of our truce. But it's as much a part of me now as I am a part of it. And I don't know why my power is seemingly no longer holding it together.

Lightning travels from cloud to cloud before forking down to the ground, and I fill my glass again to drain it in one swallow.

I'd rather be out there inflicting torture than in here wondering what the fuck is happening and how the fuck I'm going to fix it. A drop or two of blood used to keep the realm and its boundaries strong for years. Now I need buckets of it to barely make a dent.

I don't want to think about what will happen if the Shadow Realm becomes devoid of power and reverts to the wild, untamed thing it was before the war.

There certainly aren't any mortals alive who remember what it was like when the dead danced among the living. The darkness roamed the land, infecting everything it touched.

I might not be so intent on stopping it now if not for my own sense of self-preservation. I might enjoy giving the mortals who've never seen me a real reason to fear the God of Death.

Power ripples like a coming storm seconds before someone knocks on my door.

"Come!"

The faint scent of lavender and rosemary follows her in. Then there's another smell, a stronger one, and my lip curls in disgust.

"You smell like mortals."

Kaia laughs and takes a seat in one of the overstuffed chairs in front of the fireplace. The firelight dances over her dress, making it shimmer in the low light.

"I'm just back from my feast day celebrations."

"I forget your people like you enough to follow the old ways. What I don't understand is why you prolong the torture by attending all three days."

I join her in the opposite chair, conjuring myself another glass of liquor and her a glass of wine. She takes a delicate sip, watching me over the rim of the glass, and I know what she's going to say before her lips even part.

"Your people celebrate you too. You just refuse to acknowledge them."

"My people are dead."

"That should be a bonus for you. Since you hate the smell of the living."

I chuckle despite myself and stretch my legs out in front of me. "Did you need something?"

"I saw Railan when I arrived. Sparring in the training yard with Hayle and Nevon."

I already know where she's going with this, but I let her finish.

"Another breach in the veil?" I hold up three fingers, and her brows draw together. "It's getting worse," she murmurs. "What can we do?"

"I have no idea."

Kaia pauses with the glass halfway to her lips and stares at me. I've known Kaia my entire existence. Few people in this world know me better, and the concern on her face mirrors my own.

"There has to be something that can be done. A ritual or a spell. Something."

"The only thing that's ever worked is my blood." I sit forward in my chair, eyes intent on the flames dancing behind the grate. "And even that is failing me now."

She purses her lips, a small crease forming between her brows. "I haven't heard any whispers from the high court about the veil thinning."

"Still have spies embedded at my brother's court, my lady?" I say with a raised brow, and her mouth twitches before she takes another sip of wine.

"I enjoy being informed. Knowledge is power and all that."

"And what sort of information have your spies shared with you?"

She twists the glass in her hands, the liquid beginning to swirl in a perfect circle, less a result of the movement and more from her power.

"He's introducing several new demigods into society soon."

"Zanirah must be thrilled."

The wine in her glass goes still, and she flinches at the mention of the queen, her gaze drifting to the dancing flames. "She always was more content than I was to look the other way."

I snort and glance out the window when a tree in the distance catches fire. My brother is cruel in ways most of Acaria cannot fathom. He hides it well, under his fine clothes and grand palace and massive feasts and celebrations.

Most of the gods who sit among his high court play the game well, ignoring my brother's antics in favor of maintaining their lands, money, and power and avoiding my brother's infamous wrath.

But while we are similar in many ways, we are different in the ways that matter. I don't hide my cruelty behind expensive things and fancy balls and too-wide smiles. What you see with me will always be what you get.

"So it's safe to say you won't be going, then?"

I chuckle, setting my glass on the table between us with a thunk.

"No. I have more important things to do than watch my brother debut his half-mortal bastards in front of his wife."

"You say that like you feel bad for her."

There's an edge to Kaia's voice. My brother has always been a touchy subject where she's concerned. There was a time before. When things were different. But it's been so long now the memories hardly ever sharpen into crystal-clear focus for me. Maybe some things are best left forgotten to time.

"Of course I don't. The two of them deserve each other. Will you go?"

She levels me with a piercing gaze. "I have not been invited, Thieran."

I'm not surprised. My brother's wife usually handles the invitations for things like this. Aside from the twice-yearly functions that are mandatory for all the gods, neither Kaia nor I ever get invited to anything else. Most of my dark court gods are also conveniently left off the guest list.

"I enjoyed them once," she says into the silence. "Ascension balls."

"Me too," I admit.

There was something about the pomp and circumstance of

life in the high court. But that was a long time ago. Before we nearly destroyed Acaria with our petty squabbles and infighting. Before my brother showed his true colors and declared war against me. It was another lifetime entirely.

She opens her mouth and closes it again, taking a deep breath before finally speaking. "I'm the one who's supposed to hate him. Not the other way around."

"He doesn't hate you," I promise her, but I'm not sure if it's the truth. I hardly know my brother anymore. "He hates that you didn't take his side."

The King of the Gods does not forgive easily. Not even the people he claims to love most in the world.

"And why would I when…" Setting her glass on the table between us, Kaia waves the words away, her smile sad. "It hardly matters now, in any case. And you're right. We have more important things to worry about. If your blood still fortifies the realm, then at least some part of the ritual used to create it is holding."

"It does, but not as well as it once did." I conjure more liquor into my glass and take a careful sip. "I fear it's a losing battle."

"You are the God of Death." She clears her throat, staring into the flickering flames. "All the ritual was meant to do was concentrate your dominion over the dead to a specific location. Give them boundaries."

I nod. That was the idea. Though I'd never intended to be banished here along with them.

"What I don't understand is why it seems to be weakening."

"I'm sure there's an explanation." She captures her bottom lip between her teeth, brows drawing together. "There's a whole section in my temple library on blood rituals. I can pick up some of the best volumes the next time I go to Rhagana."

When she pushes to her feet, I rise with her and turn as she moves to the door, pausing with her hand on the knob.

"Until then, I'll see if my spies can find out what, if anything, the king might know about this."

"You've embedded yourself in my brother's inner circle?"

She lifts a shoulder but won't meet my gaze. "Among the queen's ladies. Useful for information should we need it."

"What other secrets do you know of my brother and his wife you aren't sharing?"

Kaia looks at me over her shoulder, her mouth quirked up at the corner. "You know I always share the juiciest gossip with you, Thieran. I'll let you know what I find out."

She disappears, the door closing gently behind her, and I wave my hand over both glasses to get rid of them. The depth of Kaia's spies might surprise me, but she's right. More knowledge where my brother is concerned is always better than less.

I'm not sure why my brother would know what's happening beyond the veil. Not even Kaia knows the worst of it. But if he does, it's better to be prepared.

I could feed the realm my blood for eternity; I'll always have more than enough to spare. But if my blood isn't enough anymore, if the Shadow Realm is really dying and I can't stop it, it will mean my end too. Because I've used more than my blood to fortify this place.

I am so inextricably linked to the realm and the power it uses to sustain itself that I know exactly what happens to me if I can't hold it together. We are one and the same. I won't survive without it. If the Shadow Realm ceases to exist, it will most assuredly take me with it.

CHAPTER SIX

Elora

W ater sloshes over the rim of the bucket and narrowly misses my feet. This chore of hauling water from the creek to the cabin would go twice as quickly if Meera didn't act like a big baby about going near the forest. She stands at the side of the cabin, her big brown eyes watching my every step while her ears are pricked for any noise.

She's the reason I still haven't made use of that big tub Hellena's husband and son brought over the other day. I bought everything I need for it: fluffy towels that were a luxury I shouldn't have splurged on and lavender-scented soap with chamomile and a blend of dried herbs the shopkeeper told me would make my dreams come true.

But getting enough water from the edge of the forest to the fireplace to the tub would take hours without Meera's help. By the time I'm done, I'm just as liable to fall asleep in the bath and drown as I am to have sweet dreams.

I dump the water into the large wooden basin beside the cabin, and Meera steps back to avoid any droplets landing on her forelegs. I roll my eyes before crouching down to wash this morning's breakfast dishes.

"You can't be angry about having a bath forever, you know. You needed a good wash." She snorts in disagreement. "Well, you smell better, in any case."

A rabbit darts out of the brush at the edge of the wood and back into cover when it sees us, and Meera shifts on her feet at the movement. I haven't seen her this skittish since I first rescued her.

She hadn't been my intended target; her master had. A man who'd raped and murdered a twelve-year-old boy.

After cutting off his dick and letting him choke to death on it, I'd seen her standing in a small paddock behind the house. Thin enough you could count every single rib. Initially I wasn't going to take her with me, but I couldn't leave her behind.

We'd laid low together for a few months. She'd gotten her strength back and meat on her bones, and I'd given her time to trust me. We've been through a lot these last few years, and more often than not, I trust her instincts.

But I need her to warm up to the forest because I won't last forever on the fruits and vegetables and oats from the village market. I want fresh game, and at better prices than I can get from the butcher.

"It's not as bad as you're making it out to be," I tell her, dunking the last dish in the soapy water to rinse and setting it on a clean cloth.

She gives me a disbelieving stare, and when two more rabbits race from the edge of the forest, we both look up. My stomach growls at the idea of rabbit stew for dinner. It would be perfect with the carrots, cabbage, and potatoes I picked up at the market yesterday.

Standing, I dry my hands on the edges of the cloth and carry the dishes inside. My dagger sits in the middle of the table, tucked into its protective leather sheath, and my brand-new bow and quiver of arrows are leaning against the corner next to the door.

The butcher warned me about not hunting in the woods when he saw me with my new purchase the day before. His words echoed the goddess's, but it was hard to take him seriously with a giant flank of venison hanging on a hook behind his head.

Obviously the forest was safe enough for him to venture inside, and I wasn't going to be warned off simply because I'm a woman. It's been a while since I've used one, but I'm decent with a bow and better with a knife.

I strap the dagger to my thigh and sling the quiver of arrows over my shoulder before heading out the door again and locking it behind me. Meera moves to block me as soon as I round the house, looking down at me in what I swear is disapproval.

"It's just a few rabbits," I tell her. "They'll make a delicious stew."

I move to go around her, and she again blocks my path with her bulk. Taking a step back, I cross my arms over my chest.

"If you're so worried about it, why don't you come with me?"

Her ears flatten, and she takes a handful of steps to the side.

"That's what I thought," I say, feinting to the left and then darting around her to the right. "I'll be back soon. If I don't survive, you know which way the village is!"

She whinnies at me, but I ignore her. I'm more interested in the rabbits than Meera's misguided anxiety about the forest. I've bathed in the creek twice more and wandered in far enough to find delicious wild berries without meeting an untimely end. A quick trip for a nice supply of meat will hardly be the end of the world.

I hear the flutter of leaves as I draw closer, and I slow my steps so as not to spook the rabbits. Rabbits are easier caught with traps because they move so fast, and it would probably be a good idea to set a few for regular meat, especially when snow begins to fall. For now, I'm hoping to take good enough aim with my bow to get what I came for.

As soon as my boot hits the dense brush rimming the forest, two rabbits shoot out from under the leaves and race away from me. They stop ahead, their noses twitching while they wait to see what I'm going to do.

Quietly, I slide an arrow out of my quiver and nock it to the bow. Drawing it back, I take aim and release. A grin curves my lips as the arrow flies true, but the rabbit leaps out of the way at the last second, and my arrow sinks deep into the mossy dirt instead.

Trudging deeper into the forest to retrieve it, I listen for more sounds of scurrying and follow them through low brush. Another rabbit pauses up ahead, and I nock a second arrow. I can tell it's going wide before it lands, and the rabbit darts away again.

I sigh. I need a bigger target.

As if summoned, a doe steps out from behind a thick tree trunk and dips her head to collect a mouthful of clover. I'd have to build some kind of larder to store that much meat without it going bad, but venison stew sounds just as good as rabbit, and I'd relish the manual labor to avoid boredom.

Nocking a third arrow, I release it. But it isn't a clean shot, catching the deer in the meaty part of her flank and sending her bounding off into the forest. Cursing under my breath, I set off after her. I don't want her to suffer, and I don't want another predator to make use of my kill, either.

The light dims the further I walk into the forest, but I notice a smear of blood on a leaf and another on a tree trunk. I have to at least be close. She couldn't have gone too far with an arrow lodged in her hip.

Heavy breathing and a faint snuffling sound draw my attention, and I slow my walk, creeping over the brush in order to not make a sound. I prepare to aim. I want a quick, clean shot. The animal's suffering isn't my goal.

A mist so thick I can't see the ground curls around my legs, and I realize for the first time just how far I've wandered into the forest. It's dark, as if the entire day has passed and it's already twilight.

There's a pained groan from the other side of a cropping of thin trees, and I push forward. I shouldn't be in this far, but I'm too close to my prize to leave it behind. And if I'm successful, I won't have to make another trip into the forest for a while.

I push through the trees, bow raised, but my deer is not alone. Another animal hunches over her. And it hasn't bothered to kill her before enjoying its meal.

It has the vague shape of some kind of wild boar, but there's something off about it. Though I can't quite place what. In the split second it takes me to wonder if it'll eat just as good as wild boar, the animal senses my presence.

My feet are frozen in place as I watch it slowly stand on its hind legs until it's fully upright. When it turns, a scream tries to claw its way from my lungs, but I swallow it down. Whatever this creature is, I've never seen one before.

It's covered in fur from head to toe, and while the bottom half resembles a wild boar, the top is entirely too human for my liking, with arms too long for its body and claws extending from three thick fingers where hooves should be.

It watches me, blood dripping from the corner of its mouth and matting the fur on its chest. When I take a slow step back, it rips the animal from whatever trance it's in, and it lunges, mouth parting to reveal razor-sharp teeth stained with the doe's lifeblood.

I dodge to the left, but I'm too slow, and a long claw catches me in the side, drawing a jagged cut across my stomach from navel to hip. I can't help the scream that escapes me, and I discard my bow in favor of my dagger. Though I'm not sure how much help it'll be against a creature like this.

It circles me, moving closer with each revolution, and a shaky breath saws in and out of my lungs. It sizes me up, eyes wild, and I know I won't make it out of these woods alive if I try to take it on in a fair fight.

Slipping an arrow from my quiver, I lunge forward with enough force to jab it into the creature's chest and then run as fast as I can as it snarls and snaps.

The fog thickens and I use it to my advantage, shrouding myself in it the deeper I go into the forest. I think I'm heading back toward the village, but it's hard to tell without any light. If I circle in this direction, I should come up on the main road near the square. It's quite a walk from there back to the cabin, but at least I won't be dead.

I hear the beast's breaths behind me, deep and guttural, muffled by the thick fog and the rapid staccato of my own panting. I'm losing too much blood. My hand is coated in it when I pull it away from my side.

The mist grows thicker and the air colder. So cold it hurts to breathe. Or is that a symptom of the wound? Jagged and weeping. My vision dims, and the hair raises on the back of my neck, but I'm drawn forward toward the smell of woodsmoke and spices.

The smell is familiar, comforting, though I can't work out why that would be.

A boulder black as midnight juts out of the soil, and a warning signals at the back of my mind, but for what, I'm not sure. Collapsing against the rock, I strain my ears for the beast's heavy breathing.

There's nothing. Not the stomp of hooves or the crunch of leaves. I should be able to hear animals, the warble of a bird or scurry of a rabbit, but it's silent save for the faint sound of a river.

My brows draw together. There shouldn't be a river here. We're too far inland, and the Avain is several days' hard ride to the east.

I'm again drawn toward the water by that invisible force. With each step, cold seeps into my bones and pain radiates from the cut in my side. If I can make it to the river, I can clean myself up, check the damage, and pray to all the gods I don't fucking die.

The river is inky black when I reach it. It's both a sight that unnerves me and feels familiar all at once. There's that smell again, cedar and cinnamon and woodsmoke. It's closer now, but I'm intent on my goal. Reach the river, don't die. Reach the river, don't die.

I stumble on the bank and fall to my knees. Everything is gray.

The leaves, the grass, the scattering of fallen branches. Like the river's leached all the color from the land and trapped it in its swirling black depths.

I can't see the bottom—I can't see much of anything—but I swear a figure moves beneath the surface. A face, a hand. But they're gone again so quickly it's impossible to be sure. I'm probably hallucinating from the blood loss. I shake my head to clear it.

Holding my hand over the surface, I have the faint sensation of recognition. But that doesn't make any sense. I've never been to this place before. I'd remember a river black as pitch and gray grass.

My stomach tightens, and I squeeze my eyes against a wave of nausea. If I pass out before I clean this wound, it'll become infected. Or worse, my blood will attract predators. After my run-in with that hideous beast, I shudder to think what other awful creatures lurk in these woods.

A noise to my left catches my attention—the snap of a branch, a sharp intake of breath. But I'm too slow to react.

Before I can turn my head, there's weight and warmth at my back, and a strong hand covered in black leather wraps around my wrist, drawing my hand away from the water.

"Wait," I croak, unsure if any sound actually makes it past my lips.

I try to stand, but my legs won't hold me. I brace myself for the impact against the hard earth, but none comes. There's more warmth against my knees and around my waist, and then I'm floating.

A puff of breath cools my cheek seconds before a deep voice whispers against my ear, "How did you cross the veil, little one?"

I have no idea what he's asking me. But I can't answer. The darkness and the pain swallow me up.

CHAPTER SEVEN

Thieran

T he wind whips around me in sharp bursts, blowing my hair across my face and my robes around my legs. This is the tallest peak in the mountain range that separates Síra from the rest of the Shadow Realm.

Just under the howling of the wind, I can make out the screams of the unredeemables as they endure whatever means of torture I've devised for them. But even that is not enough to find peace from her.

It doesn't matter where I go in my realm or what I do to distract myself; I can sense her presence everywhere. The slow, ragged sound of her breathing, the erratic beat of her heart, the dull ache from the wound in her side. I do not have as deep a connection with any other being, alive or dead. Not even Kaia, whom I've known as long as I've known my own brother.

It's fucking distracting.

With a sigh, I shift and find myself face to face with the intricately carved door of her tower room. Waving my hand over the black wood hewed from Shadow Realm trees, I hear the thunk of locks give way and watch the shimmer of my power receding.

For now, I'm keeping her presence in my realm a secret from everyone save the soul I've tasked with her care. Until I know who this woman is or how she managed to crossed the veil alive, her existence is no one's business but mine.

She's asleep when I enter, her long brown hair fanned out on the pillow behind her, framing a pale face. She's stunning, with her high cheekbones, elegant nose, and full upper lip. It's the first thing I think every time I see her.

I drop into a chair across the room and watch her chest rise and fall from the shadows.

It's been three days since I found her crouched over the River Axan with blood painting the ground where she knelt. Three days of being unable to purge her from my fucking thoughts.

There's something familiar about her, even if I can't quite put my finger on it. Like a long-forgotten memory that won't sharpen into focus.

The chamber door opens, and a lanky woman enters carrying a silver tray. She nearly drops it when she sees me, fumbling into an awkward curtsy.

I motion for her to rise and nod at the figure on the bed. "How is she?"

The soul frowns, setting the tray on a table and choosing from a selection of vials. Palming one that shimmers bright purple, she removes the cork and cups the back of the unconscious woman's head. Upending the vial down her throat, she lays her gently against the pillows and smooths her hair.

"Her wound was deep, but she seems to be responding to the potions I've given her so far."

She pulls the covers back, exposing the long, lean lines of the woman's body through the thin nightgown the soul changed her into. Reaching for the hem of the gown, she pauses, darting a look at me. When it's clear I'm not leaving while she continues her examination, she eases the gown up enough to see the wound while leaving her charge mostly covered.

Probing around the edges of the cut that still looks fresh and angry, she murmurs something to herself about magickal wounds and their potential effects on mortals. But there's more she wants to say. I can sense she's holding back.

"What else?"

"I can't say for certain because we don't know how she was wounded, but I suspect whatever blade or beast did this was a magickal one."

I cock my head at the idea. Being wounded with a god-touched weapon could explain how a living mortal was able to cross the veil instead of wandering lost in the forest. A tenuous possibility, but a possibility nonetheless.

"If you'll permit me, my lord."

I motion for her to continue with a nod of my head.

"Lady Kaia is the only one I trust with this. Her healing power is the strongest in the Shadow Realm. If anyone can examine the woman and know for certain there aren't any lasting effects from the wound, it's her."

I fix my eyes on the woman's sleeping face. "And if there are lasting effects?"

The nurse follows my gaze. "There could be any number of consequences. If power lingers in the wound, she might not heal properly. She could succumb to an infection."

And die. The unspoken word hangs in the air, and the prospect of it makes me uneasy for reasons I can't explain. Death is where I'm most comfortable. If this woman is to become a soul in my realm, I would welcome and judge her as I would any other.

But I don't want her as a crossed-over soul for me to rule. I want her as something else entirely. And that fucking irritates me too.

Rising from my chair, I cross to the door and pause with my

hand on the knob to look back at her. The soul tucks the covers back into place and smooths them with her hand.

"Do what you can to keep her comfortable. I'll speak with Lady Kaia."

The soul nods, bobbing into another curtsy before I sweep out of the room.

While Kaia has her own lands bordering the Shadow Realm, she spends most of her time in my palace. Every god in my dark court has rooms here, and they are free to use or not use them as they please. Unlike my brother's high court, I rarely require them to spend a specific amount of time in my realm.

Kaia's rooms are in the wing opposite mine, and I smell the scent of her power as soon as I turn the corner. She opens her door when I knock, but her smile quickly fades to a frown.

"What's wrong?"

I hate that she can read me so well.

"Who said anything was wrong?"

She says nothing, simply clasps her hands in front of her and waits patiently for me to explain. I take a deep breath. She isn't going to like that I've been hiding some mystery mortal—not just in the realm, but in my palace—from her for three days.

"I need your help."

"I gathered that."

"Do you have a moment?"

She steps back and ushers me inside. Most of the rooms in the palace are decorated in shades of black, from the obsidian floors to the black stone the palace was carved from to the tapestries I prefer on the walls.

But Kaia's rooms remind me of an enchanted forest, with their deep greens and purples and golds. The painting above her mantel is of a full moon rising over silhouetted trees, with gold candelabras on either side.

Her familiar jumps down from a nearby chair and winds

around her legs, purring loudly. Today it's a black cat. The last time I saw it, it was a raven.

Kaia conjures a pot of tea for herself and a glass of liquor for me, fixing herself a cup while she motions for me to sit. I take a sip of my drink, waiting until she's added sugar and milk to her tea before explaining.

"I found someone kneeling next to the River Axan the other day and brought them back to the palace."

She frowns again, tilting her head ever so slightly as she lifts her cup to sample her tea. "A soul wandered all the way to the river of sorrow from Videva? Why would you bring them back here?"

I hesitate, my fingers tightening on the glass in my hand. "Not a soul. A living mortal."

Her shoulders jerk, and her eyes widen.

"How is that possible?" she wonders. "How was a mortal able to cross the veil?"

"I have no idea." Something I find myself saying far too often as of late. "But the woman was badly injured. A long wound from her navel to her hip. I summoned a healer from the village who seems worried whatever caused the wound—weapon or beast—may have been imbued with a god's powers."

"If it was, there could be consequences," Kaia says, her words echoing the healer's. "Which healer?"

"The one with the most experience." I wave a hand in the air at her arch look. "Tall, thin, graying hair."

"You asked for her help, and you don't know her name?"

I raise a brow. "You say that like it's out of character for me."

Setting her cup on the table, Kaia rolls her eyes. "If the weapon was god-touched or even magickal, it would linger in her system. Slow or even stop the natural healing process. The power would have to be removed."

"That's similar to what the healer said. That she could succumb to an infection. Or worse."

"And you want me to have a look and confirm."

Kaia says it like an accusation, and I know precisely what she means.

"I should have told you sooner."

She sniffs, rising and moving to the door. "Yes," she says. "You should have. What do you know about her?" she asks after a long silence.

"Nothing more than what I've told you. I've spent the better part of three days researching in the library to see if it's possible for a mortal to somehow get into the Shadow Realm."

"And?"

I snort. "And according to every text I have, it isn't. I don't like the implications."

"You think this has something to do with the veil thinning? I thought it was just that it was easier for guardians and the like to get out. Not for things to get in."

I nod slowly. "So did I."

"Have any souls escaped?" She chews her bottom lip, worry etched between her brows.

I shake my head. "No. They're all presently accounted for."

We lapse into silence as we climb the tower stairs. Shifting back to the woman's room would be faster, but I sense Kaia's need to mull this over in her head, so I give her the time and the quiet.

By the time we reach the door, her shoulders are squared and her jaw set. I wave away the wards and locks, and she raises a brow.

"Were you ever going to tell me about her?"

"Those aren't for you. They're mostly for Aeris. Gods know I don't want her finding out about this until I can figure it all out."

Kaia murmurs her agreement and steps around me into the room. The healer dips into another curtsy, and Kaia offers her a kind smile. Crossing to the bed, she stops short.

"Elora."

I rush to Kaia's side, looking from her to the woman and back. "You know her?"

She shakes her head, capturing her bottom lip between her teeth. "I met her the other day. She was standing outside a little cabin on the edge of Rhagana when I arrived for my feast day celebrations. I told her not to go into the forest."

She steps closer, reaching out a hand to tuck Elora's hair behind her ear. "I wouldn't normally give that warning. But there was something about her. I can't explain it."

I huff out a breath. I know the feeling where Elora is concerned.

"What have you given her so far?" Kaia asks the healer.

Neither of them pay me any mind as they begin discussing the different tinctures, balms, poultices, and potions the soul has used and her theories about the wound itself. Kaia makes little noises of agreement while the soul speaks.

I'm drawn closer to the bed as they murmur behind me. I have no idea what it is about this woman who stumbled blindly into my realm. No idea why I can feel every beat of her heart in my chest as if hers and mine were sitting side by side.

I reach out a single fingertip, prepared to trace it down her arm. I haven't touched her once, not bare skin to bare skin, but standing this close to her, there's an unshakable pull to do just that.

"I want to do a full exam," Kaia says at my elbow, and I drop my hand to my side, curling it into a fist.

"She's had a full exam," I tell her.

"I'm sure she has." Kaia tugs back the coverlet and shifts her body in front of mine to block my view. "I'm going to give her another one to make sure nothing was missed."

When I don't move, she peeks at me over her shoulder, brows raised. "You can go, my lord. I'll come find you when I'm done."

Inclining my head, I leave the room, locking and sealing the door behind me. I would trust Kaia with my life, but it's still more difficult to leave than I want it to be.

Shaking my head, I shift to my study and slip out of my robes. Hanging them on a hook by the door, I grab my favorite dagger and shift to the middle of Síra. Surely there is someone within these desolate boundaries I can work out my frustrations on.

Anything to keep my mind off that bewitching puzzle of a mortal woman asleep in my tower and everything her presence implies about what's happening to the Shadow Realm.

CHAPTER EIGHT

Elora

L avender. That's the first thing that registers as I float on the edge of consciousness. The heady scent of lavender.

It's not unfamiliar. The entire town of Rhagana is steeped in lavender and rosemary. You can hardly turn around without seeing a bundle of it hanging in someone's window or doorway for luck or blessings or prosperity.

But I'm not sure why the smell would be so strong inside my cabin. Strong enough to invade my dreams and rouse me out of sleep. And I must be sleeping because the surface under me is impossibly soft, the blankets warm and cozy.

The weight on top of me suddenly disappears and with it, the warmth. I shiver and shift to cover myself, but my body will not obey. I try again to grasp the blanket, but my hand doesn't move save for the twitch of my fingers.

It's my first sense that something is wrong, and panic climbs my spine and wraps itself around my throat. I suck in a sharp breath and try again. Still nothing.

"She wakes, my lady."

I freeze at the sound of voices. Someone is inside my cabin with me. Someone who's restrained me or drugged me. Pramis.

It must be his guards. How did they find me so far south of Pramis's territory? And so fast?

Pramis prefers public executions. Sometimes hangings, sometimes beheadings. A few summers ago, he had a thief drawn and quartered simply for trying to explain why he stole a loaf of bread.

I swallow hard around the lump in my throat. Whatever the sun god has in store for me will not be pleasant. Not for killing one of his high priests in cold blood. No matter how much the bastard deserved it.

The voices come closer, and even though I know it won't work, I try to scoot away.

"Stand there," a second voice says, and something about it is familiar, although I'm unable to place it. "I don't know what might happen when I coax out this power."

Power?

A warmth begins at the top of my head and flows down my face and neck, over my shoulders and stomach, and past my hips and legs until it reaches the tips of my toes. It might be soothing if I wasn't braced for imminent death and unable to move.

As the warmth slowly subsides, it's replaced by a different sensation, a heavy one. Following the same path as the warmth, it prickles over my skin until I'm on fire from it. When it finally wends its way down to my toes, my whole body feels as if it's pulsing with energy, lightning in a bottle, snapping and striking.

Fingertips brush gently over the skin of my wrist and then wrap around it, anchoring me in place. A second hand presses into my shoulder as the prickling intensifies into pain. Like when all the feeling rushes back to a numb limb.

The sensation gathers from my head to my toes, but it concentrates in my stomach until it's unbearable. Sweat beads on my forehead and drips down my temples while my insides rend themselves apart and knit themselves back together with agonizing slowness. I grit my teeth against it so hard I'm afraid they may crack.

By the time it stops, I'm panting, chest rising and falling with each labored breath. The pressure on my wrist and shoulder disappears, and then someone is holding something against my lips.

I turn my head, surprised when it actually moves, and wrench my eyes open to see two women staring down at me. The one closest to me with a vial of clear blue liquid in her hand smiles even while a frown creases her brow.

"Can you drink this?"

I shake my head. "No," I tell her, and my voice is stronger than I expect it to be after being drugged and tortured for gods know how long. "What did you do to me?"

"I removed power that lingered after you were cut." She sits down on the edge of the bed, vial still in hand. "I'm not going to hurt you," she adds when I shuffle away from her, eyeing what could very well be poison. "This is just a potion for your wound."

Maybe I'm not going to be dragged away and hung for killing the priest. But that doesn't mean I'm going to drink whatever they give me. At least not without them drinking it first.

"I'm not wounded."

"You are," she insists, gesturing to my stomach. "A long, deep gash here. Do you know how it happened?"

I look down at myself, hands flying to my chest when I realize the clothes I was wearing this morning are gone, replaced by a long, thin nightgown the color of elderberries. I scan the room, looking for my things, but nothing stands out against the endless black. Everything from the shiny floor to the tapestries on the wall is black, and it feels both comforting and suffocating at once.

My gaze lands on the woman perched on the edge of the

bed. She's dressed in a royal blue gown that shimmers when it catches the light. Her bright red lips are curved into a soft smile and her black hair spirals down her back.

"I know you."

"Yes, we've met. Elora of Dremen."

It comes flooding back to me in an instant. Meeting the goddess, her warning about the forest and its dangers, my stubborn desire to catch a rabbit for dinner. An image of the creature I encountered flits across my vision, and I shudder.

It was unnatural, its body contorted until it was both man and beast, unable to tell where one ended and the other began. I shake my head to clear it of the nightmarish sounds the thing made as it feasted on the doe.

"I was in the forest hunting. I followed a deer too far in, and there was a...thing. An animal of some sort." I'm not sure how to describe it without sounding like I've lost my senses, so I don't try to. "It clawed me, and I ran. I thought I was heading back toward the village. To Rhagana."

"Unfortunately, you wandered in the opposite direction," Kaia says. "You've been asleep for three days."

I frown. That's impossible. I'd know if I lost that much time. Wouldn't I? If I've been here for three days, that means Meera...

"I have to go."

Kaia lays a hand on my arm, and I pause momentarily. The scent of lavender blooms in my nose, and a sense of calm washes over me. But it feels foreign, constricting, like a garment that doesn't fit quite right, and I shake it off until it and the lavender fade.

"I can't let you leave," she says when my feet hit the floor.

"Am I a prisoner?"

"Well, of course you aren't," she says, sounding exasperated. "But I—"

"Then you can't keep me here."

I fight the urge to bolt. I can't leave here wearing nothing but a nightgown. Especially when I have no idea where the fuck here is or how to get back to Rhagana. All I know is I don't want to stay.

There's something about this place and the way it calls to me, the way there's a new feeling buzzing under my skin. I don't know what it is, but I don't want any part of it.

"Elora, please," Kaia implores as I wander the perimeter of the room, searching for my clothes. "I don't know what will happen to you if you leave."

Her voice is sincere, but the words fill me with dread. Like she's just as worried as I am that I'm trapped here.

"You said I wasn't a prisoner."

She sighs and softens her tone. "You aren't. But that doesn't mean it's safe for you to leave."

I glance up at the other woman when I see her move out of the corner of my eye. When she passes in front of a torch hanging on the wall, her body...changes. One minute she's solid, and the next, I can see straight through her to the wardrobe on the other side. A scream tears its way from my throat, and I stumble backward until my back is pressed against the cold stone wall.

"Where am I?" I demand, the breath wheezing in and out of my lungs.

"You're in the Shadow Realm."

I drag my gaze away from the woman who's gone solid again and fix it on Kaia's face. She looks serious, but she can't be. Mortals can't cross into the Shadow Realm.

"That's not possible. The only way a mortal can enter the Shadow Realm is if..."

My hand flies to my throat, and this time I find myself battling a wave of grief. Of all the ways I might have died, gutted and eaten by an unnatural beast seems like an injustice. Although, since I can't remember it eating me, it may have been a better way to go than being tortured and killed by Pramis.

I take in the room again. It's round rather than square, with a large bed to my left, a wardrobe directly in front, and a narrow table to my right. There are sconces on the wall every few feet holding thick torches and candles in a candelabra on the table, but no windows. There's even art on the walls. Macabre and dark, but art nonetheless.

I've heard stories about the Shadow Realm all my life. None of them mentioned crossed-over souls getting their own richly decorated rooms. Truthfully, I thought I'd end up in Síra. I've killed too many people to expect to spend eternity anywhere else.

Kaia quickly steps forward and runs a hand down my arm, dropping it when I flinch. "You're not dead, Elora."

I shake my head. Nothing makes sense. All of this feels more like a nightmare than reality. "Then how did I get here?"

"That's what we need to find out. Will you please come back to bed before you freeze?"

I don't feel cold, but I am a little lightheaded. Too many thoughts swirl around in my head to make sense of it all. Giving Kaia a wide berth, I skirt back to the bed and climb in, yanking the covers around my chin like a shield.

Kaia turns to face me, but doesn't move any closer. "Your body resisted me when I pulled the power from your system, even though the power wasn't yours. Do you know why that would be?"

"I didn't even know such a thing was possible."

"You see it sometimes in hereditary witches. The power in their blood builds up over centuries and can act as a sort of protector against sickness and injury."

"Witches."

A laugh tickles the back of my throat, but I swallow it down. The idea that I could be a witch is more absurd than the notion that I somehow wandered into the forbidden Shadow Realm while still alive.

"Did your family belong to a coven? Larger ones might also have an effect if you're not a hereditary witch."

I shake my head. "My aunt was too devoted to the Goddess of Nightmares." I cast a sideways glance at Kaia. "No offense."

Kaia smiles and takes a step closer to the bed. "None taken. What about your parents? Did they practice?"

At the mention of my parents, tears prick my eyes. They've been dead for so long, and the years since have been so difficult, I hardly think about them anymore.

"Not that I remember." Swallowing around the lump in my throat, I lean back against the pillows, stuffing the painful memories of my past down deep. "So am I fixed now? You've got all the power out of my blood or whatever?"

"I think so. I want to give you some time to rest and heal before I check again. I'd like to take another look at your wound if that's all right with you. If I was successful in removing the latent power from your system, you'll heal much faster and cleaner now."

She stops next to the bed and gestures to the edge of the blanket. "May I?"

Begrudgingly, I lower the blanket and shift onto my side so she can tug the nightgown up over my leg and hip. The faster this wound heals, the sooner I can figure out how to get the fuck out of here. That is my only goal.

Kaia pokes gently at my stomach, her dark eyes fixated on my side. The searing pain I remember when I first woke up is replaced by a dull ache you might expect from a healing cut.

"I think we did our work well," Kaia says to the woman standing on the other side of the bed.

She lowers the nightgown and offers me a kind smile.

"Does that mean I can go?"

Her smile falters for a fraction of a second before she stands, smoothing her skirts with long, thin fingers. "We'll want to make sure you're healed up properly first. Then we can discuss what comes next."

It's not really an answer to my question, and the vagueness of it makes me uneasy.

"You are going to eventually let me go, right?"

"Of course."

But she hesitates, and I'm reminded of something my uncle used to say. How the only way to know if a god was lying was if their mouth was moving.

She sets the vial of blue liquid on the table by the bed and motions for the other woman to follow her out. I shudder when she passes in front of a torch and becomes translucent again.

"That potion will help you sleep. Sleep will help you heal."

Kaia doesn't wait for me to answer, disappearing through the door with the woman on her heels. I hear the thud of locks moments before a black cloud shimmers over the door, sealing me inside.

I have no idea how to get past a god or escape the Shadow Realm. But I do know I can't stay here. The land of the dead is no place for the living.

CHAPTER NINE

Thieran

The water runs red when I submerge my body beneath the surface. Technically, souls don't bleed. They are more a memory of their mortal shells than a physical body, but I find the addition of it makes for a more satisfying experience. And their screams helped drown out the incessant beating of that woman's heart.

Elora. Kaia must have worked her magick, because I can no longer feel the dull ache in my side where Elora's wound was. It's something else entirely now. A presence in the air and under my skin and in my consciousness I've never experienced before. I dislike it.

Steam curls away from my body in thin tendrils when I come up for air and press my back against the smooth stone. The hot springs aren't far from the palace. You can see the looming structure through the trees if you look hard enough, and Elora's tower is visible even at this distance, spearing up into the dull twilight sky.

If I hadn't blacked out the windows to keep people from asking too many questions, I'd be able to see the yellow glow of candlelight. It's just as well. I need her to remain hidden from as many people as possible until I can determine how she got here and if I want to let her out again.

Kaia won't speak of it if I ask her not to, and the soul is bound to me and my secrets, so she can't tell anyone even if she wanted to. It's everyone else I'm concerned about.

A branch snaps, followed by the soft sound of a feminine giggle, and I sigh. So much for my solace.

I wait a beat, and Nevon emerges from the trees, his arm wrapped around a petite nymph with pale blue skin and short green hair. They're both already naked, but only the nymph seems to care, squeaking in surprise and diving behind Nevon to shield herself.

Nevon chuckles, peering at her over his shoulder and giving her a wink. "Lord Thieran has seen more than one naked nymph in his time."

Pushing out of the water, I'm dry by the time my feet hit the banks. "Haven't we discussed you bringing Acarian nymphs back here?"

"These hot springs are the best on either side of the veil," Nevon counters. "For all sorts of things," he adds with a grin.

"You would know," I say, tugging on my breeches and tunic. "With as often as you use them."

The nymph pokes her head out from behind Nevon's elbow, her delicate features twisted into a frown. "What does he mean by that? How many others have you brought here?"

Nevon shoots me a pointed look, and I arch a brow. The youngest of my judges has bedded more creatures than I can even begin to count over the centuries. I'm hardly going to cover for him so he can bed another. Especially not after he's ruined my own hope for a few moments of peace.

"Hundreds," I say, and Nevon scowls.

"Hundreds?!" Her voice vibrates with anger. Her power has no effect here, but if we were on Acarian soil, no doubt the leaves on the trees would tremble.

"Hmm." I tilt my head, pretending to think. "Maybe more like thousands."

I set off for the palace, and it's not long before her angry tirade reaches my ears.

"You said I was the only one!"

Nevon replies with something to soothe her, but the words are lost to me as I shift back to my rooms and conjure a fire behind the wrought iron grate. The hiss and pop of it carries the solitude I was craving, but the faint buzzing under my skin is more insistent here than it was at the springs.

A knock echoes in the silence, and I cast my eyes to the ceiling. God's teeth, can I not have five fucking minutes to myself?

I stalk across the room and yank open the door, prepared to tell whoever it is to go the fuck away, but Garrick stands there with his hands clasped behind his back. He gives a slight bow when he sees me, the black cloak attached to his shoulders swinging gently with the movement.

Stepping back, I motion him inside and close the door, leaning back against it. It's hard to tell from the look on his face if he brings good news or bad, but it's a little early for his daily report, and that fact sets me on edge.

"Has something happened?"

"We found the forest guardian, my lord."

"And?"

"The deer population might be a little worse for wear, but it's been securely tethered to the veil again."

"Where did you find it?"

"My men found it wandering in the woods near Rhagana."

My brows shoot up before drawing together. It's quite a distance from where the tether snapped to Kaia's capital city. A long distance to cover in just under a week, even for a beast like that. A beast that would surely wreak havoc on a populated city center like the ones up north.

"And the veil? Any new breaches?" I haven't sensed any, but confirmation never hurts.

"None that I saw. In fact…"

He stares over my shoulder, his weight shifting slightly while he measures his words carefully.

"In fact?" I prompt when his silence carries on too long for my patience.

"The veil is stronger than I expected it to be when we crossed. And we were weaker on the other side than we've been in a long time."

I nod. More good news.

"If there's nothing else, my lord."

I dismiss Garrick with a wave, turning toward the fire as the door closes behind him.

Souls are no longer permitted to roam the land freely. Save for Garrick and the small band of souls cloaked with enough of my power to spend a few hours outside the realm should the need arise. Unless shielded with power, a soul that crossed the veil would whither and disappear.

It's yet to happen, but the failsafe exists nonetheless.

Just as the failsafe exists to keep mortals from crossing the veil to commit suicide or save a loved one. Mortals cannot survive here. This land is for the dead.

But that is no longer true. Because Elora is alive and well and inside my realm. The woman who seems to have traipsed across the uncrossable border hearty and hale and invading every sense.

Her foreign heartbeat kicks up in my chest, and I rub my palm over it. I don't know what to make of it, but I wish it would go the fuck away.

Another knock sounds, and I sigh. I am apparently destined for constant interruptions today.

Kaia stands on the other side of the door, her hands gripped in front of her. She looks uncharacteristically frazzled, and it sends a flurry of thoughts skipping through my head. All of them about Elora. The one thing I wish I could stop thinking about.

"What's wrong?"

Stepping around me, she crosses to the fire and drops into one of the chairs, conjuring herself a glass of wine. She takes a deep drink before she speaks.

"She's an interesting puzzle, your mortal."

My jaw clenches, and my eyes narrow. "She's not my mortal." I claim the seat opposite Kaia and conjure my own glass of wine. "What happened? Did you kill her by accident?"

I try for flippant, but even I hear the dread edging my tone.

"Not to worry. She's alive and well, but…"

"Puzzling?" I finish for her.

"Mmm," Kaia murmurs into her glass. "The healer was right. She had power clinging to her, slowing the healing process."

"That shouldn't be odd. It's what you were expecting."

"Yes." She nods. "What I wasn't expecting was the way she resisted me when I removed it. It's rare. It's…"

"Puzzling."

Kaia takes another drink of wine before setting her glass on the table with a clink. "She was unaffected by my calming power."

"You're sure?" My fingers tighten on the glass in my hand when she nods.

"It's difficult to interpret what happened any other way. She shook it off like she might an unwanted touch. Almost as though it were second nature."

I push out of my chair and pace over to the fire, setting my untouched wine on the mantel. Kaia would never force her power on anyone. It seems more plausible that the woman shied away from it and Kaia retreated. If it is indeed possible for a mortal to evade a god's power, I've never heard of it happening before.

"Do you think her time in the Shadow Realm could be the cause?"

I tilt my head at the idea. "I'm not sure. Perhaps. This is new territory for me. A mortal crossing before death."

"It would make sense. Things have felt so different recently. How long has she been here? Three days, you said?"

Her words snap steel into my spine, the realization hitting me all at once. We've not had a single breach or a whisper of power fading in days. Three days, to be exact. Not since Elora inexplicably crossed the veil into my realm.

I'm not sure what to make of it, but the timing can't be a coincidence.

Whirling for the door, I wrench it open and race down the hall. I hear Kaia struggle to match my pace until she shifts in front of me and brings me skidding to a halt.

"What are you doing?"

I brush past her and continue my way down the wide hall. The tower's entrance isn't far from my rooms. A safety measure in case someone discovered the mystery woman before I was ready.

"Thieran."

She grabs at my elbow, but I shake her off when we reach the tower's lower door.

"When did things start feeling different to you?"

Her brow creases, but it doesn't take long for the understanding to strike her too. "A few days ago. You think Elora arriving in the Shadow Realm and the change are linked?"

I climb the narrow stairs two at a time, annoyed to find Kaia waiting for me on the landing at the top.

"I think I want to find out."

"She needs rest. She's still recovering. Can't this wait a few days?"

She holds my gaze for a long beat before ultimately relenting and stepping to the side. I wave my hand in front of the door. It shimmers as the wards dissolve, and then a set of three locks thunk open.

"Mind your manners," she says before following me inside.

Elora isn't in bed as I expect to find her. Instead she's across the room, digging through the wardrobe. Gowns and cloaks and stockings and gloves strewn over the floor in her haste to find whatever it is she's searching for.

Her brown hair is twisted into a thick braid hanging down her back to her waist, and when she spins to face me, her hand goes to her thigh, making me wonder if she usually has a weapon strapped there. Her eyes are defiant, her jaw set and determined. Neither of which I should find attractive.

I have the fleeting image of her underneath me and begging for more, but I banish it because she is the exact kind of tempting distraction I cannot afford right now.

Her gaze flits from me to Kaia and back, and she turns fully to face me when I stop in the center of the room.

"Redecorating?"

"I'm looking for my things. I want to leave."

"You need rest," Kaia says from behind me, drawing Elora's gaze over my shoulder. "You still have healing to do yet."

"I'm not taking your potion. I have no idea what's in it."

Kaia sighs. "It's a healing drought with a little valerian root to help you sleep. We're not going to hurt you."

Shaking her head in disbelief, Elora crosses her arms over her chest and takes a step back, raking me with a frosty glare.

"I can't stay here. I have responsibilities. My cabin, my horse. She must be frantic."

I bark out a laugh. "It's a horse. I'm sure it's wandered off to find someone else to feed it by now."

Elora's mouth thins into a hard line. "My mistake in thinking the God of Death knows how to care for the living."

"I'll be sure your horse is seen to," Kaia promises before I can hurl back a retort.

The silence in the room grows thick, and before I can stop myself, I give in to the desire to be alone with Elora.

"Get out, Kaia."

Kaia hesitates, but ultimately her obedience is signaled by a ripple of power on the air. Elora drags wide eyes back to my face, but she doesn't retreat from me when I take a step closer.

"You can't keep me here." Her chin ticks up in a show of defiance, and I find the simple act far more enticing than I want to.

"You are mistaken, little one."

I unfurl my power by degrees. The familiar warmth of it wends slowly through my body until it fills every inch of me. Elora's eyes drop to my feet and the black smoke that curls around my legs. Her face remains neutral, but she takes a single step back. Wise.

"I am the God of Death, and this is my realm. I can do whatever the fuck I please."

Her green eyes are intent on mine, and her throat bobs when she swallows.

"What do you want from me?"

I reach out with my power and envelop her in it, propelling her forward until she is close enough to touch. But I don't. I can't. Not yet.

"How did you cross the veil?"

"I have no idea. I didn't even know it was possible until Kaia told me where I was."

"That's because it isn't possible."

"Apparently it is." Elora's chin ticks up. "Unless I really am dead and this is some kind of nightmare I can't wake up from."

The hope behind her words is so strong I can scent it on the air, and my brows draw together.

"Whatever you think I am, whatever you think I've done, you're wrong. Three days ago I was a normal woman hunting a deer for dinner. Then I woke up locked in a tower with people telling me absurd things about power in my blood and being trapped in the Shadow Realm."

She tries to move away from me, but my power holds her in place. Rage darkens her eyes to emeralds.

"Let go of me."

A smirk ghosts my lips, my eyes tracing down the column of her throat and catching on the rapid flutter of her pulse. I have to stop myself from leaning down and pressing my lips to it.

Fuck, I cannot give in to this hold she has over me.

I release her from my power so quickly she stumbles back a step, and I'm across the room before she can blink.

"Where are you going?" she demands.

"I will get to the bottom of who you are and how you crossed into my lands without my permission. Until I do, you will stay here where I can keep an eye on you."

"You said I wasn't a prisoner," she shouts.

"I said nothing of the kind. Kaia does not give orders here. My word is law."

Ignoring Elora's protests, I step out on the landing and seal the door behind me. The sooner I find out who she is and why she might have an effect on my realm, the sooner I can be rid of her. And I desperately want to be rid of her.

CHAPTER TEN

Elora

I pace the circumference of my tower room, trailing my fingertips over the smooth stone as I go. There isn't much to do holed up in this place. I haven't even been left with a book to read or parchment to write on. In the rare moments I'm not seething with anger at being held prisoner, I'm bored out of my fucking mind.

Every few hours, a tray of food materializes on the table, despite the fact I've yet to eat more than a few bites of any meal. Kaia typically appears sometime between breakfast and midday, though it's impossible to tell exactly what time of day it is without windows.

I pause between two torches and stare at the wall. Sometimes I swear I can feel a ripple on the air when I pass by certain spots in my wandering. Like maybe there should be windows where I see only solid black.

I press my hand to the stone, and it feels cooler than the area around it. But maybe that's my mind playing tricks on me. I keep hoping I'm dreaming. That I'll wake up from this nightmare and laugh about it all. I don't want any of this to be real, despite Kaia's continued insistence it is.

She should arrive soon for her daily visit. Part of me dreads it, and part of me has begun to look forward to it. She is my only source of contact, even if I refuse to engage much with her.

After she finishes imploring me to eat more than a few mouthfuls, she spends the better part of an hour asking me questions I refuse to answer until she sighs, apologizes about her lack of progress with Thieran, and leaves again.

On her first visit, she assured me Meera was being cared for by someone in Rhagana. That, at least, brings me a small measure of comfort.

It feels silly to miss a horse as much as I miss Meera, but I don't have any friends. Meera has been the only constant in my life for a long time. I move around far too often to form any sort of bond with people, and even if I didn't, trust does not come easy to me. I've been betrayed far too many times.

I've yet to meet someone who would not stab me in the back and step over my corpse in order to get what they wanted. Gods and mortals alike.

If I ever had happy memories, I can't remember them. From the time my parents were killed until I decided to take my fate into my own hands, everyone I trusted to love and protect me did exactly the opposite.

Life became much easier to survive when I began expecting the worst of people. When you already expect the worst, no one can let you down.

I hear the shuffle of feet on the stairs moments before power shimmers over the door and the locks give way. Kaia knocks before she enters with a hopeful smile on her face.

"You look well today," she says. It's the same thing she's said every day for the last three. "Have you eaten?"

Her eyes travel to the untouched tray on the table, and she frowns. I've disappointed her. Again. But she can ask her question a million different times, a million different ways. I'm not interested in becoming complacent here while she and the God of Death hold my life in their hands.

Despite Kaia's reassurance that I am, in fact, not a prisoner, I haven't been allowed out of this tower since waking, and whenever I ask when I will be permitted to leave, she refuses to meet my eyes.

With each passing moment, it becomes easier to believe this is all some nightmarish delusion the God of Death has concocted to punish me for all eternity. My torturous penance for killing so many people over the last decade.

"I thought we might try something different today."

I cock my head and arch a brow, but I don't move, leaving the bed as a barrier between us.

"We've spent so much time discussing power and potions and things. Perhaps we could instead just talk about you." She waits for me to speak, but I leave her to the silence. "You could tell me about your life before you arrived in Rhagana."

She crosses to the table and pulls out a chair, lowering herself into it with an effortless grace. Her dress—a mesmerizing midnight blue—ripples and settles around her legs. Back straight as steel, she folds her hands gently in her lap and looks up at me with an encouraging smile.

"Please, sit."

She glances at a chair, which pulls away from the table without a touch. The sight of it moving on its own makes me uneasy, and I take a step back, crossing my arms over my chest.

"My apologies." Kaia sighs. "You'll get used to it eventually."

That's just it. I don't want to get used to any of this. I want to get out of here. But I've spent the better part of three days searching for a way past the power shimmering over the door or even looking for a way to pick the locks. There's nothing.

They won't even give me back the things I arrived with. My clothes are probably ruined, but my dagger is priceless to me. It was the first thing I purchased after my first kill. Ogeinian steel is the best in Acaria, and the blacksmiths in the God of Fire's territory are unmatched in skill.

That dagger cost everything I had at the time. I didn't eat anything but scraps for nearly a week after. But it reminds me every day that I am responsible for carving out my own fate. Literally, in many cases. And I want it back.

"Do you have any brothers or sisters?"

Kaia's soft question pulls me out of my thoughts, and I blink. I'd almost forgotten she was there. But I have no desire to dredge up my past. I'd rather it stay buried where it belongs.

"What about your parents? Are they still in Dremen?"

The question makes me flinch, but I fix my face into a neutral mask before she can read my expression. Technically my parents are still in Dremen. But I want to leave their memories in the ground with them.

"You do realize what a complete waste of time this is, don't you?"

With a huff, Kaia brushes an invisible piece of lint from her skirts and shifts in her seat. "It wouldn't be a waste of time if you at least made an effort."

"I've already told you. I have no answers to help solve your riddle."

She pins me with an exasperated look. "How do you know if you don't try?"

"I don't know why I was able to cross the veil any more than you do."

Kaia rubs her forehead. "Elora, you might know something helpful and not realize it. I don't understand why you're being so difficult."

I force out a rough laugh. "Really? You don't know why a mortal being held prisoner in the Shadow Realm wouldn't want to help the gods keeping her locked in a tower? I knew you people were self-centered, but I didn't think you were out of touch entirely."

Eyes darkening and shoulders squaring, Kaia's voice is stern when she speaks again. "I'm not holding you prisoner. I'm only—"

"Following orders. I know. That doesn't make it better."

"I'm only trying to help," she finishes, tone softening. "Have you ever considered it might not be safe for you to leave again?"

"You're saying I'm trapped here?"

An icy chill unfurls down my spine. The possibility I might not be able to leave, even if they were willing to let me go, is a heavy one. I'd be dead without actually dying.

"I'm saying I don't know. We've never had a mortal wander into the realm before. I don't want you to get hurt."

Seemingly giving up on trying to convince me, she pushes out of the chair and turns for the door, pausing with her hand on the knob to look back over her shoulder.

"Is there anything else I can get for you?" She gestures to the tray. "Something from the kitchens you might actually eat?"

"All I want is my freedom."

"I'm working on that." She says it with such conviction I have a hard time believing it's a lie. "Anything else?"

"A book or two would be nice." Surprise lights her face, and I gesture around the room. "Not much else to do in here, in case you haven't noticed."

She nods once, closing the door behind her. There's a pause before the locks snick back into place and the power shimmers over the wood. Like I have every day for three days, I cross the room and grip the handle, wriggling it until the power warms my palm and travels up my arm to my shoulder.

I have the faint sense that if I tried hard enough, I could push through the power shimmering over the door and locking me in this tower, but I banish the absurd notion. I might be stuck in the land of the dead, but that doesn't mean I actually want to die.

Turning, I resume pacing the perimeter of the room, stopping short next to the tray. I lift the cover on the plate, and the smell of sausage and potatoes floats into the air, making my stomach rumble in protest.

It's still hot even though it's been sitting here for hours, steam curling into the air. I reach for the spoon before stopping myself. I'm torn between wanting to sate this gnawing hunger in my belly and the worry of ingesting whatever they may have put in the food.

They're keeping me prisoner. They hardly deserve my complacency too. Slamming the lid down on the tray, I stalk across the room and bury my face in my pillow to rid my nose of the scents still making my mouth water.

It worked when I was a child. After my parents died and I was sent to live with my father's brother, who delighted in sending me to bed without food, knowing the smell of it would carry to my sleeping loft.

My life might have turned out differently if my parents hadn't been killed on our way back from trading. I might have grown up a well-loved farmer's daughter with a doting mother and father. I might have married a man who looked at me the way I always remembered my father looking at my mother. Like she hung the moon and the stars.

I like to think my parents loved me just as much as they loved each other, but my memories of them are few and far between. It's my uncle who dominates my childhood. The man who raised me with his leather strap, resentful of being tasked with my care, until he finally decided to get rid of me.

These memories of my past and where I come from were laid to rest a long time ago. Resurrecting them is more painful than I would have anticipated. I want nothing more than to put it all in a box and forget it ever existed. But that seems unlikely.

Instead I'm stuck here at the mercy of a god who, at worst, seems to think I'm capable of something I'm not, and at best, doesn't care if I languish here for an eternity. I would give anything to escape the Shadow Realm unscathed and get back to my life.

But even assuming Kaia really is trying to talk Thieran into letting me out of here, making sure it's safe for me to leave this place and never look back, I'm under no illusions he'll actually listen. The God of Death isn't exactly known for his mercy toward the living.

Which is why I might need to take a different approach. If I can stumble into the Shadow Realm, surely I can stumble out again.

The key is getting out of this fucking room so I can figure out how to do just that. Even if that means playing nice with the God of Death.

CHAPTER ELEVEN

Thieran

I trail my fingertip over the spines of the leather-bound books lining this particular shelf until I find the one I want. Plucking it from the stack, I carry it back to a table already laden with books and flip to the page on wards and cloaking rituals.

A quick scan tells me this text does not have the information I'm after, but I settle in to read it anyway in case there's a clue to where I could look next. My research on how a mortal might have crossed the veil would go much faster if I could access the library in Fontoss. It's the most comprehensive library in Acaria, with perfectly preserved books dating back as far as the written word.

Better yet, I could use access to the Fates who maintain it. It's said the Fates are older than the gods. Created from the darkness and the light. The past, the present, and the future in human form. They know the destiny of every being in this land, mortal or immortal. They hold the entire history of our existence between them.

But the last thing I need is to run into my brother and have him ask too many questions. The only reason I enter Acaria's capital city is to attend the high court functions where I'm required to make an appearance. And since the winter ball isn't for another several weeks and the memorial banquet takes place in the spring, my presence there would draw notice.

I hardly want anyone to know I'm searching for answers on the power sustaining the realm and why the veil seems to be thinning enough for a mortal to cross without dying. Or, more to the point, for a mortal to stop the power from leaking out.

She's been here nearly a week, and still, everything seems to be holding. There aren't any new breaches, and the boundaries between each territory inside the realm are stronger than they've been in years.

But beyond that, I feel an unmistakable change. I can't explain it, but it's this feeling buzzing under my skin. Something I haven't felt in so long that I forgot it ever existed.

Tossing the book on top of the map and pieces of parchment spread out over the long table, I grunt in frustration. This passage is as useless as all the rest.

According to everything I've been able to find, what has happened should not be possible. I should not have a living, breathing mortal woman barricaded in my tower.

The door creaks open and Kaia enters, her footsteps echoing into the soaring ceilings. She falters when she sees me, irritation and anger evident on her face. I expect her to veer off into the shelves to get whatever she came for, but she makes her way to me instead.

"Any progress?" She indicates the pile of books in front of me.

"Not yet." I scrub a hand over my face and shove it through my hair. "I'm sure I'd find something in Fontoss."

She blinks curious eyes, tilting her head to study me. "You're going to Fontoss to search?"

"Of course not." I wave away the suggestion. "Much too

risky. But if there are answers to be found, that's where I'd find them."

"And if there aren't answers to be found?"

"Then the Shadow Realm is dying."

And I am dying with it.

The color drains from Kaia's face, her fingers worrying the edge of the map closest to her.

"There has to be another explanation," she says, voice tight. "Something you're not seeing."

I sweep my arm over the table, gesturing to the precarious stacks of books I've been scouring for days.

"Do enlighten me."

"The incantations, the rituals used to create the realm and the veil, the binding spells used to seal the living out and the dead in." She picks up the book closest to her and flips through it. "They were permanent."

"Apparently they weren't."

Kaia is silent for a long moment, staring at the book in her palm with unfocused eyes. "And what of Elora in all this?"

At the mere mention of Elora's name, the slow, steady thump of her heartbeat in my chest becomes more prominent. It's much easier to ignore when I'm distracted.

"What of her?"

"You can't keep her up there forever, Thieran."

Sighing, I push back from the table and cross to the floor-to-ceiling window between bookcases. Smooth stone gives way to jagged rock and then waist-high grass stretching as far as the eye can see. It sways in a gentle breeze.

"I know you don't approve of how I'm handling this, but—"

"Oh, good," she says. "I was afraid I was being too subtle."

I bark out a wry laugh. "You can't honestly say you haven't noticed things feel different since her arrival. That whatever is happening to the realm has slowed, if not stopped, in the days since I plucked her from the riverbank."

I hear her draw in a slow, deep breath. "You're right," she agrees, albeit reluctantly. "Things have felt much different—stronger—than they have in years. So what are you planning to do? Keep her here forever?"

Again I'm forced to notice Elora's heart beating in time with my own, and I do my best to shove the sensation away. At present, I have no other choice. I'd much rather be rid of her, but if my choices are to sacrifice the Shadow Realm or harbor a mortal I want nothing to do with, I'll choose the latter every time.

"If that's what it takes."

"You could at least let her out of the tower."

"But not out of the realm?" I turn to stare at Kaia, brow raised. "You're advocating keeping her prisoner?"

Kaia averts her eyes. "I know as well as you do what the world was like before the Shadow Realm was created, before you ruled the dead behind the veil." Wrapping her arms around herself, she squeezes. "There are many things I would do to keep that from happening again."

There's nothing I wouldn't do to save the Shadow Realm—and myself with it. Even if it means giving a mortal woman her own rooms in my palace. If I have to keep her here until I either find out what's causing the weakening and stop it or find another solution, I suppose the least I can do is give her a bit more freedom.

"Why don't you spend more than thirty seconds in her presence?" Kaia says before I can speak. "Then you might see things as I do. Talk to her, Thieran." A stack of books materializes in her hands, and she holds them out to me. "Bring these as a peace offering."

I read the titles on the spines and raise a brow. "Novels?"

"You've got her caged in there like an animal. She's bored."

Before I think better of it, I tuck the books under my arm

and shift to the landing outside her room, dismissing the wards and locks before pushing through.

She yelps, spinning to face the door with a knife in her hand. She relaxes when she sees me, but not by much. Amused, I set the books Kaia gave me on the little table by her bed. She'll need a lot more than the knife on her breakfast tray to get past me.

The door closes behind me with a wave of my hand, and she steps back when I move further into the room.

"That won't do much for you." I nod to the knife still clutched in her grip. "If your goal is to kill me."

She flips the blade deftly through her fingers but doesn't set it down. "Not kill, catch off guard. What are you doing here?"

"I'm visiting my charge," I say, irritated by her tone. "Lady Kaia visits."

"Kaia knocks."

"Lady Kaia does not rule this realm." I grip my hands behind my back. "I do."

Elora snorts. "What does ruling a realm have to do with manners? Although, considering how you've trapped me here and refuse to let me go, I gather manners are not your strong suit."

"Careful, little one."

She scowls, and the knife twists through her fingers again. "What do you want?"

Her question is cold, dismissive, and I take another step forward. "I have some things I'd like to ask you." I pull out one of the chairs at the table with a flick of my wrist. "Sit down."

Glancing at it, she shakes her head. "I'd rather stand."

I briefly consider forcing her into the damn thing but think better of it. She's more likely to answer my questions if I'm civil about it. And I want to size her up before I make my decision.

"Where were you born?"

"Dremen."

"And is your mother a witch?" It's Kaia's theory, not mine, but I want to see Elora's reaction to it all the same.

She jerks at the question. "My mother was a farmer's wife, not a witch."

The two aren't necessarily mutually exclusive, but her use of the past tense does not escape my notice. "Was?"

Shifting on her feet, Elora breaks eye contact, staring at a distant point over my shoulder. "She died many years ago."

The pain in her voice is genuine, and the next words out of my mouth surprise even me. "I'm sorry for your loss."

Her spine straightens and her gaze snaps to mine. "It was a long time ago."

"And you have no idea how you were able to cross the veil?"

"No," she says, exasperated. "I've told Kaia this already. If I did know, I'd have gone right back out again."

"And you think you can?" I step closer, lips twitching in a barely contained grin when her back hits the stone wall behind her as she tries to flee from me. "What if you're trapped here forever?"

Her throat bobs when she swallows.

"How old are you?"

"Eight and twenty. Is there a point to these questions? Or are you just bored today?"

"Such a mouth on you, little one. You'll want to take care not to try my patience."

"I'll take my chances. My lord."

She sneers the last two words, barely flinching when I close the distance between us and cage her against the wall.

"It would be unwise to forget you are a trespasser in my realm. And your punishment is in my hands." I brace them both on the wall beside her head.

"I'm a prisoner here, not a trespasser."

"You crossed my border uninvited."

Her chin lifts, breath warm against my cheek. "And have

remained locked in this tower for six days. It would appear I am already being punished."

I drop my head, my lips brushing the shell of her ear and raising goosebumps along her cheek and down her neck. "Believe me, little one. When I punish you, you'll know."

Taking a few steps back, I give her a minute to regain her composure before I ask the one question that's been hovering at the back of my mind for days. "Did someone send you across the veil?"

Of all the reactions I might have expected, her laughter isn't one of them. It rolls out of her, low and deceptively sweet. It's a stark contrast to her sharp tongue and quick wit. The sound of it has me moving closer again.

"Is that really what you think? That I'm a spy? A spy for who, exactly?"

"The high court has been—"

She laughs again, her cheeks going pink with it as she clutches her stomach and doubles over. Irritation prickles over my skin.

"You think I'm a spy for the high court?" she asks, wiping tears from her eyes.

"Stranger things have been known to happen," I say through gritted teeth.

She dismisses my words with a wave of her hand. "I have no interest in helping the gods do anything. Not them, and definitely not you. The closest I've ever been to a high court god was when..."

The words die on her tongue, and she sucks her bottom lip between her teeth. But I desperately want her to finish that story.

"Go on."

"Let's just say I had a little run-in with a high priest."

The priest who tried to bargain for his fate swims across my vision. I scanned through his deeds only briefly, but I don't recall seeing her face among his victims. She doesn't strike me as the kind of woman who would get on her knees for a favor from a god. But I've been wrong about women and their motives before.

"Interesting."

Her eyes narrow, and she cocks her head. "What's interesting?"

I shrug. "That you would seek a favor from a god. And that you would spread your legs for it."

She springs forward, gripping my arm and spinning us both until my back is pressed against the wall. I could overpower her if I had a mind to, but I'm intrigued by this turn of events, so I let her have the upper hand. For now.

Anger lights her eyes, and she presses the blade of the knife against my throat.

"I do not seek favors from gods," she snarls. "Or the rapists they choose to represent them."

"No?"

I smirk down at her, and she increases the pressure on the blade until she breaks my skin. Her eyes drop to my throat and follow the trail of blood dripping from where the knife point makes contact.

This close, her scent assails me. A hint of lavender, no doubt from one of Kaia's soaps, but something else. Something uniquely her. It's intoxicating in the worst way.

"So your encounter with the priest was what?" I ask, drawing her bright green eyes to mine again. "A friendly chat?"

"I'm the one who killed him."

I can tell by the look on her face that she expects her confession to surprise me. But imagining her with a blade in her hand in a similar position to the one we're in now makes far more sense than picturing her on her knees begging for mercy.

"A lucky blow, I'm sure."

Her eyes darken, and just like the other day, I'm tempted to yank her against me and claim her mouth, to trail my lips over every inch of her skin until she's begging me for more. I think I might like to hear Elora beg. But I'll tuck that away for another time.

"I haven't landed a lucky blow since the day I vowed never to be a victim again."

"Until today."

Anticipating her before she can shove the blade further, I wrap my fingers around her wrist and pivot, slamming her body against the wall. I apply pressure to her wrist, and the knife clatters to the ground.

She struggles against my hold, but I keep her firmly pinned, hands on her wrists.

"You are nothing against me," I remind her, and she goes still.

"I am not nothing." Every word is laced with venom, and her body tenses.

"What are you going to do, little one?" She struggles against me, and I tighten my grip just enough to have her go still again. "You can't kill the God of Death."

"But it might be fun to try."

I chuckle. "I may actually enjoy that. I imagine you would be fun to spar with."

"Was there anything else you wanted to ask me? My lord."

I hate the way she sneers my title. I've never particularly cared for it, but she hurls it like an insult with razor-sharp barbs. Dropping her wrists, I put distance between us.

I'm damn well ready to be rid of her, but the fact of the matter is until I discover another solution, I need her right now. The truth of it sticks in my throat.

I don't love the idea of giving her free rein over the palace. She's liable to sneak into my rooms in the middle of the night and slit my throat just to watch me bleed out and knit myself back together. But the more comfortable she becomes, the more

I'm able to study her, and the easier it may be to understand her effect on the realm. And that is knowledge I can't do without.

"I've decided to let you out."

"You're letting me go? Back to Rhagana?" The hope in her voice almost makes me regret my next words. Almost.

"No. I'm releasing you from the tower. Lady Kaia will be back shortly to show you to your rooms."

When I turn for the door, she matches my pace, slapping her hand against it when I reach for the knob.

"You cannot keep me in the Shadow Realm indefinitely. You have to let me go sometime."

I flash her a grin that has her taking a step back. "Are you sure about that?"

Disappearing through the door, I wave my protections back in place and shift to where I sense Kaia's presence. She doesn't look all that surprised to see me, but her eyes widen with my next words.

"You can give her rooms close to yours." As far away from me as I can manage without putting her in the nearby village.

"You're actually going to give her rooms?" Kaia asks. "And you want me to do it?"

"She likes you. Or at least she tolerates you more than me."

And I need a plan to get more information from her to solve my little problem before I lay eyes on her again.

"All right." Kaia smoothes her skirts, a small smile lifting the corner of her mouth. "I'll ask the servants to prepare the rooms next to mine."

I nod and turn to go.

"Thieran. This is a good thing you're doing. This is the right thing. You won't regret it."

I nod before shifting to my study and conjuring a glass of liquor. Throwing it back in one swallow, I hiss as it burns a trail down my throat. I've already begun to regret it. But it's too late now. The only way through this mess is forward.

CHAPTER TWELVE

Elora

U nable to sit still long enough to get lost in one of the books Thieran delivered, I pace the width of my room. I'm not sure how long it's been since he disappeared, but long enough that this tingling sensation where he touched me should have subsided.

That foreign humming sensation in my veins that's been present since I woke here has only gotten louder, more insistent. It's fucking distracting. And I can't afford to be distracted now.

He said he was letting me out of here. Maybe not out of the Shadow Realm, but out of this tower. And with that freedom, I can find my own way out. All I need is the time and the space to find my way back to Rhagana.

Once I'm free, I'll take Meera and ride far away from the forest's edge, as far north as I dare, before sheltering again. I need distance from the God of Death, and whatever plans he has for me he isn't sharing, but there's still the sun god to worry about. I imagine Pramis is busy looking for his priest's murderer.

But I've been in bad spots before. Being trapped in the land of the dead might keep me safe from Pramis's wrath, but it's hardly a life I want to live.

A knock startles me, even though I know Kaia is coming for me, and I spin toward the sound just as she enters, a bright, cheerful smile on her face. I try to match her easy grin because I need them both to trust me enough to let me roam freely, but it feels foreign on my face.

"Come with me."

She turns and disappears in a swirl of skirts. I hesitate, unsure if this is some kind of trick rather than reality. I wouldn't exactly put it past Thieran to amuse himself by fooling me into thinking I'm free when I'm not.

When she doesn't return, I advance slowly toward the door, toeing the threshold and then edging my way onto a narrow landing. I wait to be zapped or flung back into the room or whatever other awful tricks the God of Death might devise against escape.

"Elora?" Kaia's voice echoes up the stairwell.

Surprisingly, nothing terrible happens to me for crossing the locks and wards, so I follow the winding stairs to find Kaia at the bottom. Her smile widens when she sees me, and she gestures for me to follow.

"Where are we going?"

"To your rooms." She all but sings the words, her voice brimming with something that sounds like triumph.

"Rooms." I peer behind me at the tower we've just left. "So I'm really being let out of there?"

Kaia waves a dismissive hand. "That wasn't a room. It was a prison cell. I have the servants preparing a set of rooms down the hall from my own. It's a nice, private part of the palace with a pretty view of the forest."

I barely manage to swallow a snort. Nothing about that forest is pretty, not now that I know what lurks within it. And with the dull light streaming through the windows, I can't imagine the rest of the Shadow Realm is all that exciting.

As we make our way down the hall, a familiar smell hits me. Cedar and cinnamon and woodsmoke. It's a scent that clings to Thieran and invades my dreams, and it gets stronger the closer we draw to an ornately carved door at the end of the hall.

A heady pulse flutters behind my sternum, seductive and captivating, but I shake it off. That's a new feeling too. Along with Thieran's touch came the unmistakable sensation of something else. Something that belongs to me but doesn't at the same time.

I thought it to be another way Thieran was trying to intimidate me, another show of power. But it pulses stronger the closer we draw to what I'm sure are Thieran's rooms, and now I wonder if it's something else entirely. Is it possible for Thieran to have marked me in some way when he pinned my wrists to the wall?

It would explain why I can't stop feeling his touch on my skin or why the sensation of something calling to me won't go away. I rub my fingers over my wrists where his skin came in contact with mine, and it heats under my fingers.

Annoyed with it, I yank the edges of my tunic down over my hands and cross my arms over my chest. It doesn't matter what it means or why he seems to have this strange power over me. As soon as I figure out the way back to Rhagana for my horse and my things, I'll be rid of him.

And the next time I step into the Shadow Realm, I hope to be dead.

"You'll have free range of the palace for as long as you're here, of course," Kaia says, leading me down a wide staircase covered in thick carpet.

"Generous of him to let a prisoner wander around without a guard."

Kaia huffs, her heels clicking when the carpet gives way to

black obsidian floors polished to a reflective shine. "You're not a prisoner, Elora. You're a guest." She falters on the last word, but I don't bother arguing with her.

I'm allowed out of the tower, but I haven't been permitted to leave the realm altogether. He might have agreed to set me up in a nicer suite of rooms and let me wander around, but he isn't walking me to the veil and ushering me through. Or, better yet, delivering me back to Acaria himself.

What does that make me, if not a prisoner?

"Are you the only other god who lives here?" I ask, jogging to catch up.

"Most of the dark court gods spend time in their own territories in Acaria. I prefer the solitude and the quiet of the Shadow Realm. As much as I love my people, I thrive in the dark."

As do most members of Thieran's dark court, according to the stories. The courts were decided centuries ago when the gods formed a treaty after the great war. One court to rule the light and one to rule the dark, with a king at the head of each.

"You have nothing to fear from any of them. They're loyal to Lord Thieran."

Her smile is quick and sincere, but it doesn't soothe my worries. It sparks new ones. Thieran asked me if I was a spy for the high court, and now Kaia makes it sound as if the King of the Gods might consider me a threat if he knew I'd been able to cross the veil.

The thought makes me shiver. The last thing I want to be is a target of the king.

"You're safe here, Elora. You'll have private rooms, space to explore, and whatever else you desire. You have only to ask."

We pass a series of open doors, their contents lit both by the same torches that rimmed my tower room. Wide windows look out on the endless gray of the Shadow Realm. The last door reveals what appears to be a throne room, an imposing black throne sitting at the far end of the long room.

It sits alone without a mate. The God of Death and King of Shadows has no queen.

"So I can go anywhere I want?"

"Within reason, yes. You wouldn't be able to visit somewhere like Síra, of course. There's nothing there you need to see anyway."

I bite back a chuckle. I imagine the Goddess of Witchcraft has no idea how many men I've sent to Síra. It's probably the place I'd be most comfortable, surrounded by the screams and blood of the tortured. Just like the forest, her warning about Síra only makes me want to visit it more.

Stopping at the base of another wide staircase, she turns left, gesturing at doors as we pass. "If a door is open, you are permitted to use the room."

"I thought I could go anywhere I wanted?"

"You can," she assures me, leading me past a large painting of a three-headed dog standing over a figure shrouded in black smoke. "But this is Lord Thieran's palace and his rooms and his rules. Don't worry. There are plenty of places for you to explore."

A wide, tall window takes up most of the wall at the end of this hallway, and I get my first good glimpse of the Shadow Realm. It's nothing like I expected it to be, nothing like the stories I heard as a child growing up.

I expected mangled, twisted trees covering a scarred landscape. The stories my uncle told were full of fear and fire and smoke so thick you would choke on it. But this is nothing like that.

There's no color here. Everything exists in shades of gray. But the terrain isn't all that dissimilar from Acaria. Hills slope gently away from the palace, stretching across the land to a forest of blackened, barren trees.

The grass is tall, swaying in a gentle breeze, and a large path curves through it. Wide enough for a horse and carriage—if such a thing exists in the Shadow Realm.

Everything about this place continues to surprise me.

"You have a similar view from your room." Kaia stands at my elbow, and I can sense her watching me carefully. When I don't speak, she nods at the window. "Videva isn't far. That road leads from the kitchens to the village. If you ever wanted to explore there and introduce yourself."

"A village full of dead people?" The vision of a town made up entirely of translucent mortals sends a shiver through me.

"Of souls, yes. Many of them work in the palace. Only souls from Videva are eligible to serve at court."

"Lucky them," I mutter, but Kaia ignores me. "What do they do when they're not serving?"

"Most of them choose to occupy themselves with mortal pursuits."

I turn to her, eyebrows raised. "They die just to continue their work in the afterlife?"

"Eternity is a long time, Elora. They make goods and trade them with each other or with Lord Thieran."

"In exchange for favors?" I wonder what the God of Death asks from his souls.

"Sometimes."

She doesn't elaborate, moving away from the window and stopping before a large set of double doors thrown open to reveal an impressive dining room. The black marble table with space for at least two dozen gleams in the firelight, and the high-backed chairs give the room a regal feel.

"You've only to come here and ask and food will be provided to you. Whatever you wish."

"And if I wish to eat in my rooms?"

She sighs. "Whatever you wish, you have only to ask. Come, I'll show you to your rooms and let you settle in."

We retrace our steps to the wide staircase and follow it up, curving down yet another long hallway. The longer we walk, the more I wonder if they're tucking me somewhere so far away I can't find my way out again.

"These rooms are mine," she says, indicating a door as we near the end of the hall. "You are welcome to visit anytime. And these"—she stops in front of a door carved with vines, and my fingers itch to touch them—"are yours."

I give in to temptation and trace my fingertip gently over the swooping, swirling pattern before turning the knob and pushing the door in. Before I can stop it, a small gasp escapes my lips. I thought my tower room was big, but I was mistaken. Two of them could easily fit inside this one, and it's only a sitting room.

A long, deep brocade couch faces away from the door, with two matching chairs sitting opposite. Black curtains frame floor-to-ceiling windows with the view Kaia described, and from this vantage point, I can see the shape of roofs in the distance, smoke curling up from chimneys in thin wisps.

A fire already burns in a stone fireplace big enough for a grown man to stand in, and candles spear out of elaborate silver candelabras on the tables. An ornate chandelier hangs from the ceiling over the seating area. Its candles are unlit, but I can picture them casting colorful prisms against the walls.

Everything is decorated in shades of black, from the polished obsidian floors to the heavy brocade curtains to the tapestries stitched with a pattern of vines and leaves similar to the one on the doors. Despite the lack of color, it feels homier than I would have anticipated.

Kaia crosses the room and opens the double doors beside the fireplace, revealing a bedroom and a bed big enough for three grown people to sleep in without touching. I can't imagine needing so much space simply to sleep, but I cannot wait to sink into the softness.

I've never known such luxury, and though I hope to only be here a few days—less if I can manage it—I might as well enjoy it before I set off on my own again.

The fireplace in this room mirrors the one from the sitting room, hand-carved with ropes of thick vines and flowers I don't recognize.

"Do you like it?"

"I...It's very beautiful," I say, catching myself before admitting I love anything about the Shadow Realm. This is nothing but a nicer prison cell, whatever Kaia wants to believe about it.

"Did you eat any of your breakfast after I left?"

I shake my head. Even if I'd wanted to, Thieran didn't give me much of an opportunity.

"They'll send the midday meal soon."

As if on cue, there's the faint sound of a tinkling bell, and then the same tray that's materialized in the tower room three times a day for the last three days appears on the corner of the bed. I stare at it with wide eyes.

"The power that delivers the tray is tied to you," Kaia says, as if that's the only explanation I need.

"So if I'm wandering the grounds at mealtimes, a tray will just randomly appear next to me?"

Tongue tucked in her cheek, Kaia bites back a smile. "That would be a fun experiment, I think. Hopefully, you'll cease your hunger strike and the answer to that question won't be necessary."

My eyes drift to the tray on the edge of the bed.

"There's nothing...in it?"

"You think we'd poison you?"

Her voice is incredulous, maybe a little insulted. But I square my shoulders against it. The gods have always been capable of far worse.

"Drugging someone doesn't seem like that big a leap from kidnapping."

Kaia sighs, her mouth pressing into a thin line. "I'd love for you to have dinner with me tonight. Then you can see you have nothing to fear from what we feed you."

The mere idea of food, coupled with the smells drifting from the tray, has my mouth watering. If I don't start eating again soon, I likely won't be able to make it out of the palace, let alone all the way back to Rhagana on foot.

"All right."

"Wonderful. Dinner is served in the dining room at eight. I'll see you this evening."

"Wait," I call when she turns to go. "Do you know where my things are? The clothes I was wearing when I was brought here?"

Kaia hesitates. She's not stupid. I'm sure she knows I arrived with weapons. Or she can at least guess. But without a word, she gestures toward the bed, and a fabric-wrapped bundle appears beside the tray.

"You're safe here," she says again, catching my eye with a meaningful stare.

"Thank you."

She doesn't walk through the door as I expect her to, instead disappearing from view with a shimmer on the air. I blink at the empty space where she stood before deliberately turning from it and crossing to the bed.

Untying the smooth leather tie on the bundle, I pull back the fabric to reveal my clothes, the ones I arrived in, laundered, mended, and folded neatly. Beside them is my dagger, tucked into its sheath.

I waste no time strapping it around my thigh. The weight of it instantly makes me feel more myself. A welcome feeling after so many days of being so hopelessly out of my depth.

But I have a plan to remedy that as quickly as possible. As soon as I can find my way back to Rhagana, I'll disappear. Then I hope never to see the Shadow Realm or its king ever again.

CHAPTER THIRTEEN

Thieran

Crouching beside the River Loret, I scoop a handful of dirt from its banks and let it cascade through my fingers in a steady stream. The breeze carries it away from me, but even so, I feel the power pulsing through it.

This is how the realm used to feel whenever I soothed it with my blood. Like a flower with its bloom twisted toward the sun, soaking up the light. I cannot account for the change. Not in a way that makes sense to me.

It seems too good to be true that the mere presence of a mortal woman would have such an effect, yet the proof is all around me. In the beat of the wind and the timbre of the swaying branches and the thrum of power pulsing in my veins.

I've searched book after book, scroll after ancient scroll, only to come away without answers again and again.

Pushing to my feet, I survey the horizon. I should be happy the solution is such an easy one after so long without answers. But I only feel dread where there should be peace. It seems too simple to last.

But my skepticism cannot dim the effects she's having, and I'm not the only one who's noticed. Hayle mentioned a change in the air only yesterday, and all the boundaries in the realm are holding fast.

It's good I've given this woman rooms. It appears she may be with us indefinitely. The idea makes my lip curl. I'd rather be rid of her completely, what with the way her scent clings to the air long after she's left a room and washes over me when I least expect it.

And if it's not her scent or the sight of her through a window or around the corner of a passage, it's Kaia going on incessantly about whether Elora is comfortable or lonely or adjusting or if we really can keep her here forever.

As of right now, we have no other choice. Until I can uncover a better way to maintain the stability of the Shadow Realm, Elora stays. However much I might wish to never see her or smell her or think about her ever again.

The idea that I'm at her mercy as much as she's at mine irritates me, and I shift back to my rooms with a scowl on my face. The last thing I ever want to be is at the mercy of another, let alone a mortal woman. One who, I imagine, has spent most of her time since being released trying to figure out how to escape.

Not that she could. I've warded the palace grounds so she can't wander beyond them without an escort. I've no idea if she can cross the veil and make it back to Rhagana or what will happen to my realm if she does. Until those questions have answers, she doesn't go anywhere unless accompanied by a member of my court.

A knock echoes as I pull on fresh robes, adjusting the collar and sleeves.

"Come."

The door swings in on Railan's broad frame, and he leans his shoulder casually against it as he takes my measure. Railan's skill at reading people and their intentions makes him an excellent judge. In every other instance, it serves only to irritate me.

"What do you want?"

He lifts a brow, taking a step back as I move toward the door and then matching my pace down the hall.

"I thought I sensed you were grumpier than usual."

I snort. "And is that all you wanted? To point out what a bad mood I'm in?"

"You don't need me to point that out to you." He grins, white teeth flashing against dark skin, and I roll my eyes. "I was coming to tell you we just welcomed a new batch of souls."

I stop short. Punishing unredeemables would be the perfect distraction to my little mortal problem. But Railan anticipates my question.

"No one bound for Síra in this group, but we did send quite a few to Irios."

"Traumatic end?"

Railan's eyes go soft and he nods. "Fire. They were trapped."

"Sounds like the healing fields are exactly what they need, then."

"Indeed. Only a few wanted to drink from the Grense, so I imagine they'll be there a good long while."

We continue to walk in silence toward the dining room, but I can sense there's something else on his mind.

"Spit it out, Railan."

"I saw the most curious thing this morning." He pauses for what I can only assume is dramatic effect. "A mortal woman wandering the palace grounds. A live one."

I purse my lips as we descend the stairs toward the dining room. I'm not trying to keep Elora a secret anymore. If I wanted her hidden, she'd still be in the tower room. But I haven't exactly heralded her presence either.

"Yes," I reply. "I imagine you did."

"Is that it? No other details you want to share? Like how exactly a mortal woman crossed the veil?"

"I have no idea how. But her presence here is a necessity." For now.

Reading my meaning, Railan stops short, then catches up with long strides. "You think she's responsible for the change in the realm? For the reason the veil stopped weakening?"

"It didn't simply stop weakening. It's gotten stronger. And yes. I think she's responsible, even though I don't know how or why."

"So you're keeping her here."

It isn't a question, and I cast a sideways glance at Railan in an attempt to gauge his opinion on the matter. His face gives nothing away.

"I have little choice until I can figure out another solution."

He nods, brow furrowed. "What do you know of her?"

"Born in Dremen, parents are dead, not quite thirty." I tick the scant few things I know about her off on my fingers. "Stubborn, reckless. Irritating."

"Interesting," Railan murmurs, but I ignore the implication in his tone.

"She isn't interesting. She's a necessity."

"And when she's not a necessity?"

"I'll release her back into Acaria to live what I hope is a long life far away from me."

"I'm sure you will."

He doesn't sound at all convinced, but I don't have time to reason out his meaning, the sound of voices reaching my ears as we round the last turn for the dining room.

First a woman's voice, Kaia by the pitch of it, and then a deeper one that sounds vaguely like Railan. The man says something low and deep, and it's followed by a feminine voice I recognize all too well. I sigh.

"If you'd told me about her, I could have steered Nevon away from her. He'd enjoy a mortal to flirt with. And more."

The idea of Nevon touching Elora stops me dead in my tracks, forcing me to stamp down an immediate rush of jealousy. No. I shake the thought from my head. Not jealousy. It can't be. It's a useless emotion, and certainly not worth wasting on a mortal's attention.

Pausing at the threshold, I survey the scene. Kaia is in her normal seat near the head of the table. She's in a gown the color of plums, her hair swept off her face to cascade down her neck.

Elora is seated across from her. Not in a gown, though I made sure to instruct the servants to have some put in her wardrobe, but in a pair of black breeches and a white tunic, a black corset fitted over top. Her rich brown hair is twisted in a thick braid, and I have the briefest vision of wrapping it around my hand, yanking her head back to expose her neck.

Her eyes and her smile are trained on Nevon, his hands moving quickly as he speaks. She laughs, and the sound of it winds through me in a way that both entices and irritates.

Railan clears his throat behind me, propelling me into the room, and when Elora's eyes find mine, there's the subtlest shift in the energy before Railan distracts her with an exaggerated bow. Reaching for her hand, he lays a gentle kiss on her knuckles, eliciting a smile that is amused rather than coy or shy.

A smile that makes me want to punch him in the throat and shove him out of my way. Fuck's sake, this woman is a problem.

For a moment, I consider leaving and taking dinner in my rooms. I still have Garrick's latest report to go over, some souls from Meren to review, and an unopened letter with the sun god's seal I've been ignoring since yesterday. But I won't run from her. Not in my own damn palace.

Instead I round the end of the table and take my seat, closer to her than I might have liked, and Railan takes his usual spot at my right hand, directly to Elora's left.

Her gaze meets mine again. There's challenge in it, and more of that energy shifting on the air. I wish I knew what it was about this woman that both intrigues and vexes me. But she occupies far too many of my thoughts already to worry about solving riddles that don't need answers.

"You are a vision," Railan says as the doors at the end of the room swing open and servants trail in carrying bowls of steaming soup and baskets of warm bread.

She shifts in her chair when a translucent hand sets her bowl in front of her, but her tone is polite with her thanks. Then she turns those mesmerizing green eyes to Railan and sends him a wide smile.

"I bet you say that to all the mortal women who stumble across the veil."

With a laugh, Railan leans closer and drops his voice. "You would be the first."

"And hopefully the last."

My tone is clipped, cold, but I can't help it. I want those eyes on me again. And something about Railan and Nevon being so close to her sets my teeth on edge.

"I don't think you have anything to worry about, my lord," she assures me, her tone dripping with sugary sweetness. "I doubt any mortal would willingly cross the veil to spend time in your company. Pleasant as it is," she adds, spooning up a bite of soup.

To his credit, Railan bites back a laugh, but Nevon's is loud and deep.

"Don't mind the God of Death," Nevon tells her, drawing her gaze. "He never knows how to behave among the living."

"Elora," Kaia says before I can snarl a reply, "are you settling into your rooms?"

Shifting in her seat, Elora nods. "I am. They're very comfortable." She flicks a glance at me but says to no one in particular, "Thank you."

"Good. I'm glad. You know if you need anything, you have—"

"Only to ask," Elora says. "I remember."

Silence descends over the table, leaving only the clink of spoons against porcelain. When the servants come to clear away the soup and set a fresh course of roasted vegetables and grilled pheasant, Elora stares down at her plate with a frown.

"Is something wrong with it?" I wonder, cutting into a carrot.

"Where does it come from?"

"You don't know how vegetables are prepared?"

Kaia shoots me a sharp glare, and I notice Elora roll her eyes.

"I've prepared enough myself to be familiar with the method. I thought nothing grew in the Shadow Realm. Everything is supposed to be dead."

"I'm not dead," Nevon assures her with a cheeky wink.

"And neither is the whole of the realm," Railan adds.

"Videva." Kaia takes a sip of wine. "I told you the souls in Videva live as mortals would in Acaria. That includes tending gardens and livestock, hunting birds and game."

Elora tilts her head. Studying her plate, she spears a leek and brings it to her lips, taking a careful bite. She chews slowly, deep in thought, and I watch her throat as she swallows.

"What else do mortals get wrong about the Shadow Realm?" she wonders.

"Almost everything."

Railan smiles at her before shooting me a look, imploring me to explain. I lift a shoulder. I've never been one to correct the mortals and their stories about me or my realm. Whatever they believe about the fate that awaits them is none of my concern. I am responsible only for attending to them once they cross over.

"I'd like to see it. The realm."

Her tone is light, but she's concentrating too hard on carving a bit of pheasant off the bone. It would seem my guest has already discovered she can only wander so far from the palace.

"I can take you."

"No."

The word is harsh, commanding, and Nevon sits back in his

chair with a huff while Railan watches me with calculating eyes. I shouldn't have said it, not in front of Elora. But the idea of her being alone with Nevon anywhere in this realm, especially where I cannot see her, has me gripping my spoon so hard I'm in danger of bending it in half.

"Railan can take you." Railan's eyebrows shoot up. "If he has time."

"It would be my pleasure." He turns to Elora, who's studying me. "Tomorrow?"

"Tomorrow would be fine." She drags her gaze away from mine and offers Railan a warm smile. "Thank you."

Kaia fills the silence with talk of her upcoming solstice festival and the rituals her priestesses are hard at work preparing. But I hardly hear a word she's saying, my eyes fixed on Elora as she wraps her pretty, full lips around a bite of carrot.

This woman is my own personal torment, and I remind myself I need to stay as far away from her as possible.

CHAPTER FOURTEEN

Elora

A breeze sings through the high grass, teasing the hair coming loose from my braid and tickling my neck. I pull up the fur-lined hood of the cloak I found in my wardrobe to shield myself from the worst of the chill.

It's colder here in the Shadow Realm than it was when I left Rhagana. The gods don't seem to notice, though, with Kaia in her stunning, shimmering gowns and Thieran in his swirl of black robes.

Railan and Nevon wore the same to dinner the night before, but it didn't look as imposing and otherworldly on them as it does on Thieran. Or perhaps it was less the robes and more the way he was looking at me. As if he wanted to consume and obliterate me all at once.

I shiver at the memory, drawing the cloak tighter around me and banishing the thought from my head. Instead I turn my attention to the palace, studying it from my new vantage point.

It's an impressive structure, jutting out of the ground as if carved from the rock it sits on. It looms three stories above the earth, and towers spear up into the pale gray sky at every corner, fat and round.

I can't see the tower that used to be mine from where I stand, but I imagine they're all the same, with their winding staircase and circular rooms. These, at least, have windows.

I've not been able to wander far from the palace in any direction. More wards and protections courtesy of my captor, no doubt. But no matter how far I go, it seems to call to me, beckoning me back. It's a disconcerting feeling to be so enamored with the place I most want to leave.

I've spent days exploring the inside to test Kaia's promise I can go where I please as long as the doors are open. I've barely seen a fraction of it, the hallways twisting and turning into new passageways until I'm certain I'm lost and will never find my way out again.

Most of the rooms I've encountered so far seem to belong to the other dark court gods, their symbols carved into each door. They seem to sit unused, since the only other people I've encountered are two of the three judges and the servants. Which is just as well. The fewer gods I run into before my escape, the better.

It's not the inside of the palace I need to concern myself with, anyway. It's the outside. I won't find my way back to Rhagana for Meera and my things if I can't explore beyond Thieran's protections. How to get past them without an escort is a problem I can concern myself with another day.

I feel the ripple of power on the air seconds before Railan appears beside me. He's almost as tall and broad in the shoulders as Thieran, but his quick, easy smile makes him far less intimidating. Thick, white locs swing forward to frame his dark face when he bends to press a kiss to my knuckles.

"My lady," he says easily, straightening and turning to survey the expanse of smooth, shiny rock stretching out from the palace until it fades into waist-high grass.

"In some Acarian territories, it's against the law to use a divine title with a mortal."

"Is it?" he wonders, lifting a brow. Then his frown fades into another kind smile, and he shoots me a wink. "Good thing for both of us we're far from Acaria."

"How far?"

"Far enough to keep the living and the dead separated."

I snort, and he chuckles softly.

"Present company excluded, of course. Now." He gestures in front of us. "What would you like to see today?"

Shifting on my feet, I grip the edges of the cloak in my fingers, stroking the soft fur. I've been practicing how to say this next part since Thieran decreed Railan follow me around the realm like a guard.

Keeping my voice light, I look up at him. "I'm sure you have plenty of better things to do today. I thought maybe you could just escort me beyond the boundary."

His eyes are alight with something like mischief. "What boundary?"

I flick my fingers at the dancing grass. "I can only make it about five paces into the grass before something raises the hair on my arms. Then it's another three paces before I suddenly feel as if I never want to leave the safety of the palace."

I glance over my shoulder at the structure at our backs. Even now, it feels vastly more comforting than what lays before us, but it's a trick of Thieran's power and nothing more. I have to get out of here, and this is the only way.

"You can feel the power on your skin?"

The surprise in Railan's tone draws my gaze. "I can. It feels the same as when I cross a boundary between territories."

"Interesting," he murmurs.

"What's interesting?"

"Nothing important." He turns fully to face me, offering me his arm. "But my orders are to go with you and show you whatever you like. My duties can wait a bit today," he assures me when I open my mouth to protest.

Nodding, I give him a polite smile. I don't want to push too hard and have him refuse to take me at all. I've a good enough memory, and I can sketch out a rough map in my rooms later.

"All right." I lay my hand over his forearm, and the warmth that zips up my fingers and fills my body has me releasing the cloak. "I'd love to know if Irios is as beautiful as the stories say."

His smile is the last thing I see before the world fades away, and I'm surrounded by muted golden light and a warm wind. It's like seeing the sun through your eyelids, coupled with the sensation of falling off a cliff. My stomach drops, and my lungs constrict until I can hardly breathe.

The only thing grounding me is the feel of Railan's arm under my hand, warm and solid. When the golden light fades and the world rights itself to solid ground once more, I sway, unsteady on my feet.

"I'm sorry," Railan says, gripping my elbow before I fall to my knees. "I should have warned you."

I squeeze my eyes shut, hand pressed to my stomach until the worst of the nausea passes.

"Maybe next time we can just walk," I say, forcing my breath out between pursed lips.

Railan chuckles. "The Shadow Realm is vast. It would take quite a long time to walk from one end to the other."

"Days?"

He shakes his head. "Months."

I refuse to let the gravity of those words sink in. There has to be a way out of here that doesn't involve me wandering aimlessly for months. And I will find it. That's the point of today's little excursion. Map the Shadow Realm, find the best path back to Acaria, ride as far away as I dare.

I'll sweet-talk Railan and whoever else into as many tours as it takes to get out of here and back to my life.

"Well?" Railan asks once my legs stop wobbling. "What do you think? Is it like the stories?"

The healing fields of Irios stretch before me, and I blink to make sure my eyes aren't deceiving me. Unlike what I've seen of the Shadow Realm so far, Irios is a riot of color. The absence of color everywhere else makes these almost blinding.

The vibrant green of the grass disappears into the horizon, and flowers in every color imaginable blanket the fields. A grove of trees sits to the left, their branches heavy with fruit.

Releasing Railan's arm, I wander over to the closest one, reaching up to cup a pear in one hand. I make to pluck it, then pull my hand back at the last second. This fruit isn't for me, and I have no idea what might happen if I eat it.

Reaching around me, Railan plucks the pear from the branch and tosses it into the air, catching it with his opposite hand and holding it out to me with a flourish.

"Oh, but I—"

"There's nothing in the Shadow Realm that will hurt you if you consume it."

I reach for the pear, rubbing my thumb over its pretty yellow skin. "Not even the water from the River Grense?"

"The river of memories is only meant to make you forget. Not to harm."

Some days forgetting seems better than remembering. But I shake that thought away and hold the pear up to my nose. The scent of it makes my mouth water, and I take a big bite before I talk myself out of it.

The flavor is bright and sweet on my tongue, the flesh crunchy and juicy. It tastes like home, and a memory from my childhood rises unbidden. Me toddling through the orchard on our farm, chasing after my mother, who wears a basket strapped to her waist as she collects fruit from our trees to sell.

She carves a slice off a pear plucked fresh from a tree and hands it to me, brushing my curls out of my eyes as I nibble the fruit. She fades away quickly, too quickly, and I blink back tears at the loss of her.

Staring down at the pear, I wait for the grief I haven't felt in so long to pass.

"Good memories are stronger in Irios than anywhere else in the Shadow Realm. It helps with the healing," Railan explains.

I nod. Unwilling to take another bite, I let the fruit roll from my fingers to the ground and watch it absorb into the earth like water.

"How long can a soul stay here?"

Stepping around the tree and further into the field, he sweeps his arm out in front of him, and I see souls wandering in the bright green grass for the first time.

"As long as they need to."

"And then what happens?" I ask, my voice barely above a whisper as I watch two souls cross paths as if the other weren't even there.

"Some move to Videva to live their eternal lives in the company of those like them. Others choose to reincarnate."

I tilt my head to study the woman closest to us. She wears a plain white dress, and the gentle breeze that's warmer here than at the palace blows her blond hair around her shoulders.

"Do you have to be reincarnated?"

"No."

I purse my lips. I've never thought of reincarnation as a choice before, assuming all souls cycled through the Shadow Realm over and over. Stories on the matter differ based on who's doing the telling, but my aunt was adamant that life was meant to be lived again and again until you got it right. Whatever right was.

The idea of it always exhausted me. Why gamble on living life again and potentially going through the same torment a second time?

When Railan walks further into the field, I follow, and with each step I feel calmer, more relaxed. He glances at me and smiles.

"That's exactly how the healing fields are meant to make you feel."

"What?" I ask, my voice soft and dreamy.

"At peace. Comforted."

Pulling the fresh, warm air deep into my lungs, I let it out slowly, gently. I do feel at peace here, but that isn't the point of today's excursion, and I need to keep my wits about me.

"Where are we in relation to the palace?"

He bends to pick up a bright pink flower I've never seen before, tucking it behind my ear before responding.

"Northeast of the palace. Irios is surrounded by dense forests and heavily warded, as it requires the most protection."

"More than Síra?"

Mistaking the curiosity in my voice for concern, he reaches out to rub a hand down my arm. "Don't worry. Síra's borders are well fortified and holding. You're safe from the tormented."

"I'm not afraid of what lurks in Síra."

He laughs unexpectedly, bright and big. "Of course you're not. And it's all starting to make a bit more sense."

"What is?"

He opens his mouth to speak but freezes, his back going straight and his shoulders squaring. He cocks his head as if listening to a sound only he can hear, and it takes a long moment before he relaxes again.

"It would seem we have a batch of new souls that have just arrived and are in need of judging." Holding out his arm to me, he raises a brow when I don't immediately take it. "I must go."

The idea of disappearing with him again makes my stomach roil, and I take a step back, shaking my head.

"I'm hardly in danger here, right? Couldn't you leave me to explore the fields and come back for me later?"

He twitches, brows drawing together before nodding once. "All right. But don't wander far. Meren is that way"—he points over my shoulder—"and I wouldn't want you getting into trouble."

"Of course not."

Railan hesitates, but I give him what I hope is a convincing smile. I have no intention of staying put, but he doesn't need to know that.

"I won't be long," he assures me before disappearing with a shimmer on the air.

I wait a few minutes to make sure he doesn't return to see if I've kept my word. When nothing happens, I spin on my heel and start off in the direction he told me not to go.

I've never heard of Meren in any of the stories about the Shadow Realm, and my curiosity is piqued. Maybe it's nothing but a barren wasteland; maybe it's the key to getting out of here. But I can't know either way until I see it for myself.

Railan's claim that it would take months to traverse the Shadow Realm on foot from one end to the other flits through my mind, and I nearly stumble over a small rise. That may be true, but why would he warn me away from Meren if it wasn't close enough to walk to?

I don't know if it will help me get out of here, but at this point, more pieces to the puzzle of how to escape this place are better than less.

The healing fields stretch out in front of me with no end in sight, rolling with gentle hills that remind me of the farmland I rode through after leaving Pramis's territory. That seems like lifetimes ago, yet it's only been a few weeks.

I carefully pick my way down into a little valley and prepare to climb up the other side. Tossing the edges of my cloak over my shoulders, I'm beginning to wish I'd left it behind. Sweat beads between my shoulder blades and drips down my spine as I crest the next rise.

I squint toward the horizon and think I see a point where the color begins to fade back to shades of gray, but it's so far away it's impossible to tell if it's really there or my eyes are playing tricks on me. Determined to find out one way or another, I begin my journey again.

When the air shimmers with power, I stop short and mutter a curse under my breath. I haven't even moved completely out of sight of the pear tree, and already Railan is back to collect me.

But it isn't Railan who materializes close enough to touch.

Thieran crosses his arms and stares down his nose at me. "Where exactly do you think you're going, little one?"

CHAPTER FIFTEEN

Thieran

Elora opens her mouth to answer me, but thinks better of her reply and snaps it shut. Inhaling deeply, she lets it out in a huff of breath and smiles. If she's going for polite, she's missed her mark because her smile is all sharp edges and hard angles.

I'm the last person she wants to see right now. And something about that is immeasurably pleasing.

"My lord," she says in that way I hate. I wonder if she knows I hate it or if it's just luck on her part. "I didn't expect to see you here."

"Yes," I drawl. "In my own realm. So surprising."

Her eyes narrow at my sarcasm then dart over my shoulder, and she forces her smile wider. She looks wild, ribbons of hair blowing around her face. As much as I might wish to see her in a gown, I like the look of her in her leathers, fierce and challenging.

The thought brings a scowl to my face, and she takes a step back. I'm here because I sensed her wandering where she shouldn't be, not to have fanciful thoughts about what she chooses to wear. No matter how perfect her curves look wrapped in leather breeches and a corset that begs to be untied inch by torturous inch until...

"You didn't answer my question," I bark, watching her mimic my stance with her arms crossed over her chest. "What are you doing out here?"

"That wasn't your question, my l—"

"I swear to the gods," I say through gritted teeth, and her smile turns smug. So she is doing it to irritate me. "Where are you going, Elora?"

"That way." She gestures with her chin. "Railan had urgent business to attend to."

I sensed the souls' arrival on the air the same way he did. What I did not sense was her return to the palace. It took me longer than I would like to locate her, forcing me to unearth my connection with her after burying it so well these last few weeks. That steady thump, thump, thump of her heart next to mine.

"And why are you going that way?"

She tilts her head, eyes searching mine. "Seemed like as good a way as any."

I know it for a lie the second the words pass her lips, and my patience where she is concerned is fraying. She wanted past the boundary I put in place around the palace, and I let her have it, even though I knew why.

"You cannot escape the Shadow Realm."

Gripping her arms hard enough to leave bruises, she swallows hard. "What makes you think I'm trying to escape?"

Taking a step closer, I circle around until I'm standing behind her. Elora's body goes stiff. She doesn't move away from me, but her heartbeat has quickened considerably. Though she's trying not to show it, Elora's afraid of me. And I like it.

I lean toward her, my lips ghosting the shell of her ear, my chest brushing against her back.

"I can smell the desperation on you. Sickly sweet and utterly useless. Even if you could discover how to get past the wards without an escort and figure out which direction to go without getting lost and manage to walk there before summer..."

Her jaw clenches, and I reach up to catch a strand of her hair before it can blow across her face, twirling it around my finger.

"Even if you can manage to do all of that, you'll never make it. Do you know why?"

"Why?" Her voice is a hoarse whisper.

Angry, but there's something else there too. Something that makes me take a step closer, pressing even tighter against her.

"Because it doesn't matter where you are. I can sense you in every corner of the realm. Wherever you go, I'll find you."

I linger longer than I need to before taking a slow step back. Elora doesn't move; she simply draws her arms tighter around her, eyes locked on the horizon.

"What is Meren?"

It's not the question I expect her to ask. In truth, I was waiting for her to beg for her freedom, to plead for a bargain or a favor. She might be proud and stubborn, but no one is that prideful when their life is on the line.

"Where did you hear about Meren?"

"Railan mentioned it before he left." She gestures toward the horizon. "Said it was that way."

I move to stand in front of her, drawing her gaze. "I can't imagine he told you to seek it out."

Her green eyes are defiant. "He told me to stay away from it."

Sighing, I pinch the bridge of my nose. There has to be a better way to safeguard the Shadow Realm than being saddled with this woman for the rest of eternity. In fact, the alternative is beginning to sound more and more attractive.

"If he told you to stay away from it, why are you walking in that direction?"

"It isn't as if I have anything better to do."

Sorrow flickers through her eyes for a moment, so briefly I

wonder if I imagined it. Damn this woman and all the ways she plagues me.

"Fine, then." I wrap a hand around her upper arm. "If a tour of Meren will shut you up."

"No. Wait. I—"

Her words are swallowed up by the wind as I shift with her to the edge of Meren's lands. She sways when I release her, dropping her hands to her knees and sucking in deep lungfuls of air.

"There are faster ways to kill me, you know. Next time just drive a blade into my heart."

Laying my hand on the back of her neck, I push healing power into her until she's steady enough to shrug me off and push herself upright.

"Thank you."

"Do my ears deceive me? Thanks? I had no idea the viper could speak without biting."

She casts her eyes toward the sky and pulls her cloak tighter around her. It's colder here in Meren than in Irios, and the region is painted with the same dull shades of gray as the rest of the Shadow Realm. It's not meant to be an altogether pleasant place.

Her eyes take in the landscape, a mix of grass and trees like Irios and craggy rock like Síra. Meren stretches from the far east boundary to the center of the realm, bordering Irios to the west and Síra to the south.

"I don't understand."

"Understand what?"

"The stories." She bends down to brush her fingers over the dirt, tracing shapes in it and then wiping them away. "They talk only of Videva, Irios, and Síra. What is Meren?"

"An in-between place."

Her brow creases in a frown, and I step away, resisting the urge to smooth it with my finger. Or my lips.

"In between what?"

"In between punishment and forever."

Elora swings around to look at me, hands going to her hips, one cocking. The dagger strapped to her thigh glints in the light, and my eyes are drawn to it. I don't know what she thinks she'll ever be able to do with a blade here, but damn it all if I don't like seeing it there.

"Can you be more specific?"

I drag my gaze slowly up her body. Her cheeks are pink when my eyes finally land on her face, and I grin.

"More specific about what?"

Huffing out an annoyed breath, she swings her arm out to indicate the vastness before her. "About your mysterious extra territory."

I shift on my feet. I've never had to explain Meren or its creation to anyone before. My dark court doesn't question the choices I make regarding my realm, and I'm not entirely sure my brother or his high court know it exists either. Or would even care to know.

The Shadow Realm was created to serve a single purpose. Keep me and those who supported me during the war as far away from Fontoss as possible. I didn't object because Fontoss was the last place I wanted to be and my brother the last person I wanted to spend my time with.

"Meren is for souls in transition."

"I thought that's what Irios was for. Transition from what?" she asks when I give a small shrug.

"What does it matter?"

The stare she gives me is dry and unamused. "Humor me."

"The Shadow Realm was created with three lands. Irios for souls to find healing and peace from mortal lives filled with pain and grief, Síra to punish those who cannot be redeemed, and Videva to wait until life beckons again."

Elora nods, tucking a strand of hair behind her ear. "As the stories say."

"The judges and I quickly learned mortal existence is more complicated than that. It isn't always so black or white, good or bad."

"So you created a place for the shades of gray. For the in-between."

"I did. Not all bad deeds are committed by bad people. So in Meren they're given the opportunity to work off their soul's debt before transitioning to Irios to heal or Videva to wait."

"They can transition to Irios?"

Her voice is full of wonder, and I take a step toward her without thinking. "They can. They can drink from the Grense and forget too. Once their debt is paid."

"You recognized their humanity." Her eyes drop to my mouth, lingering there for a long moment before she turns and puts distance between us. "I didn't know the gods were capable of such a thing."

"We're just full of surprises. Alas, I cannot indulge you any longer. I have better things to do." I hold out my hand for hers, but she merely stares at my palm.

"I'd rather walk."

Rolling my eyes, I reach for her arm, but she dances out of my grasp. "I'm not walking all the way back to the palace when we can shift."

"You shift. I'll walk."

"You're being ridiculous."

"It's disconcerting to be in one spot and then in another in the blink of an eye. To say nothing of the horrible feeling of being turned inside out and then righted again."

"Come here." I hold out my hand again. "Now, Elora."

"I don't mind walking. Besides, your power is cold, and I—"

Irritated, I grab her hand and yank her up against me. Cupping her face in my palms, I push warmth and calm and healing into her before shifting away from the edge of Meren and into the hallway outside her rooms.

She squeezes her eyes shut for the journey, her hands gripping my wrists, nails digging into the skin. When it's done, she sags against me for a brief moment before righting herself. But she doesn't step out of my embrace, and I don't release her.

Her gaze snags on my mouth again, and her lips part. The beat of her heart picks up, and her throat clicks when she swallows hard. I give her a moment and the silence, curious about what she might do with both.

Slowly, the mesmerized look in her eyes fades and she stumbles back, grappling behind her for the doorknob to her rooms. When she proves unable to open it, I put us both out of our misery, my body brushing hers as I reach around her to push the door in.

Skimming my nose against her temple as I retreat, I inhale her scent before stepping back.

"Do me a favor, little one." She scowls, and it only deepens when I grin. "Try not to get into any trouble."

"I make no promises."

"I didn't imagine you would. That's what the wards are for."

I shift to my study, where Garrick and Nevon are both waiting for me. While Garrick launches into his daily report about the Shadow Realm, my mind drifts back to Elora. It's more fun than I anticipated to throw her off balance and make all the thoughts tumble out of her head.

And if I'm going to be stuck with her, I might as well learn to get my amusements where I can.

CHAPTER SIXTEEN

Elora

T ucked into an alcove overlooking the palace's northern grounds, I study the crude map I've managed to draw of the Shadow Realm over the last few days. Between additional tours with Railan and lots of sweet talking with Nevon, who I imagine would flirt with anyone who stood still long enough, I've gathered enough information to sketch out a sizable portion of the realm.

There's only one problem. That's not true. This entire situation is nothing but problems, but my map has a singular issue. It's woefully incomplete.

I've marked Irios and Meren and what I can see of Videva from the highest window in the south tower. But it's impossible to know how big each of those territories is. I know the forbidden forest stretches along the entire border of the Shadow Realm, separating it from Acaria and disguising the veil.

I've only seen a full-scale map of Acaria a handful of times in my life. I can't recall the entire thing with crystal clarity, but I remember the depth and breadth of the forest. It runs the length of the six different territories belonging to members of Thieran's dark court.

If the rendering was an accurate one, then the map I've drawn is roughly only half finished. And even with Railan's patient tours and Nevon's help in filling in the gaps, I still have no idea where any of the rivers are.

According to the stories, the Shadow Realm has three rivers. The River Grense, meant to wipe a soul's memory were they to drink from it, to offer them a fresh start. The River Loret, which guards the entrance to the realm. The souls of the dead are said to cross there and pay their toll.

And then there's the River Axan. The river of sorrow. The stories of the river's purpose vary. Some say a method of torture for the damned, and others a toy for the vengeful God of Death to cast souls into when he's bored. Just to hear them scream, they say.

Carefully folding the map, I shove it into my pocket. I didn't think much about the God of Death before I ended up in his realm. Some mortals are plagued by constant thoughts of him, my aunt included, but to me, he was nothing but an inevitable conclusion.

Whether I lived fifteen years or fifty, my fate would be the same. I was always meant to end up in the Shadow Realm. We all are. I just never thought I'd end up here alive. With no way out again.

Suddenly the fate I'd resigned myself to doesn't seem as comforting. Not when I still have so much life to live and the God of Death himself is far more interesting than I want him to be.

Shoving away from the wall, I pace into the hallway and back to the window. He plays games, he tricks, he lies to get his way. That is what people say of the God of Death. And I can hardly dispute that. Not when he's keeping me prisoner for reasons that are entirely his own.

If Kaia knows what they are, she won't say—and neither will Railan. They're both evasive when I ask why Thieran insists on keeping me here, telling me it's for my own good or changing the subject completely.

I don't know if what Thieran said was true, if he can sense me anywhere in the realm and prevent my escape. Whether it is or it isn't, I'd rather incur his wrath by trying than become complicit in my own captivity.

All I need to do is find the direction of the River Axan. It's rumored to be black as pitch and seductive, calling out to wandering souls. A black river is the only thing I remember about my arrival in the realm. Before Thieran scooped me up and I woke in the tower.

If I find the river and can map it from beginning to end, I might be able to pinpoint a general direction to walk. Then I can put Thieran's claim that he can sense me anywhere to the test.

I'll ask Nevon more about the realm's rivers at dinner. He'll tell me almost anything if I lean close and flirt well enough. I'm woefully out of practice in the art of flirting, but it seems to be working where he's concerned. And it has the added benefit of twisting Thieran's face into a pinched scowl.

Serves him right for touching me so intimately when he brought me back from Meren the other day. He did it only to unsettle me, and I hate that it worked. Almost as much as I hate the dreams I've been having about him ever since. Of his lips and his hands and his...

I squeeze my eyes shut against the thoughts. No. I absolutely will not go there. That's what he wants. To distract me. To keep me here. And it won't work.

Spinning away from the wall to head back to my rooms, I stop short at the unmistakable sound of metal on metal. Rushing back to the window, I peer out, able only to see a bit of the smooth balcony below and the grass beyond.

I'm beginning to wonder if I imagined it until I hear it again. It can be no other sound. I'd recognize it anywhere.

Moving quickly down the hall, I try to place myself in the palace. Around the next corner and ten paces down the passage is a door leading to the expansive balcony. Maybe I'll be better able to determine where the noise is coming from once I'm outside.

The air is cold in the looming shadows of the palace, slapping against my face and stinging my eyes, but I'm too afraid to miss finding the sound to go back inside and get my cloak. It rings out again, followed by a grunting shout, and I follow it along the wide stone to the stairs at the far end.

Taking them down, I follow the edge of the palace, quickening my pace when I hear the clang again, louder this time. As soon as I round the corner, I discover the cause of the noise.

Four men face off in pairs in the center of a grassy patch framed on all four sides by a low stone wall. Thieran, Railan, and Nevon, with a man I can only assume is the third judge since he's a mirror image of Railan and Nevon both.

All the men, lean and broad, heft long battle swords. Thieran swings his in a flourishing figure eight, finishing in an attack position, and I find the entire thing far more attractive than I have a right to. A fact that only serves to irritate me further.

Crossing the yard to the ring, I wave to Nevon when he spots me and send him a flirty smile. He returns it, jogging to the wall as I approach and holding out a hand to me. I lay mine in his big palm, and he instantly leans down to kiss the back of it.

"Come to watch us hack at each other, then?"

"Only if you promise to put on a good show."

His grin is wide and boyish, though I imagine he's many centuries old. "Of course we will. Won't we, boys?" he asks, turning back to the others. "A good show for a pretty lady."

"I'm not interested in putting on a show," Thieran says with a growl. "For her or anyone."

I boost myself onto the wall, dangling my feet over one side and gripping the edge with my hands. "If you're not good with a sword, my lord, just say that."

Railan bites back a laugh at my challenge while Thieran's lip curls back over his teeth. He brandishes it again, and I ignore the flutter in my belly as he circles Railan.

Railan is patient, but Thieran is more so, circling and circling until suddenly he strikes at a dizzying speed. Feinting to throw Railan off balance, Thieran lands a blow on Railan's bicep that actually draws blood, the wet of it soaking into Railan's sleeve.

At my soft gasp, Nevon pats my hand. "Don't worry. We heal fast. And my brother's had worse."

There's not much of a pause before they're circling each other again. It's Railan who goes for the strike this time, but Thieran is faster, spinning out of the path of Railan's blade at the last second and bringing his sword down against Railan's side.

The judge steps quickly to the left, but not before the tip of Thieran's sword dots across his abdomen, drawing more blood. I'm not sure if Thieran is doing this for my benefit or if he's always this bloodthirsty in practice, but he flicks a glance in my direction before his ice-blue eyes dart away again.

"Nevon." I let my voice carry. "Are you as good with a sword as our Lord Thieran?"

Nevon stands straight at the goading tone in my voice. "Of course. Maybe even better."

Thieran tosses his sword from one hand to the other and back again, the muscles in his forearms flexing, and the flutter in my belly resumes.

"But I'll need a favor from you, dear Elora."

I drag my gaze away from Thieran's intense one and smile down at Nevon, eyebrow cocked. "A favor?"

He taps his cheek. "A kiss to carry into battle."

"It's not battle, you twit. What the fuck do you need a kiss for?" Thieran snaps.

Because I can hear the irritation in Thieran's voice as clearly as I can hear the wind in the trees, I lean over and press a kiss to Nevon's cheek, his grin widening.

"The only thing I'll ever need to win," he says, taking a step back, hand over his heart. "The affections and faith of a beautiful woman."

When I look up again, Thieran is watching me intently, and I grip the wall tighter. He finally tears his gaze away from mine when Nevon draws closer, sword at the ready.

They face off, Thieran's eyes finding me every few seconds until Nevon makes his first move. If Railan is good, Nevon is better. Balanced, focused, and fast, he glides effortlessly from one position to another, relentlessly battering Thieran until the god has no choice but to focus solely on his opponent.

Nevon spins, his blade coming dangerously close to Thieran's throat. I know neither of them can die, that whatever wounds they have will eventually heal as Railan's cuts already have, but that doesn't stop my heart from lodging itself in my throat every time their blades dance and sing.

If Thieran were seriously injured, the time it takes for him to heal might give me enough of a head start to escape the realm before he can track me down. But still, the thought of watching his blood spill isn't as exciting as I want it to be.

"They can't really die, you know." Railan steps up beside me, but I refuse to meet his curious stare.

"I know that. What do I care if the God of Death is injured trying to show off?"

"That is the question, isn't it?" Railan says softly, drawing my gaze.

"He's my captor," I remind us both. "His...incapacitation would be rather a bonus for me, I think."

"Mmm," Railan murmurs. "Then why do you look so concerned?"

"I—"

The distinct sound of a blade striking its target and a stream of muttered curses focuses my attention back on the men in front of me just in time to see Thieran ripping his tunic off over his head.

"By all the fucking gods, Nevon. Did you have to go so deep?"

There's a large gash across Thieran's chest from breast bone to armpit, and my heart punches into my throat for reasons I don't want to examine. Before I can even reason out what I'm doing, I leap from the wall and run to the center of the ring, pushing onto my tiptoes to inspect the wound.

Does it need to be cleaned? Tended to? Wrapped in bandages? I press a finger to the edges of it, and Thieran grits his teeth, reaching for my hand and squeezing my fingers in his grip.

"Don't make it worse, for fuck's sake. The healing is bad enough."

"You could charm the swords. So they don't cut so deep." I huff out a breath. "Or at all."

"Don't tell me you're worried for me, little one." He steps closer, crowding my personal space. "I've already told you, you can't kill the God of Death."

"I wasn't worried," I assure him, but his smile only grows bigger at whatever he sees on my face. "I'm only jealous it was Nevon drawing your blood and not me."

"I've been wondering if you're any good with that dagger you keep strapped to your thigh." His eyes drift down to my hips, and my face heats.

"Good enough to protect myself and put food on the table."

"So you say," Thieran replies, his eyes never leaving mine. He takes another step closer, the heat from his body warming my skin. "One day I may make you actually prove it."

I lift my chin, which only brings our lips closer together, and my eyes drop to his. "I'd be delighted," I say, my voice barely above a whisper.

Someone clears their throat behind us, startling me out of whatever trance I've fallen into. I leap away from Thieran, eyes dropping to his chest and the unblemished skin there. There's not even a speck of blood to be found, as if the wound drew it all back in before knitting itself together again.

"I interrupted your exercise," I mumble, taking three more steps away. "I'll let you get back to your afternoon."

And with all the grace and calm I can muster, I turn away from the God of Death and the judges who watch us and flee.

CHAPTER SEVENTEEN

Elora

There's an eeriness to nighttime in the Shadow Realm. At nightfall, the usual twilight hue of the sky succumbs to inky black, bathing the landscape in total darkness. If the sky holds stars, they're impossible to see. No sun, no moon. Nothing to rise and set and send you traveling sure-footed in the right direction.

I press the map I've only just completed this afternoon flat against the quilt on the bed. The edges are worried and threadbare from my nervous fingers, but the decision is made. I'm leaving tonight.

Thieran manipulated me too well with his story about offering redemption to souls in Meren and his healing power after we shifted. And I embarrassed myself with my antics in the training yard the other day. Worried for the God of Death, my captor. I snort.

Just because he hasn't continued to confine me to a window-less tower doesn't make him any less of a warden. His hospitality still has strings and boundaries. And I am no longer interested in being controlled by either.

Which is why I've spent the last few days preparing as best I can and avoiding Thieran altogether. A feat, now that he seems intent on seeking me out. The man made a study of ignoring me for weeks, and suddenly he's there every time I turn a corner.

It hardly matters, though. In just under an hour's time, I'll be well on my way back to Rhagana for my things and then as far away from the Shadow Realm as I can manage. Maybe I'll go all the way to the northern coast and sail away to somewhere new.

A land where the gods don't have power, where people would only blink in confusion at the mention of Thieran, the dark God of Death.

The pretty mantel clock Kaia conjured for me the other day trills the time. An hour past midnight.

Moving to the window, I push the curtain aside enough to peek out. I see no movement from my vantage point, no light in the windows on this side of the palace. As far as I can tell, everyone is abed at this hour.

Kaia is in Rhagana tonight preparing for her solstice celebrations, and since her rooms sit right next to mine, her absence makes this the perfect time for me to escape. She's nice enough, but she seems as committed to keeping me here as Thieran is, even if she is less intense about it. Though I can imagine no one is more intense than Thieran.

Satisfied no one is roaming the palace grounds at this hour, I let the curtain fall back into place and cross to the bed.

Aside from the dagger strapped to my thigh, I have a carving knife I took from dinner tonight tucked into my boot. I will not be caught off guard by another forest beast and end up right back where I started.

I'd prefer my bow, but since it was never returned to me, I have to assume I discarded it in the forest while running for my life from an animal that wasn't quite an animal. It doesn't matter. I can buy another one once I get back to Acaria and find a target for my blade and someone willing to pay for the work.

Running my fingertips over the fur-lined cloak, I consider

leaving it behind for the millionth time. I'd prefer to leave the Shadow Realm taking only what I arrived with, but it's even colder in the dark than it is in the subdued light of day. And though I think I've found a route that will lead me out of here much faster than Railan's ominous months, it won't do me any good to be slowed down or weakened by the realm's eternal chill.

Decision made, I swirl the cloak around my shoulders and fasten it across my chest. It's almost quarter-past, and I need to hurry. I want to be well away before anyone stirs.

On my way to the door, I crouch in front of the fireplace, using the poker to shove aside the embers for my prize. I hope I remembered all the steps and ingredients; it's been lifetimes since I read about this cloaking charm in one of my aunt's books as a child and again when I was running from the boy who broke my heart.

A trinket or bit of jewelry steeped in a tea made with mint, comfrey, cinnamon, obsidian shards, and a lock of hair from the wearer for three nights. There was something about the full moon in there, but since I can't see the moon, I have to hope it was full enough for it to work.

Once aged under the full moon, I sealed it with fire. Holding up the coin, blackened with soot, I study it closely. It looks no more extraordinary than it did three days ago when I found it, but I tuck it into my pocket anyway.

I'm not a big believer in mortal magick, but I figure it's better than nothing to shield me from Thieran's senses. Between the coin and the late hour when everyone in the realm should be sleeping, the odds feel like they're decidedly in my favor.

Pushing to my feet, I cross to the door and ease it open. The hallway is empty, as I expect it to be at this time of night, and I step out. Padding toward a set of back stairs I discovered in my first week here, I keep to the shadows, avoiding the halos of light from the torches. I attempted to extinguish them the night before, but they must be magicked, because no matter what I tried, they wouldn't go out. Not even water would douse them.

The door to the back passage groans softly when I open it, and I freeze. No one else has rooms on this side of the palace that I know of. Or no one currently in residence, anyway. But that doesn't mean I want to announce my departure.

When I'm sure the coast is clear, that no one is coming to drag me back to my room and lock me inside, I slip through the door and make my way down. There are no torches to light my way here, so I drag my fingers along the smooth stone wall to keep my balance as I follow the winding staircase down and down until it ends at another door.

This one opens without issue, but the wind instantly rushes into the tight space and whistles up the cylinder, tossing my braid around my face. Darting out into the night, I close the door behind me and press my back flat against it.

That's the first phase done. Now all I have to do is make my way to the weak spot in the wards I found when I was walking with Nevon after dinner.

It's so dark I can't even see my hand in front of my face. The pitch black of the palace's face swallows up any light there is to be had—and there isn't much. My natural instinct is to use the stone in my pocket to light a torch, but I can't risk it. Not yet. Not until I've been cloaked by the trees and am out of view of the palace.

I memorized this route. I can do this. Follow the wall of the palace until it gives way to the balustrade lining the balcony off the dining room. From there it's fifteen paces straight on until I reach a statue in the shape of a winged horse.

The wards stand guard beyond the row of statues Nevon was showing me earlier. I'm still not sure what to make of Railan's surprise that I can sense a god's boundaries, but whether it's unusual or not, I'm going to use the skill to my advantage. It's the way I found the weakness in the first place.

Wandering with Nevon while he droned on about the creatures depicted on the statues, many of them I'd never seen before. Myths from a forgotten era long before I was born. We'd passed the horse, and I'd felt it.

It was more a loss of sensation than a sensation itself. The power felt weaker, that feeling of buzzing energy disappearing for a scant moment before returning as we continued our walk.

I thought maybe I'd imagined it until I returned a few hours later to be sure. The feeling was the same. More than that, I was able to put my boot through the hole to the other side.

I thought I'd have to wait a few more days to find a way past them, make up a cunning excuse to Railan or Nevon, who's too easily distracted by a pretty smile and a flirtatious caress. But this was better. Now no one could suspect what I was doing because no one was the wiser.

My fingers hit air, then the carved stone of the balustrade, and I breathe a sigh of relief. I'm getting closer. I might as well be walking with my eyes closed for all the visibility I have. But I push forward, fingers bumping each pillar of the balcony's railing in turn.

When it ends, I pause. I have to walk straight ahead to hit my target, except straight could be any direction when you can't see where you're going. It's disorienting, wandering in the pitch black. But the only way out is forward, and I'm hardly one for giving up before I've really begun.

Inhaling the brisk air deep into my lungs, I rub the coin in my pocket for luck and close my eyes as much to center myself as anything else. One foot in front of the other, heel to toe, I count fifteen paces from the balcony's edge across the smooth rock of the palace grounds.

I reach out a hand in front of me, feeling around for the statue's base. Panic rises in my chest when my hand hits only empty air. It has to be here somewhere. I couldn't have wandered that far in the wrong direction.

Taking another lurching step forward, my shoulder collides with the hoof of the rearing horse, and I mutter a stream of curses, rubbing at the spot with my palm. Good to know I'm not a totally hopeless case.

I shift one step to my right, grinning when I run my fingertips over the horse's outline, from kicking hooves to elegantly curved wings to smooth flank. A sudden longing hits me in the center of my chest, but I shake it off. I'll be reunited with Meera again in a day, hopefully less, and then I'll never leave her again.

Tracing the square base of the statue, I navigate around it and finally feel the hairs pricking up on my arms. I'm so close. Just a few steps to the left and...there. The smallest void in Thieran's wards.

Fingertips running over the outline of the coin in my pocket, I inch closer to the barrier. I didn't try to go through it before, afraid someone might see me, and I have no idea if I'll actually be able to slip through. I'm navigating only on instinct and what little hope I have left.

I reach my right hand up to where the wards remain intact, and my palm presses against a flat surface. If I didn't know there wasn't anything in front of me but air and the grass beyond the expanse of rock, I'd think I was touching a wall.

My fingers inch across the mirage, slowly, so slowly, until they dip forward and through the weak spot. I push my entire arm through and wait for something to happen. But nothing shoves my limb back. No lights come on in the palace. There's nothing but the labored sound of my own excited breath.

I twist my body sideways to slip through the narrow opening, turning and pressing my hands against the barrier from the other side. Grinning in triumph, I glance briefly toward the palace. The windows are still dark; the air remains quiet.

A step back and my feet hit springy earth; two more and the

waist-high grass tickles my fingertips. Pivoting deliberately from the palace, I begin my trek through the grass toward the trees. I'm at least a hundred paces from the edge of the forest, and I'm blind until I reach it.

I can't risk lighting a torch in full view of the palace, but I don't enjoy wandering around in the dark toward a forest full of gods only know what, so I pick up my pace and take off at a steady jog. Arms out in front of me, it's several minutes before my hands hit scratchy bark.

Sighing with relief, I wrap my arms around the tree's trunk and rest for a minute, my heart pounding in my chest. I'm so close to freedom I can taste it. The thought of being away from this place nearly tears a sob from my throat, but I swallow it down. There's still so much ground to cover. Too much to celebrate just yet.

I edge my way further into the forest, carefully toeing the ground so as not to trip and fall. I have to make sure I'm far enough in before I light any torches. The light will go a long way to speeding up my journey, but not if it alerts someone to my presence here.

Once I'm satisfied I've wandered far enough, I drop to my knees, searching the forest floor for a thick tree limb. I have no idea if Shadow Realm trees even catch fire, let alone burn up, but the ground is littered with them, and I can always discard one for another until I'm beyond the veil and have the moon and stars to guide me.

Finding one twice as thick as my wrist and long as my arm, I tuck it between my legs and gather a bundle of moss into a little pile. Striking my stone against the dull metal coin until it sparks, I shift my body to shield my work from the wind.

Once, twice, a third time, until finally a shower of sparks falls onto the moss and catches, glowing steadily in the dark until a small flame dances in the center. If I was after feeding myself, I'd add twigs and sticks and branches until I had enough of a fire to keep warm and cook, but I don't need that much light or heat tonight.

Dipping the tip of the tree limb into the flames, I hold my breath, waiting for it to light. If this doesn't work, I'm stuck in these woods until the sky lightens enough for me to see the direction I'm going. And that won't give me nearly enough time to follow the river I've marked on my map to the veil.

When the bark catches, I release my breath in a whoosh, glancing back toward the palace. I can't see it from here, but it's bathed in darkness, and I am now ringed by light.

Shoving to my feet, I push further into the forest to put distance between myself and the palace. The silence all around me is almost as unsettling as the endless dark. There should be animal noises—the hoot of an owl, the scurry of a fox—but there's nothing. Only my shallow breaths and the occasional pop and sizzle of the torch.

I tug the map free from my pocket, spreading it open with one hand and smoothing it against my thigh. The River Axan curves like an L, according to Nevon, which means as long as I'm walking away from the palace in this direction, I'm sure to run into it.

Once I find it, I only need to follow it until it becomes shallow enough to leap across the rocks Nevon says are there. His story was meant to be a cautionary tale about a demigod who tried to cross the river to bargain with Thieran to save his lover. On the last rock, the demi slipped and fell and was pulled beneath the surface by the Shadow Realm's river guardians. Never to be seen again.

All I heard was there was a way across the river and back to Acaria.

Pushing ahead, I keep a close eye on the torch in my hand. The fire doesn't appear to be burning the limb down too far. And isn't that handy?

If not for being held prisoner here, I might have found the

Shadow Realm far more interesting, might have liked to explore it more thoroughly. Except maybe Videva. Unsure if my parents might be there, toiling away with the other souls, and too afraid to ask, I thought it best to avoid it completely.

My body grows weary, my feet aching as I continue my journey. With no stars to track my progress, it's impossible to tell how far I've gone. Am I walking too slowly? Is this the right direction? Will I just wander aimlessly in circles, as the stories claim?

I stop short at the sound of what might be rushing water, clearing my mind and straining my ears. There it is. The faintest sound, like a babbling brook. It's difficult to orient it in such utter darkness, but it sounds like it comes from ahead of me, and I pick up my pace.

I would happily walk for years if it meant I could get away from this place, away from Thieran. The God of Death haunts my dreams in ways I wish he wouldn't. I'm eager to put time and space between us, maybe find a good, strong man at some distant tavern I can take to bed. Sate this desire coiled tight in my belly I should not feel and drive the King of Shadows from my thoughts forever.

The sound of the river grows louder, and my face splits into a wide grin. It babbles over rocks and laps against the banks. If it's dancing over rocks here, that must mean I'm not far from the shallow patch.

And that much closer to freedom.

CHAPTER EIGHTEEN

Thieran

S he's made it farther than I expected her to, and I find myself impressed not just by her skill but by her sheer determination. She's a puzzle to me, this mortal woman who consumes so many of my thoughts whether I want her to or not.

I trail behind her through the trees, watching. I could see her clearly without the flames flickering on the tree branch in her hand, but the soft light plays over her face, highlighting the high curve of her cheekbones and delicate slope of her nose. Her top-heavy mouth is shadowed in the low light, but I remember the sight of her lips up close. When she nearly kissed me in the training yard.

If I didn't know any better, I'd say she was worried for me. For a fraction of a moment, at least. The look in her eyes as she prodded her long, thin fingers around the edge of the wound while it healed is seared into my memory. Alongside the way her lips parted when her gaze dropped to my mouth, the way her body leaned subtly into mine, the way her fingers flexed in my grip.

These are all things I've tried time and time again to erase, and stubbornly they cling on. So much so that I find myself following her scent around the palace. But each time I draw close enough to corner her, she flits away again.

I might have given up on this pointless, frustrating, fruitless endeavor if not for learning of her plan for tonight.

She's been clever, I'll give her that, but not clever enough to escape my notice entirely. How could she be? I've been singularly focused on her for days. I keep telling myself I only need a taste, a moment with her, and I can forget this whole thing simmering between us. The more I think it, the less I believe it to be true.

There's nothing much either of us can do about the fact that she's stuck here, so we might as well have some fun. I imagine Elora would look quite the picture riding my cock, taking her pleasure from me, moaning my name. Begging for more.

She quickens her pace, and I'm forced out of my thoughts and back into the present moment. We're close to the River Axan, almost in the same spot where I found her bloody and weak.

I assume she's looking for the shallow stones, but the story of the demigod come to claim his love is only a myth mortals tell each other to soothe themselves into thinking it's possible for love to span worlds and lifetimes. For someone to be so giving of themselves they would risk their very soul to save another.

I know it to be a lie. Mortals and gods alike are cruel and selfish, myself included. I didn't have to let Elora get this far. I've given her false hope that she'll get to leave here tonight, that she'll be free of me.

But I need her. She's the thing holding my realm together, and I'm not about to let her go and risk its downfall. I've long since known I'd do whatever it took to keep the Shadow Realm strong. Including preventing the only solution I currently have from leaving.

Elora follows the curve of the Axan's banks, her cloak billowing out behind her. One day, I might actually get to see what she looks like in a gown. Not that I mind the way her breeches leave absolutely nothing about her curves to the imagination.

Grunting in frustration, Elora retraces her steps, holding the torch up to a piece of parchment in her hand and studying it. A map, I assume. She really has been putting her time with Railan and Nevon to good use. Though I'm sure she got more information out of Nevon than anyone else. The man can hardly keep it in his breeches around a beautiful woman.

I wouldn't say Elora was his type. He tends to prefer nymphs and sirens, but he isn't all that picky either. The idea of him touching her, of her touching him, seeds jealousy in the center of my chest, and I banish it with a wave of my hand. I doubt Elora would go for Nevon, but I'll make sure my youngest judge knows she's off limits.

Shoving the map back into her pocket, Elora sidles closer to the bank, peering down into the water. She stands there for a moment and then takes several steps back, the hood from her cloak falling to her shoulders to reveal the mussed strands of her thick braid.

She cocks her head and takes another step back, as if she's judging the distance between the banks. She can't really mean to jump. It would be impossible for her. She'd land smack in the middle of the river, and wrestling her from the ravenous river guardians would be a feat, even for me.

They have one purpose in this realm, and that is to keep in any soul who does manage to slip beyond the borders of their assigned territory from reaching the veil. I hardly want to be plucking her lifeless body from their clutches. Gods know what would happen to the realm then.

Elora takes two more steps back, crouching to drive the edge of her makeshift torch into the river's spongy banks. By all the gods. The infernal woman really does mean to make the leap.

Sighing, I step out from my hiding spot, intending to call her name and put an end to this whole charade. But her muscles bunch, and she takes off toward the bank before I can draw breath.

Something about watching her prepare to leap over a river dangerous enough to kill her in the blink of an eye shoves my heart into my throat. I shift to the river bank, wrapping an arm around her waist and hauling her back against my chest as her feet leave the ground.

She struggles against me, kicking her legs and clawing at my arm. When she finally remembers her dagger, her hand dives for it, but I'm faster, wrapping my other arm around her and securing her in my grip.

"Am I destined to save you from rivers for the rest of your life?"

At that, she goes still, all the fight draining out of her.

"Thieran."

There's so much anger in the single word. And still I can't help but enjoy my name on her lips. It's the first time she hasn't called me my lord with a sneer in her voice.

"Will you behave if I set you down, little one?"

"No."

Her honesty makes me chuckle, so I shift us back to the palace and dump her unceremoniously into the middle of her sitting room. Her hand reaches for her dagger again, and my arm shoots out to grip her wrist, tugging her forward hard enough to have her crashing into my chest.

I drag my hand up the outside of her thigh, enjoying the way her eyes darken and her jaw sets. Flipping the catch on the strap holding it in place, the weapon comes off in my hand. I linger a bit longer than necessary before releasing her and stepping back.

"Any others?"

She crosses her arms over her chest, chin lifting defiantly.

"I'll strip you naked to search for them if I have to." And I'd enjoy it too.

After a beat, she bends down and pulls a knife from her boot. Thinking better of throwing it at me, she holds it out to me handle first.

"I have to say I'm impressed. Truly."

She scoffs. "I'm not looking for your approval."

"I suspect not. You got farther than I thought you would."

Her eyes narrow on my face, and her fingertips dig into the skin of her arm. "How long have you known?"

"Since you asked the kitchen maids for comfrey, cinnamon, and...what was the other one?"

"Mint," she says through gritted teeth.

"Mint. That's right. I only needed to ask what you were in the kitchens for to get an answer. Though, to your credit, they were hesitant to give up your secret."

"If you hurt them—"

"Don't insult me. I wouldn't hurt the souls in my realm for being kind to you. How were they to know what you planned to do with them?"

Her body visibly relaxes, and she drops her arms to her sides, eyes looking everywhere but at me.

"You can't keep me here forever. I figured out how to get out once. I'll do it again."

"You got out because I let you."

I don't mean to make the confession. Why not let her think she was capable of escaping me if that made her feel better? But the words are out now, and I can't take them back.

"What do you mean, you let me?"

"I was born hundreds of years before Acaria even existed." I take a step forward, a grin tugging at the corners of my lips when she takes one back. "I maintain this entire realm with my power and barely a thought. I can walk into any Acarian city and force mortals to their knees with a snap of my fingers. And you really think I accidentally left a gap in the wards meant to keep you exactly where I want you?"

It takes her a moment to piece my meaning together, but when she does, she jerks upright, green eyes darkening and narrowing to slits. She lunges forward, drilling her finger into my chest. If looks could kill, I'd be dust under her heel.

"This entire time you've been playing me for a fool. Letting me sneak into the kitchens for herbs and tricking me into thinking I'd found a chink in your shield. And for what?" she snarls. "To amuse yourself?"

"Something like that." I smirk. "It was fun watching you try, impressive watching you nearly succeed."

I grab her wrist again when she draws her hand back to strike me, trapping it against her thigh and wrapping my arm around her waist. When I yank her onto her tiptoes, her chest brushing mine, she stops struggling.

"But you should absolutely stay away from the River Axan. I'd rather not have your death on my hands."

"No. You much prefer being my captor."

Her eyes dip down to my mouth, and she swallows. Anger still rolls off her in waves, but there's something else there— desire, maybe—and I can't help but grin.

"Careful, little one. Or you'll make me think you don't mind being stuck here with me as much as you say you do."

"You arrogant son of a—"

I silence the rest of her words with my lips, as eager to taste her as I am to shut her up. Her fingers grip the edges of my robes, and I expect her to shove me away, but she doesn't.

Instead she pushes higher onto her toes and tugs me forward, her teeth biting into the flesh of my bottom lip.

I release her wrist in favor of wrapping my hand around her throat. Using my thumb to angle her head back, I take the kiss deeper and slide my tongue against hers. She sighs in a way that arrows straight to my cock, and I urge her back until her legs hit the back of the brocade couch in front of the fireplace.

I want her under me and begging, and I'll take her on whatever surface I can get her. She doesn't fight me when I lift her onto the rounded curve of the feather-stuffed cushion. If anything, she pulls me in closer, her back arching when my hand skims down her side, tracing the shape of her breast.

"I hate you," she whispers against my jaw as I find the catch for her cloak and undo it, pushing the heavy fabric off her shoulders.

"Good." I tug at the laces of her corset while her lips and teeth and tongue explore the column of my throat. "This will be more fun for both of us that way."

She stills against me, but it takes her a moment more to shove me away. Her chest rises and falls with each heavy breath, and she presses the flat of her hand against her corset to keep it in place.

Her lips are red and swollen from my kiss, and I reach up to drag my thumb over her lower lip, dropping my hand when she flinches.

"Get out," she says softly, and I incline my head, quietly crossing to the door. "This won't happen again."

I pause with my hand on the knob. "You'll behave and not try to escape anymore?"

"No." She shakes her head, gesturing between us. "This. This won't happen again."

"We'll see."

I step out into the hallway before she can respond and shift to my rooms. Tonight won't be my last taste of Elora's lips, and there's so much more of her I want to sample.

But I'd be wise not to forget she serves a purpose here. Because I felt a change in the realm's power when she got so close to the veil. And I can't afford to lose her. Because losing her will cost me everything.

CHAPTER NINETEEN

Elora

With a rattle, a tray appears on the table by my bed. The smell of venison and eggs and freshly baked bread makes my mouth water. Kaia tried—unsuccessfully—to get me to come out of my rooms for meals once she came back from Rhagana. But I need time and space to think.

The more I stay confined to my rooms, the less I have to see, hear, or interact with Thieran. I torture myself enough with the memory of the way I let him kiss me, the way I kissed him back. The way I would have let him do more if I hadn't come to my senses when I did.

I wish I could say it was the effect the shifting had on me, but I'd be lying. There's something about the God of Death I can't explain. As much as I hate him—and I do hate him with a burning passion for trapping me here—I want him too. And I hate that just as much.

Annoyed with myself, I shove the covers back and swing my legs over the side of the bed. Quickly pulling on a dressing gown, I carry the tray into my sitting room and set it on the low table.

I briefly consider skipping breakfast, but my stomach grumbles in protest, so I force myself to sit. I will make another attempt at escaping. I'll make as many attempts as it takes to get away from this place. I will not become Thieran's pliant little prisoner while he plays whatever sick game he's playing with me. But there's no need to starve myself in the meantime.

Scooping up a bite of scrambled eggs, I sigh when they melt on my tongue. I've only met the woman who runs the kitchens once, when I went to ask for the herbs for my ritual that didn't work, but she was a force. And she knows her way around food. I've never eaten so well as I have in the Shadow Realm.

Before coming here, I spent most of my time eating at taverns or cooking game over a campfire. Neither of which compare to the magick Ygris makes in the kitchen. Slathering fresh butter on bread that's still warm from the ovens, I take a bite and sigh. The food might be the only thing I'll miss about this place. That and the bed.

Popping the last bite of bread into my mouth, I pour myself a cup of tea from the pot and bring the steaming cup to my lips. It's been almost a week since Thieran caught me by the river and brought me back here, and I've pouted for long enough. It's time to hatch a new plan.

I'll have to be more careful with this one. If I can't outwit Thieran, maybe I can get around him. I'm not generally one for using my body to get what I want. I prefer the speed of my dagger instead. But seducing Nevon wouldn't exactly be a hardship, and if I can convince him to let me out of here with a lover's plea, it will have been worth it.

The whinny of a horse catches my attention, and I shove away from the couch to cross to the window. I must have imagined the sound because I see nothing but grass and the trees beyond. If I crane my neck and look to the right, I can make out the edge of the wide swath of cleared land that is the path to Videva.

It curves around the sheet of smooth stone and ends at the kitchens. Each day, the souls who serve here journey from the village to the palace and back again. It would all feel so ordinary and mundane if the occasional glimpse of a transparent hand or head didn't still make me shiver.

I should explore the village myself. There could be something useful there for me. As Kaia is constantly reminding me, souls in Videva live and work as they do in the mortal world. It would likely be a better source for herbs or anything else I might need to aid in my next escape. And hopefully less of a chance Thieran will track me there and interrogate whoever supplies me.

I've avoided it for a reason. The idea of seeing my parents there sends a wave of grief through me, and I draw my dressing gown tighter around me. They've been dead so long, and I was so young when they were killed, I'm not even sure I would recognize them. Or if they would recognize me. Or if they're even still in the Shadow Realm at all.

Stepping away from the window, I stuff the grief and the uncertainty back down. I have too many other things to think about without twisting myself into knots over the parents I lost so long ago. Whether or not they're in the realm hardly matters now. I don't intend to be here much longer.

I cross back to my breakfast tray; there's a bit of venison left and my tea. I'll be all the stronger for it if I finish both before setting off into the palace today. It's time to stop hiding. Because the last thing I want is for Thieran to think he's cowed me into submission.

My steps falter at a knock on the door, and I change course, pausing with my hand on the knob.

"Who is it?"

"Good morning." Kaia's voice is soft and cheerful.

The door swings open on her smiling face, and I nearly join her. Everything about Kaia is infectious, from her smile to her laugh to her sunny disposition. It's irritating. I'd have expected the Goddess of Witchcraft to be a little...darker.

"I'm glad to see you up and about." Her eyes dart over my shoulder, and her smile widens. "And that you've had breakfast."

"Thank you for seeing to that."

"It wasn't me," Kaia assures me. "The staff think very highly of you, and they were concerned when they didn't see you in the dining room."

That news surprises me. I wasn't aware any of the servants thought of me at all, let alone enough to worry I wasn't being fed.

"May I come in?"

I step back and Kaia breezes past, followed by her usual faint scent of lavender and rosemary. Her skirts rustle with her movement, the glittering overskirt catching in the dancing candlelight.

She settles on one of the chairs across from the couch, folding her hands in her lap. I suddenly feel underdressed and unkempt. Tugging on the sleeves of the dressing gown, I smooth a hand over my hair and reclaim my seat.

I reach for my teacup, pausing as I consider. "Would you like some tea?"

Kaia smiles again. "That would be lovely, thank you."

I add some tea to the porcelain cup Kaia conjures and hand it to her, watching as she drops in two sugar cubes and swirls her finger over the surface to stir it. I doubt it will ever be any less jarring to watch the gods use their powers. If I had my way, I'd never keep company with a god again.

"I'm sorry, Elora," Kaia says, lowering her cup to her lap after taking a careful sip.

"Sorry for what?"

She plucks at a fold in her skirt, smoothing it with her fingertips. "For the time you must spend here."

"It might be easier to stomach if someone would tell me

why." She purses her lips, and I set my cup back on the tray with a loud clatter. "Or how long I might be held against my will."

She flinches at that, and I allow a bead of satisfaction to bubble up. I've known Kaia wanted to keep me here as much as Thieran does, and now I know, at least on some level, she feels guilty about it. It's not much of a consolation, but it's something.

"I wish I could give you more answers." Her gaze slides to mine, and her smile is apologetic. "But I can't. I hardly understand it myself. Only that…"

Her words trail off, like she's weighing how much to share and how much to keep from me. She shakes her head. Decision made.

"It isn't so bad here, is it?"

There's a note of hope in her voice, but her face falls when I snort. I might like Kaia, and I might appreciate how kind she's been to me, but I won't let her paint a pretty picture over this.

"It would be better if I weren't a prisoner."

Or in such close proximity to the god who refuses to stop invading my thoughts.

"I want to make you smile, Elora. You like to read, don't you?" she continues before I can remind her my freedom would give her the kind of genuine smile she wants. "I don't think you've found the library yet. You've been so focused on exploring beyond the palace."

She quirks a brow, and a mischievous look comes into her eyes that makes me wonder if, in some small way, Kaia approves of my escape attempt. Or can at least respect it.

"It's quite large, the library," she says in an effort to convince me. "Plenty of things to choose from."

I imagine the God of Death doesn't just stock his library with novels about women falling in love and having adventures in far-off lands. No doubt he has books about history and gods and rituals and the power used by both in there. And those I can use just as much as the entertainment of a good novel.

"That sounds nice. Let me—"

I'm interrupted by another knock, and when I don't immediately rise to answer it, Kaia pushes up from her chair and crosses the room. It could be Nevon; he tried to call yesterday and entice me to take a walk with him. I should have taken him up on it, but I was too busy sulking. Today, though, I'll say yes in a heartbeat and make sure I lay my flirting on thick.

But it isn't Nevon's face revealed when the door swings in. It's Thieran, and I make a noise of disgust in the back of my throat. He has the nerve to smirk at me, his eyes traveling over my body from head to toe and making me acutely aware for the first time how thin this dressing gown is.

"Get dressed," he commands. "I have a surprise for you."

So sure I'll obey, he turns from the door in a swirl of robes, and something about his tone and his order and his mere presence makes me bristle.

"No, thank you."

He pivots to face me again, eyebrow raised.

"I tire of your surprises."

He steps into the room, ignoring Kaia when she subtly shifts to block his path to me with her body.

"Don't make me dress you myself and haul you outside kicking and screaming." He pauses for a beat. "Or maybe do. I'd enjoy it so much."

"Thieran." Kaia's voice is a low warning, but he isn't deterred.

"Ten minutes. Meet me at the bottom of the stairs."

He's gone again before I can speak, and Kaia huffs out an annoyed breath with her hands on her hips.

"I swear I have no idea what he's up to," she says. "But you'll have to get dressed to visit the library anyway. I'll go with you, and we can go there right after his...surprise."

"You don't know what it is?"

She shakes her head, moving to the door. "No. He wasn't at breakfast this morning. And Railan said he'd left early." She looks at me when I don't move to change. "Better to get it over with quick, I think."

Disappearing into the hall, Kaia closes the door behind her with a gentle click. I'm not eager for Thieran's surprise, though I have to assume he uses that word loosely. I can't imagine he's interested in doing something nice for me. But I do want to see the library, so I'll consider this my medicine first.

It doesn't take me long to change my dressing gown for a fresh pair of breeches and a tunic. I quickly lace up my corset and draw the strings tight, tying them into a neat bow. Thieran's had more gowns delivered since my arrival, but a curious amount of corsets have also appeared since he kissed me, in an array of colors and cuts and styles.

I run my fingertips over the fabric before closing the wardrobe doors and meeting Kaia in the hallway. We walk down to the stairs in this part of the palace in silence, and Thieran is waiting for us at the bottom.

"You're coming too, then?" he says to Kaia.

"I am. You're not usually one for surprises. I want to make sure you mind yourself."

Thieran scoffs but doesn't object, reaching for my elbow. He raises a brow at Kaia, and she gives a slight nod before we disappear. The air that envelopes us is warmer than Thieran's power usually feels, and it's devoid of the nauseating tumble I've felt before.

When we arrive, Thieran brushes a hand up my arm, and my body warms further, calm settling into my bones. I glance up at him, but he doesn't make eye contact. He's made the shift not just bearable, but comfortable for me without being asked.

A ploy, I'm sure, to try and earn my trust or something. The man is always thinking ten steps ahead of me. Infuriating as that realization is.

Kaia appears beside us a second later, and I realize for the first time that we're standing at the edge of a farm somewhere on the outskirts of Videva. From this vantage point, I see the village is far bigger than I imagined, stretching out from us to the horizon.

A small, neatly kept farmhouse sits just back from the road, with a pasture to the left. Beyond the simple wooden fence, a herd of goats grazing on the short, colorless grass surrounds a single cow.

"What's the surprise? You'd like me to make myself useful by becoming a farmhand?"

Thieran casts his eyes to the sky and moves to open the wooden gate, motioning me to go ahead of him up the short path to the farmhouse. Intrigued, I skirt around him, tilting my head to study the house.

There's something oddly familiar about it, the slant of the roof and the striations in the wood, worn from the elements, though it's never rained or stormed in the Shadow Realm as long as I've been here. Flowers in what I imagine would be a riot of color overflow a garden bed right by the front door, and I stop short as a memory barrels through me.

Me on my knees, digging in the dirt and singing a made-up song while my father rips weeds out of the ground beside me. His smile is indulgent when he looks over at me, and he runs his hand over my tumble of unruly curls.

Grip this one here, poppet, he says, using his strong hand to show me how to grab a fledgling weed. *And tug it free so it doesn't kill the pretty flower.*

This place. It looks just like the home I was born in. Right down to the simple lace curtains hanging in the front window. I take a step back as Thieran raises his fist to knock on the door.

"Wait. I can't." I hate the tremble in my voice, and I clear my throat. "If it's all the same, I'd rather not have this particular surprise."

He frowns. "What are you talking about?"

"If..." I take a deep breath. "If my parents are in there, I don't want to see them."

His face softens, and he steps toward me, resting his hands on my shoulders and giving them a gentle squeeze. "Your parents aren't here. And even if they were, I wouldn't do that to you." He pauses, dropping his hands. "Or to them."

It's an answer that only brings up more questions. Does he mean they're not here in this house? Or not in Videva? Or not in the Shadow Realm at all because they chose to reincarnate? But I don't have the time to voice any of it because he raps on the door, and it swings in almost instantly on a girl much too young to be my mother.

"My lord." She drops into a deep curtsy. Then her eyes light up when she sees Kaia, and she does another bob. "My lady. What an honor. Would you like to come in for some tea? Or we've fresh bread just from the fire."

"No, thank you," Thieran says in a tone that is gentle and kind.

It surprises me, but now that I'm looking closer, I can see the girl is not afraid of the God of Death as I would expect her to be. And isn't that a curious thing.

"I've come to show my...guest," he decides, sweeping me with a look somewhere between amusement and challenge, "around the stables."

My whole body lights up at the word. Yes, I miss Meera terribly, but I also miss a good, hard ride through an open field, the wind in my hair, and a strong, sure horse under me. This surprise might be worth the time spent in Thieran's presence after all. Assuming it isn't a trick and he actually lets me ride beyond the wards.

"Of course, my lord."

The girl steps out and leads us around the side of the house, away from the pasture. A soft sigh escapes me when I see the small stable and paddock. A draft horse towers over the fence and chuffs when he sees us. His coat is shiny and his mane is clean.

When Thieran reaches up to run a hand down the horse's nose, he leans into him and not away. Another surprise. Thieran murmurs something to him I cannot hear as we step through the paddock's gate and cross to the stable.

"In the last stall, my lord. A bit skittish still, but we've put down fresh hay and water."

"Thank you," Thieran says in obvious dismissal.

The girl drops another deep curtsy, and then we're alone in the barn. It's small, with only three stalls and tack hanging on pegs on the back wall. The first two stalls are empty, but even without the girl's direction, it's clear the third stall is occupied. And by a horse who doesn't altogether like its living arrangements.

Stepping up to the stall, I inhale sharply. It can't be. Jerking around to look at Thieran, I see him leaning one shoulder against the stall next to me, his arms crossed over his chest.

"I-it's not possible," I breathe.

"Obviously it is."

I shake my head, blinking back the tears stubbornly gathering in my eyes. "But how?"

His smile is teasing and a little arrogant. "Magick."

Power shimmers at his fingertips until a swirl of black smoke pours from them and spins into a tiny cyclone. I turn back to the stall when the horse nickers, and when our eyes meet, Meera takes a step forward.

I run my hand down the side of her neck and press my forehead to her nose. It's only been a few weeks, but it feels like years.

"Is it a trick?"

I don't realize I've said it out loud until Thieran scoffs. "The things you think of me. Of course it's not a trick. That is your horse, isn't it?"

Meera huffs in agreement, bumping my shoulder, and I smile. "It is."

"Well then. I've made it so you can come see her whenever you like, and there's plenty of space for you to ride without getting…lost."

Even Kaia snorts at that.

"Thank you," I whisper, not trusting my voice with more.

"You're welcome," he replies. "Hopefully this means you'll stop sulking in your rooms."

I shake my head but don't dignify him with an answer. I'm too happy to rise to his prodding. He turns to go, and I immediately start thinking of saddling Meera and giving us both a workout in the empty field beyond the paddock.

"Elora," he says, pausing at the entrance to the barn. "Do try and make it to dinner tonight. Your absence is noted. And unappreciated."

Now that gets my attention, but he and Kaia are both gone in a breath.

"What a puzzle he is," I tell Meera, moving to the back wall, pleased to see my old saddle and blanket among the selection. "But let's not think about him today. Let's have a good ride and get reacquainted with each other."

Meera stands patiently while I saddle her up, adjusting the straps and stirrups before vaulting onto her back and finding my seat. It feels foreign and familiar all at once as I lead her out into the field behind the barn.

I lean over her neck and give her a pat. "All right, my girl, I'm not after testing Thieran's limits today. Not after he's given me such a lovely gift. There'll be time enough for that later."

Sitting straight in the saddle, I urge her into a trot and then a canter. It's been weeks since I sat a horse, but the smooth, strong lines of her are like a dance I'll never forget. Eager to feel the bite of the wind on my face and the speed and the freedom, however short-lived, I take her up to a gallop and we fly.

CHAPTER TWENTY

Thieran

"Having any luck with those?"

I look up from the book in my hands to see Kaia walking toward me across the deep red carpet. Her hair is swept up off her neck and secured with jeweled combs that catch the light, and her arms are full of more books.

She's been bringing me whatever she can find from Rhagana that might aid in my search for answers about the Shadow Realm and its continued weakening. I've slacked off on my research in the last week or two since it seemed Elora's presence had given me everything I needed.

But the feeling on the air when she came so close to the veil the night she tried to escape—the night I let her get too close to succeeding—there was something about it. Something heavy and constricting. The veil reacted to her presence in a way I've never seen it react to anyone. Even me.

And I have no idea what to make of it. So I've thrown myself back into searching for answers, poring over whatever Kaia brings, debating whether to risk a trip to Fontoss to see if it has what Kaia's resources cannot give me. Only now my focus has shifted from how Elora crossed to how it's possible for a mortal to sustain the realm.

So far I've come up empty. And until I can find more information about why a mortal's presence seems to be having such an effect and what that really means, I've got to keep Elora here. And it's better for all of us if she's comfortable enough that she doesn't try to escape again.

Which is why I endured a trip into Acaria and nearly lost an arm collecting her horse. That confounding beast tried to take a bite out of me more than once while I had the stable hands prepare her. Stubborn and temperamental. Like her owner.

Never mind that Elora's smile and the raw emotion in her voice made it all worth it. Or that the sound of her laughter drifting across the open field smooths out a jagged part of me each time it carries on the wind. Or that she seems happier and more content when I see her at dinner every night.

She's even dragged Hayle, the most private of my judges, out of wherever he often hides. I don't think I've ever seen the man smile or laugh so much in all the centuries I've known him. And so far I've done a perfectly admirable job of not punching him in the face every time Elora brushes a hand over his arm.

She is settling in and behaving herself, spending most days with her horse and most nights in her room, although I occasionally sense her wandering the halls. She hasn't tested the wards again. If she does, she'll find them stronger than before.

She has become exactly what I need her to be. Pliant. And it seems entirely too good to be true. She's up to something. She has to be. I only wish I knew what it was.

After reading the same paragraph three times, I close the book with a snap and toss it on the pile.

Kaia glances up from the pages she's thumbing through. "No luck?"

"How did we manage to perform one of the biggest blood

rituals in our history and only write the damned thing down in a single book?"

A smile tugs at the corner of Kaia's mouth, and she starts flipping through the pages again. "Probably a healthy dose of self-preservation. Binding souls and mortals in the way we did isn't exactly something we should want to repeat often."

I huff out an annoyed breath and lean back in my chair.

"Any news from your spies in Fontoss?"

Pursing her lips, she slowly closes her book and sets it gently on the top of a stack. She carefully aligns its edges with the book beneath it before speaking.

"Preparations for the winter ball are well underway."

"Getting started early," I say, eyebrow raised. "The ball isn't for another six weeks."

"Seems like the king might be planning a big surprise."

That brings me upright, curiosity piqued. "Any idea what kind of surprise?"

She shrugs, moving to the window and staring out into the pitch black. "My spy didn't know. Only that the queen seems to be spending more time with the king than usual. And she seems...happier when she returns."

"Kaia—"

"Don't," she replies, trying and failing to keep the note of sadness from her voice. "It's been a long time. I'm fine."

She's never been fine where my brother is concerned, but I let the matter drop. If my brother is up to something, something he apparently intends to unveil at the winter ball we're all required to attend, then I need to know about it.

Whatever feelings Kaia might have when it comes to knowing about my brother's personal life are hers to deal with. They are her spies, after all. I wonder briefly if she is purposely torturing herself with the information. Some sort of penance for what she perceives as a betrayal, no matter how hard I've tried to convince her otherwise.

"Do—"

"Iluna is here."

I blink at the sudden change in topic, turning in my chair to stare at Kaia's back. "What? How do you know that?"

"I can see lights on in her rooms." She points across the courtyard at the glowing windows that are normally dark. "I didn't know she was visiting."

"Neither did I." A shadow moves across the window. "She doesn't usually come until after the winter ball."

Kaia looks up at me. "Think she'll come to dinner?"

Rising from my chair, I stride toward the door. "Only one way to find out."

Kaia quickens her steps to keep up with my pace down the hall. "What do you plan on telling her about Elora?"

I stop short at the top of the stairs. Elora. Aside from Kaia, my dark court spends so little time in my realm I haven't had to worry about Elora meeting anyone else or answering their questions about her.

I'm not accustomed to explaining myself to people, and I rarely bother, but I don't want this information getting back to my brother before I understand it myself. Not that I expect any members of my court to go running to Fontoss with gossip.

Except maybe Aeris, who lives for stirring up trouble.

"I'll think of something."

The low hum of voices from the dining room reaches my ears before I step into the doorway. Railan and Hayle are seated on one side of the table, heads bent together in conversation with my ferryman, Basal. Nevon sits across from them, occasionally adding his thoughts while he sips his wine.

Elora is nowhere in sight, and without thinking, I reach out across the palace and grounds to search for her, the tightness in my chest loosening when I find her in her rooms. She hasn't missed dinner since I brought her horse here. I don't want her to miss it tonight, even if her presence might complicate things where Iluna is concerned.

I consider going to fetch her, make sure she comes, but the Goddess of Night steps into the doorway. She's dressed in her preferred black fitted gown, silver jewels gleaming at her wrist and throat like stars.

Stopping in front of me, she drops into a curtsy, but her eyes are smiling when she stands again.

"My lord."

"You're earlier than usual. Any particular reason?"

"I tire of mortals more and more often these days. You understand that better than anyone."

I see Railan raise a brow over Iluna's shoulder. This should be fun. Taking my seat at the head of the table, I send Nevon a questioning look and glance at the empty chair next to him. Seeming to understand my meaning, he lifts a shoulder and takes another sip of wine.

The servants are just filling glasses when a figure steps into the doorway. I hardly recognize her at first. She's abandoned her leather breeches and tunic for a gown of deep violet. Even at this distance, I can see how it's sharpened the green of her eyes.

She fidgets with the fabric of her skirt with nervous fingers, eyes darting around the table and snagging on Iluna's unfamiliar face before landing on me. She holds my gaze for a long moment, breathing deeply. Then something snaps her out of her trance, and she takes what has become her usual seat next to Nevon.

Beside Kaia, Iluna wrinkles her nose as Elora sits, smiling up at the servant who pours her a glass of wine.

"You've a mortal living in the Shadow Realm?"

Elora flinches at the disgust in Iluna's question, and anger rises unbidden.

"Yes," I reply, challenge in my tone.

Iluna opens her mouth to speak but thinks better of it and

closes it again. I'll explain Elora when I'm ready and not before, but I won't tolerate a member of my court insulting her.

I signal the staff to begin serving, and normal chatter resumes as platters of lamb and vegetables are brought out. I nod to Iluna as she strikes up a conversation, making appropriate noises when my input is required, but my attention is on Elora.

On the way the dress clings to her curves, how her breasts swell against the gently scooping neckline. My mouth waters when I wonder if she's wearing one of the corsets I bid the servants put in her wardrobe—bright silks against soft skin.

The more I study her, the harder it is to tear my eyes away. Watching Elora has become my new favorite pastime. And the way her hair, customarily bound in a thick braid, hangs in waves down her back makes me wonder what it would feel like to thread my fingers through it, to grip it in my fist as she slides her mouth up and down my cock.

She leans in to whisper something in Nevon's ear, her hand resting on his bicep, and he throws his head back with a laugh. I frown. Something is different about their interaction tonight. Nevon is notoriously flirtatious. The man would flirt with anything moving if he thought it would charm them into his bed.

But where Elora usually dances around the edges of his flirtations, tonight she's flirting back. Sitting closer, her body turned slightly toward him. When he speaks, she tilts her head, drawing his eyes down the column of her throat to her breasts.

I grip my wineglass so hard I'm surprised it doesn't shatter.

All through the meal, I watch them, half-listening to Iluna talk of her feast day celebrations and how she tires of them more and more each year. She's saying something about attending the winter ball when Nevon leans over and whispers in Elora's ear, making color rise to her cheeks.

She nods, pushing back from the table and shooting a look

in my direction. Nevon stands, reaching for her hand and leading her from the room.

It takes every ounce of strength I have not to shove out of my seat and immediately go after them. They've gone on walks after dinner before. But this time feels different.

This time I can't get the image of Nevon touching her out of my head. I replace it with an image of smashing his face into the nearest wall until he's a bloody heap on the floor, which makes me feel better. But only marginally.

"I think the queen is—"

Unable to stomach the wondering anymore, I jerk to my feet, cutting Iluna off mid-sentence.

"Pardon me," I murmur, rounding the table and following Nevon and Elora out the door and down the hall.

I search for her again, teeth grinding together when I sense her with Nevon on the edge of the forest. The bastard is taking her to the hot springs. The same location he's fucked countless others. Before I can stop myself, I shift to the edge of the springs and wait.

It takes only a moment before the sound of their feet on the forest floor reaches my ears. I hear the low rumble of Nevon's voice, followed by the airy sound of Elora's laughter. Jealousy constricts my chest until I can barely breathe.

Above my head, the trees illuminate with a delicate glow, casting a soft golden light on the bubbling water and setting a romantic mood. A scant second later, Nevon and Elora emerge from the trees. Nevon stops short when he sees me—and the look on my face. Elora's breath rushes from her lungs in surprise.

"Am I interrupting something?"

"Actually," Elora says, lifting her chin in that defiant way that makes me want to claim every fucking inch of her for my own, "we were coming here for some privacy."

She may not know it, but that was precisely the wrong thing to say to me.

"Nevon," I growl in warning. "Go away."

He hesitates, but ultimately releases Elora's arm and shifts back to the palace. When we're alone, she takes two steps forward, the light haloing her crown of dark hair and shimmering off her skin.

"What are you doing? Nevon and I are friends and—"

"Oh, yes." Her eyes narrow at the bite in my tone. "You were very friendly at dinner."

I take a step toward her and she takes one back, so I advance again and again until her back is pressed against the nearest tree.

"First you hold me prisoner, and now I can't even have friends?"

"You think Nevon was bringing you here for an idle chat?" I gesture to the springs behind me, steam curling up from the surface. "You were going to do what? Exchange recipes and talk about your new wardrobe?"

My eyes drop to the tops of her breasts, and she takes a deep breath, making them rise and strain against her corset.

"It's none of your business what we talk about. Or do. Or where we do it."

I inch closer, my body brushing hers and making her shiver.

"That's where you're wrong, little one. Everything about you is my business. Where you go. Who you speak to." I trail my fingertip over the edge of the fabric at her shoulder, grinning when goosebumps rise across her skin. "Who you fuck. And you will not be fucking Nevon or anyone else in my realm. Understand?"

She tilts her head up to meet my eyes, bringing her mouth in line with my own. I feel the warmth of her breath against my lips, and my finger travels farther south along the edge of her gown, making her breaths come faster.

"You're not in control of me," she whispers. "I can fuck whoever I want."

I drop my head until my mouth is a hair's breadth from hers and whisper back, "Wrong again."

She closes the distance between us in an instant, fusing her mouth to mine. She doesn't touch me, her hands hanging by her sides and curled into fists, but she takes greedily from my mouth. Her tongue lashes against mine, and she groans low in her throat when I nip it with my teeth.

Her hands come up to my chest, fingers curling in the fabric of my robes, and I snake my arm around her waist, tugging her into me. I wait for her to push me away like she did in her rooms. When she doesn't, I give in to my desire from dinner and slip my hand into her hair, fisting it and roughly tugging her head back.

The act draws a needy moan from her, and I tilt my head to drag my teeth along her jaw and down the exposed column of her throat. Her heartbeat pounds a furious rhythm under my lips, and she tilts her head for me even more.

Smiling against her skin, I scrape my teeth over the spot where her neck joins her shoulder, and she sucks in a sharp breath, shuddering in my arms.

My hand slides down to grip her ass, squeezing it roughly and drawing her against me, grinding the hard length of my cock into her hip. She whimpers, and the sound makes me ache to be inside her, to feel her moving around me.

I bunch her skirt in my hands, revealing the long, smooth line of her leg. The image of trailing my lips over every inch of her from the tips of her toes to the top of her head slams into me, but there isn't time for that now. I need to be buried to the hilt in her like I need air in my lungs.

She helps me with her dress, then her hands dive into my robes when I lift her into my arms, pressing her back against the tree. She shoves into my breeches, a desperate sigh falling from her lips when I press a line of kisses across her breasts. Her fingers wrap around me, and I drop my forehead to her chest with a groan.

Stroking me root to tip, she squirms against me, my fingers digging into the soft skin of her ass. Smacking her hand away, I line myself up with her entrance and catch her gaze. Her eyes are heavy with lust, her lips red and swollen from my kisses, her cheeks flushed with desire.

I thrust my hips forward, the tip of my cock sliding inside her, and she wraps her legs around my waist.

"I hate you," she whispers, her legs tightening around my waist, trying to draw me further inside her.

"I know," I reply, slamming into her and capturing her cry with my lips.

She's exquisite, her pussy rippling around me with each brutal thrust, her breath catching in the back of her throat. Trapping her body between me and the tree, I trace a path across her jaw with my teeth, tugging her earlobe roughly.

"Fuck," she rasps, the word caught somewhere between a curse and a prayer.

"Come undone for me, little one," I command, grinding my pelvis against her clit until she shudders. "Let me feel you."

I don't relent in my pace, pushing her closer and closer to the brink, reveling in the sting as she digs her fingernails into the skin of my neck. She stiffens in my arms, body going taut, breaths ragged. I want to feel her explode. I need to feel it. To feel what I can do to her.

Then she finally, blissfully, squeezes tight around me, her orgasm tearing through her with a sob. I grit my teeth against my own release until she finishes contracting on my cock. When her body goes limp in my arms, I give her one last punishing thrust and follow her over the edge.

Her teeth scrape across my jaw, and my hips jerk, making her groan and ripple around me again.

"That was the worst sex I've ever had," she pants against my skin, eliciting a low laugh from me.

I'm tempted to take her back to my rooms, taste every inch of her, and mark her as mine in every way I know how. But she gives my shoulder a weak shove, and instead I step back, setting her on the ground and tucking myself into my breeches while she adjusts her skirts and runs a shaky hand through her hair.

Holding out my hand for hers, she hesitates before laying her fingers in mine. I shift us back to her rooms, arriving in front of her plush bed. Her eyes dart to the neatly made quilt and piles of pillows, color rising to her chest and crawling up her neck.

"Next time, I'll take my time with you."

She draws in a deep breath and looks up at me, but doesn't move away. "There won't be a next time."

I grin. "We'll see."

CHAPTER TWENTY-ONE

Elora

Skimming my fingertip over the spines of the books, I shuffle one out from the shelf and stack it on top of the others already in my hands. I carry my prizes down the winding wrought iron staircase and claim one of the over-stuffed chairs by the window.

After my unfortunate slip with Thieran in the forest, I all but begged Kaia to show me where the library was this morning. I needed a distraction so I didn't spend all my time thinking about Thieran, and plotting my next escape seemed like the best one.

The library is far bigger than I expected, with three stories of floor-to-ceiling bookcases joined by curving staircases and occasionally broken by expansive windows. I've never seen so many books in all my life.

Thieran has quite the collection. Everything from novels to Acarian history to books about magick and power and the gods. Nothing seems off limits. If Thieran knows I'm in here, he doesn't expect me to be able to learn much.

But I am determined to hatch a better escape plan, and the first part of that is to not rely on my memory when it comes to charms and anything else I might need. I will scour these books until I have answers, no matter how long it takes, and then I'm going to be meticulous in my execution.

No more asking the kitchen servants for help. I go to the farmhouse most days to see Meera and take her for a ride. It'll be the perfect cover to venture farther into the village and buy or trade for whatever I need. I don't have much to trade with, but surely there's something of value in my rooms the souls in Videva might want.

I drape my legs over the arm of the chair, wincing when the movement drags my back over the opposite arm. The skin between my shoulder blades is scratched and raw where Thieran pressed me against the tree trunk.

I shouldn't have kissed him, shouldn't have let it go farther than that. Shouldn't have enjoyed it so fucking much. The goal was to seduce Nevon, give him easy access with that uncomfortable dress. And it had been working too. Nevon wanted to show me somewhere beautiful and private.

The hot springs were both. But Thieran ruined it with his growling commands and rough hands and wandering kisses and hard... I shake the memory of last night from my thoughts. I need to focus.

Returning my attention to the book at hand, I skim through the pages, looking for the passage on wards. There are two different kinds of wards—those created by gods and those created by mortals.

Mortal wards can be broken by performing a banishing ritual. Pluck hyssop from the ground by the root and mix with the wings of a beetle, salt, and the dried, crushed bones of a hummingbird. Add the ingredients to a jar of water and let steep under the sun for three days.

I have no idea how one would go about collecting enough beetle wings to make this work or if the Shadow Realm has hummingbirds, but mortal wards are not my issue. I'm dealing with a god. A very ancient and powerful one.

The book gives several more recipes on how to break mortal wards, but its paragraph on immortal ones is less helpful, essentially advising me to ask nicely or rot on the wrong side of the barrier. Neither of which is an option. I doubt I could seduce Thieran to release me in the same way I might have Nevon.

Tossing that book to the floor, I pick up the next one and flip quickly through the pages. Ready to set it down, I pause when I see a passage about shielding mortals from the divine.

The ritual is meant more to protect a mortal from a god's advances, but the end result is the same. Thieran wouldn't be able to detect me in the Shadow Realm—an important aspect of a successful escape.

It's nothing like the one I tried last time, and the ingredients and instructions seem simple enough. Combine all the dried herbs and oils into a jar and seal it with wax from a white candle. Then leave the potion to cure for a fortnight.

It's longer than I wanted to wait, but it's better than nothing. And the herbs and oils should be easy enough to get at any apothecary. Assuming Videva has an apothecary. I can't imagine the souls of dead mortals require many healing remedies.

I mark the page with a bit of parchment and move on to the next book. Being shielded from Thieran is all well and good, but it means nothing if I can't get past his barrier. Knowing he intentionally created a hole in the wards just to toy with me has embarrassment twining with anger and heating my face.

Yet another reason I shouldn't have let him take me in the forest. No matter how good it was or how much I want him to do it again. It's been a long time since I've been with anyone, certainly not someone who makes me feel the way Thieran does. All hot, desperate need.

But that's hardly the point. We are enemies in this. And fucking him against a tree in the forest doesn't change that. If anything, it's an even better reason to get away from him before he completely addles my brain.

This book contains a few passages that might be useful about the gods and the source of their power. But the more I read, the more it seems like fanciful conclusions rather than proven fact.

It takes me more than two hours and three trips to different parts of the library before I have a pile of books that makes me feel as if I've made progress. I still don't have an answer on breaking through the wards, but I think I'm headed in the right direction.

Standing, I stretch my arms over my head, my back protesting at the movement. I thought about asking one of the servants for a salve, something to make the scratches heal faster so they stop reminding me they exist every time I move.

But the idea of anyone guessing why I might need it is exactly why I refuse to ask. The look Kaia gave me over breakfast when I casually asked her to show me the library was bad enough. She knows. Whether Thieran told her or she guessed, Kaia knows we've been together.

There is nothing I can do about that. So I'll just have to live with the embarrassment and the subtle look of what I assume was disapproval in her eyes. I do not answer to Kaia. I don't answer to anyone, whatever Thieran might think.

Hefting the books I need in my arms and tucking them under my chin, I climb carefully down to the first floor, pausing when I hear movement in the stacks to my right.

A swath of black skirt appears at the edge of the shelf before she does. Her hair, black as midnight, is twisted in a series of elaborate braids that remind me of a den of snakes. She has a small silver tiara dotted with black onyx and rubies secured on her head, and her lips are painted a deep red.

Iluna, the Goddess of Night, does not look happy to see me. Her boldly painted lip curls back over her teeth, and she sweeps a disapproving gaze over me from head to toe. It's unclear whether she dislikes me because I'm a mortal or because I'm currently in the Shadow Realm. Or both.

So far my reception by the other immortals in the realm has been a warm one. I don't need this goddess to like me, but I have no idea what danger I could be in if she doesn't. Would Thieran stop her from harming me if it came to it? Iluna isn't exactly known for her tolerance of mortals.

She takes a step toward me, and I take one back. Annoyed with myself, I stand my ground as she continues to cross to me.

"It's customary to curtsy to a god," she says, clearly waiting for my deference.

I should just do it, drop a quick bob and get out of here as fast as I can. But my pride won't let me. One day it will, no doubt, be my undoing.

"My arms are a bit full for that today. Maybe some other time."

The scowl on her face deepens, and she crosses her arms over her chest. The air shimmers around her, the faint scent of pine and ash reaching my nose before the air stills again.

"I've never known Lord Thieran to keep a mortal pet before. Especially not one who can read." Her eyes drop to the books in my hand, scanning the spines. "Or one so interested in power and the gods."

"He's just full of surprises. And I'm not a pet."

Her laugh makes me bristle, but I manage to bite my tongue before I really get myself in trouble.

"A prize. An oddity." She approaches me, studying me like a bug under glass. "What other use could Lord Thieran have for a mortal in the realm if not for his amusement?"

"You'll have to ask him."

"Oh, I intend to." She turns to go, pausing and spinning slowly around to face me. "Mortal, be sure to stay out of my way while I'm here. The smell is unbearable," she adds, wrinkling her nose.

I bite the inside of my cheek hard enough to taste blood, and when the air shimmers again, she disappears from view, leaving only the scent of her power behind.

I am still trying to understand why Thieran insists on keeping me here or what he plans on doing with me. But I do know I'm not anyone's pet or plaything. And that Iluna is the perfect reminder of why the gods aren't worth worshipping.

Shifting the weight of the books in my hands, I make my way out of the library and down the wide hall. With a note of concern in her voice, Kaia assured me when I asked who the strange woman had been at dinner last night that Iluna doesn't tend to stay long when she visits the Shadow Realm. I can only hope Kaia's right, because everything about the Goddess of Night makes me deeply uncomfortable.

From the way she looks at me to the way she looks at Thieran and everything in between. She hates mortals; that much is obvious. But she especially seems to hate my presence in the Shadow Realm. Maybe even my proximity to Thieran. Unfortunately for both of us, I have no control over that.

Huffing my way up the stairs to my rooms, I barely manage to open the door without dumping the books on the floor and sag back against it. I refuse to let Iluna force me into hiding, but staying out of her way as much as possible until she leaves might be the smartest thing I can do.

Crossing to the sitting area in front of the fireplace, I line up the books I brought back from the library in a row. Selecting the one with the page marked for the shielding ritual, I grab a piece of parchment and quickly copy it down.

I'll go see Meera tomorrow for a ride and a visit and then take a trip further into Videva for some of these supplies. I'll spread them out over a few days so as not to draw suspicion. Then I'll set to work combining everything and letting it cure.

Rising, I cross to where I flung my cloak the night before and slip my list into the inside pocket. A figure catches my eye through the window. Thieran.

His black hair, normally swinging to his shoulders, is tied back, sharpening the square set of his jaw and aristocratic slope of his nose even more. His robes are open, billowing behind him in the breeze, and I trace the long, lean lines of him as he stalks through the high grass toward the palace.

He mounts the stairs to the balcony, and from this distance, I can make out something smeared across his cheek and forehead. Blood. It's sprayed across his face and glistens on his clothes.

There's something primal about seeing the God of Death covered in someone's lifeblood, and it threads desire through me in a way it probably shouldn't. As if he can sense me watching him, he glances up at my window. His mouth ticks up at the corner, and he spreads his arms wide, giving a little mock bow.

Heart thundering in my chest, I grip the edges of the curtains and yank them closed, blocking out the God of Death and the memory of his lips and teeth and tongue on my skin.

Though I can no longer see him, I turn pointedly from the window and cross back to the sitting area, stoking the fire and claiming a seat on the soft brocade couch. Picking up the next book about wards, I flip to the first page.

I can only hope a fortnight is the longest part of this new plan. Because the longer I stay in the Shadow Realm, the more likely I am to fall prey to the God of Death. In more ways than one.

CHAPTER TWENTY-TWO

Thieran

The curtains sway back and forth on Elora's window, and I grin. She can pretend all she likes that she isn't intrigued by me. But I'm through pretending. I know the taste of her skin and the feel of her clenched around me and the sound she makes when she comes.

And I want to know more. I intend to know more. She'll submit to me again. She'll beg me to fuck her. Because the wanting between us is mutual. Even if she isn't ready to admit it to herself yet.

I debate shifting to my rooms to save myself the time, but I need to work off the heady rush of my latest torture session. I only went to Síra to sentence more souls and check the boundaries after Garrick's latest report left me wondering.

All was well until a soul being sentenced forgot his place. He'd learned it before I finished carrying out his first of many punishments. There's something centering about hearing the screams of the damned, tearing into the flesh of those who deserve it.

And this man did. He was only reaping what he sowed, the

maiming and torture he'd inflicted on dozens of others turned back on him. Every day. For the rest of eternity.

Some souls aren't worth redemption. They don't deserve the second chance Meren provides. And I enjoy reminding them of such whenever the opportunity presents itself.

Climbing the wide stairs to the balcony off this wing of the palace, I see Railan waiting for me at the top, hands clasped behind his back. His eyebrows shoot up at my appearance, and he shakes his head at the blood smearing my face and clothes.

"I was wondering where you'd gone when you didn't shift back with me after sentencing."

I lift a shoulder. "The last one spoke out of turn. And I had to remind him of his place."

Railan chuckles softly. "Had to? Or wanted to?"

"Can't it be both?"

"With you, it usually is."

He stares off into the distance, toward Síra. You can't see it from the palace; the Shadow Realm is too vast, but even so, I can picture its landscape and the jagged mountains surrounding it.

An icy wind howls constantly through the unforgiving peaks, broken only by the occasional scream or frantic prayer or desperate plea. But once they're sentenced, nothing saves them. Their fate is permanent.

"I saw Garrick's latest report."

Eyes fixed on the horizon, I nod. "Your thoughts?"

He hesitates, weighing his words as he takes a deep breath. "It looks a lot like the early reports we used to get. When we first noticed there was a problem with the veil. With the power running through it."

That was precisely what worried me about Garrick's report too. I've spent hundreds of years fortifying the Shadow Realm with my blood and my power. Until one day it wasn't enough.

Decades ago, Garrick brought me the first report that souls

in Meren were coming too close to the veil in the east. As if they could sense its power in a way they hadn't been able to in all my centuries in the realm.

I'd fortified them. The veil and the borders around both Meren and Síra. Because if Meren falls, Síra isn't far behind. It worked well for a long time. Until it didn't, demanding more and more blood and power to hold it together.

Then Elora arrived, and the realm has been stronger than I've been able to make it in years. If it's starting all over again, then I was wrong about her. I don't want to be wrong about her.

"I think," Railan says, pulling me back to the present, "we should be careful about Elora and what she might mean. For the realm."

I turn to face him, eyebrow raised. There's a clear double meaning in his words. I could ignore it, but as Railan is likely to have already guessed what happened between Elora and me in the forest the night before, it seems pointless.

"I've always been careful where the realm is concerned. It has been my top priority since it was created."

"I know that." He shifts from one foot to the other, still not meeting my gaze. "I spoke to Nevon this morning. About your... appearance at the hot springs."

"Did you? I hope he enjoyed his walk."

Railan snorts softly. "Seems to me he was hoping to enjoy a lot more but was interrupted."

"Yes," I reply, unable to keep the jealousy from my voice. "He was."

Railan opens his mouth, then closes it again, shaking his head. "I'll make sure Nevon gets the message. Thieran," he adds when I turn to go. "I hope you know what you're doing."

"The closer I am to Elora, the more I can watch her. The more I can watch her, the fewer chances she has to escape."

I can tell by the look on his face he doesn't quite accept my

178

logic. The reason is sound enough, but even I know it's not why I want her close.

Railan gives me one last look before disappearing, and I push into the palace, glancing down the hallway leading to Elora's rooms. I know she's down there. It would be easy to go to her, coax her into a bed. Take my time with her. Make her scream for me again, feel her nails on my back and her legs around my waist. But as much as I would enjoy the distraction, I have other responsibilities.

Veering down the opposite hall and crossing the wide expanse of the palace's center, I take the last set of stairs up, turning toward my rooms. I smell her before I see her, the faint scent of pine and ash hanging in the air.

Iluna steps out of the shadows and into the halo of light from a torch, the jewels in her tiara glittering when she moves. Even the fitted bodice of her black dress is dotted with tiny blood-red stones.

I had hoped for a little more time alone, maybe enough to sneak away to the hot springs for a bath. My hand on my cock and Elora on my mind.

"My lord."

Iluna bobs a curtsy, and her smile is sharp. I assume she's here to ask me about Elora and finish whatever she'd started to tell me at dinner last night. Before I cut her off and never came back.

"Iluna. Can it wait?"

"It could. But I think you'll be interested in what I have to say."

Passing a hand down my front, I exchange my dirty robes for fresh ones and clean the blood from my face. Not the leisurely washing up I was looking forward to, but the result is the same.

"My study," I say before shifting.

She appears behind me moments later, and I round the desk,

waiting for her to take a chair opposite. When she does, I conjure two glasses of wine and offer her one.

"The suspense is killing me," I say, growing impatient as she adjusts her skirts, taking a sip of her wine before folding her hands in her lap.

"I spoke with Aeris before I came."

My eyebrows wing up, but she pauses for dramatic effect before continuing. It is one of my least favorite things about her.

"She said a forest guardian crossed the veil and found its way into Acaria a few months ago. Into her territory."

"Not quite that long ago, but I'm aware. It's been handled."

She takes another sip of wine, eyes traveling over the room, but doesn't make to speak again.

"Is that all?"

"If the problem with the veil is getting worse—"

"The veil is fine." For now. "I know you can sense it almost as well as I can."

She purses her lips and tilts her head. Dark court gods possess a connection to the Shadow Realm as I do; it just isn't as strong as mine. Even Kaia, who spends more time here than she does in Acaria, isn't as entwined with the realm as I am.

"It does feel strong."

I nod in confirmation. She doesn't need to know about Garrick's latest report or his concerns. Or that Railan shares them. Both because it's probably nothing and because my problems are my own. The Shadow Realm is my responsibility, and I am handling it.

"Was there something else?"

She takes a deep breath, studying me with wide, calculating eyes meant to look innocent. I'm not sure Iluna has been innocent a day in her life.

"About the queen?" I prompt.

"The queen?"

I force myself not to roll my eyes, fingers tightening on the glass in my hand. "You said something about her last night at dinner. Before I had to leave."

"Oh." The look on her face turns sour. "Yes. The queen. She's already begun preparations for the winter ball."

I know this information already, but I don't want to jeopardize Kaia's spies, so I simply lift a brow and feign surprise.

"So early? The ball isn't for several more weeks."

Iluna gives a knowing nod. "It's a curious thing, isn't it? Normally she hates the winter ball, but this year I've heard she's ordered extra food and decorations."

Iluna launches into a rundown of all the early preparations she's heard about from her high court sources, and I wonder if she's still fucking the Goddess of Wisdom and War behind closed doors while they pretend to hate each other in public. It was never an arrangement I understood. Until now.

Elora's declaration that she hated me only made me want to fuck her harder. Only made her seem to fuck me harder in return. I want more of that fire from her. It's intoxicating. Addicting enough to get lost in.

"—a mortal."

"What?"

Iluna huffs. "Are you even paying attention to what I'm saying?"

"Of course," I lie. "You said something about seeing Elora at dinner."

"I said I was surprised to see a mortal in the Shadow Realm. I can't recall ever seeing one before. At least not a live one. However did she manage to get past Basal?"

Knowing she's gauging my response as she reaches for her wine, I keep my expression neutral.

"She has something I want. We have an arrangement."

It's not entirely untrue, but it's not the whole truth either. Elora hasn't exactly been keen on our one-sided bargain, as evidenced by the fact she was more than likely trying to seduce Nevon in an attempt to escape.

I find the idea both clever and repulsive.

"What could you possibly want from a mortal?" Iluna scoffs, taking another sip of wine.

I'd have shared her sentiment once. I'd likely share it still were it about anyone else. But Elora is different. She has been since she stumbled across the veil and into my world.

"I have my reasons. That should be enough."

Setting her glass down hard enough that it clinks against the wood, she sits back in her chair with a huff. Iluna doesn't like being on the outside looking in. But if she's taking a high court lover to her bed again, she doesn't need any more details than absolutely necessary.

"I think I'll be cutting my time in the Shadow Realm short, if that's all right with you."

I gesture between us with a flick of my wrist. "You know your presence here is never required. You are free to come and go as you please."

Iluna pushes to her feet and turns toward the door.

"I only hope you'll remember one thing." She pauses with her hand on the knob, peering back at me over her shoulder. "The truce between my brother and I is tenuous. And as a member of my court, you've always known the consequences for upsetting that balance."

She gives a curt nod, her tiara sparkling in the candlelight, before stepping through the door and closing it behind her with a snap. If my brother finds out about Elora before I'm ready, I'll handle him. But I'll make sure whoever decided to parade my business around as idle gossip pays for their transgression.

CHAPTER TWENTY-THREE

Elora

The wind bites as I draw my cloak tighter around me, and I warm myself with thoughts of the years I spent living in the north by the sea.

It's never cold in Acaria's northern territories, the constant sun broken only by the occasional storm before it clears again and the sky returns to its sparkling blue. It was the perfect place to start over. Living on the streets in Dremen, with its dreary winters and mountains of snow, would have been unbearable.

But, like everywhere else, it was full of people only willing to look out for themselves. I learned a valuable lesson living in the land of the God of Sea and Storms. The only person you can ever count on is yourself.

The young girl is out tending to the goats when I arrive, and I lift my arm in greeting. She smiles and moves toward me across the small field, the goats trailing in her wake.

"It's good to see you again, my lady," she says, patting the head of a goat, who nudges her hand.

"It's just Elora. Please," I add when the girl hesitates.

"Elora," she says shyly. "I'm Corinne. And my parents are Elspeth and Jerund." She gestures toward the small farmhouse.

"You're here with your parents?" I want to ask how, but the question feels too personal. It's none of my business how she or her family died.

Corinne smiles sadly. "We used to live in Lady Orella's territory."

I killed a lecherous village elder in the Goddess of Love and Lust's capital city once. After cutting off his hand to remind him to keep it to himself.

"There was a great storm. It rained every day for a week. The river overflowed, and...everything was lost. Including ourselves."

"I'm sorry, Corinne."

The words are empty, hollow sounding to my ears, but she smiles brightly and her cheeks pink.

"That's very kind of you, my la—Elora," she amends at my raised brow. "Is there anything I can help you with today?"

"No, thank you. I think I might saddle Meera up and explore the village."

"Oh, how wonderful. I hope you enjoy your time there."

She moves away, calling for the goats to follow her, and I can't help but smile as they dutifully trail in her wake. The draft horse nickers at my arrival at the paddock gate, and I run my hand down his nose, slipping him one of the apples I brought with me.

Meera pokes her head out of her stall when I step into the barn and huffs at the sight of me. She's annoyed I've stayed away for a few days, lost in my research. But it was time well spent, because I found a few more passages that are starting to paint a picture of how I might actually get past Thieran's wards.

I have one more angle I want to research, but before I make another visit to the library, I need to stretch my legs and stop avoiding Videva.

"I'm sorry," I croon, unsheathing the dagger strapped to my

thigh and cutting the other apple I brought in half. "I should have come sooner. But I have a gift for you."

Holding the apple on my outstretched palm, I offer it to her. She gives me a long, meaningful look before nipping it from my hand and munching away. I move to open the stall door, and she gives the other half of the apple a pointed stare.

Chuckling, I let her take that one too. "You're so spoiled. What am I going to do with you?"

"I ask myself that question every day."

Thieran's voice makes me jump, and I whirl around to face him. No robes today, just a pair of black leather breeches and a black tunic. His dark hair frames a pale face, and those ice-blue eyes seem to glow in the dim light of the barn.

He crosses his arms over his chest and leans a shoulder against the wide entrance, his gaze raking over me from head to toe and eliciting a shiver.

I have successfully avoided being alone with Thieran since our romp in the forest. I see him at dinner every night, but there's always the presence of other people shielding me. Although Iluna has finally left. Thank the gods.

"Did you need something?"

"Is that a requirement to speak to you?" There's a teasing note to his voice, but something else too.

"Today it is. I'm busy."

He moves toward me, and I feel his presence at my back like the heaviness of a coming storm. How did I not know he was there before? He never fails to invade every sense I have whenever he's near.

"Busy doing what?"

I sigh, eager to get away from him and move on with my day. "I'm taking Meera into the village, and then we're going for a ride."

"I'll take you."

His expression says his offer might have caught him as off

guard as it's caught me, but he doesn't rescind it.

"That's really not necessary. Meera and I can wander on our own. I'm sure you have…better things to do."

"I insist."

"I don't need walking," I snap, Iluna's words ringing in my ears.

Thieran raises a brow. "Explain."

I move to push around him to fetch Meera's saddle, but he grabs my arm and pulls me up against his chest.

"Now, Elora."

"Whatever Iluna thinks, I am not your pet. And I—"

"When did she say that to you?"

I lift my chin against the embarrassment that blooms bright inside me at the memory of her insult. "The other day when I saw her in the library."

His eyes darken to storm clouds, and he loosens his grip on my arm but doesn't release me. "I have never seen you as such. Iluna is—"

"Just like all the other gods." His eyes narrow on my face. "Tell me, my lord, why did the gods choose to rule over the very people they seem to despise? Surely we'd all be better off without you."

"Some of us had good intentions once," he murmurs, finally letting go of me. "Come, I'll give you a quick tour of the village before the hour grows too late."

"I can go by myself."

"You could," he agrees. "You won't."

He holds out a hand for mine, and I cross my arms over my chest. "Walking won't kill you, you know."

He shakes his head with a dry chuckle, curling his hand into a fist and dropping it to his side.

"As you wish," he replies, gesturing ahead of us to the door.

The walk into Videva is shorter than I expected and altogether a mistake since I can't stop myself from noticing how tightly the leather of his breeches stretches over his muscular thighs or how well-fitted his tunic is across his broad shoulders. I should have let him shift us.

I know he's powerful, strong. You'd expect nothing less from a god. But I also know the feel of those arms around me and the effortless way he pinned my body to that tree. I wish I didn't. Or at the very least, I wish I could stop thinking about it.

The road widens when buildings come into view, lining either side of the packed earth. The people wandering from shop to shop stop when they notice us, dropping into deep curtsies or bows as Thieran passes.

I expect a healthy dose of fear on their faces. But like Corinne, I see only reverence and surprise, and I wonder how often Thieran actually visits his subjects.

"They respect you," I say, stepping out of the way of a soul carrying a large basket on her hip.

"They're simply stuck with me, that's all. An unavoidable consequence of being dead."

"Most people are stuck where they find themselves through no fault of their own. They live their entire lives where they're born, having children who will do the same and continue the cycle. It doesn't mean they don't create happiness for themselves."

"You didn't."

"Create happiness for myself?"

He shakes his head, stopping beside me when I pause to study a display of dried herbs hanging from the eaves of a squat, wide building.

"You didn't live your entire life where you were born."

My mother's kind face swims across my vision, then my uncle's cruel one, and I hug myself tightly. "Some circumstances are beyond our control."

He doesn't comment, leaving me to the silence and following me to the next shop that catches my eye.

We spend nearly an hour wandering up and down the streets of Videva, with Thieran pointing different places out to me or people stopping us to offer gifts. It all feels very normal, like any large village in Acaria, and I have to remind myself I'm trapped here against my will.

I decide not to gather any of the things on my list for my shielding ritual, instead making a note in my head of all the shops that have what I need. Thieran's presence is slowing me down. I could have half of what I require by the time we're finished and heading back to the barn, but instead I have nothing.

I should have insisted on going by myself. The sooner I get out of here, the better, and the potion I need for the shielding ritual has to cure for a fortnight before it's of any use to me. I can't afford to lose more time than I already have to my research.

Turning toward the farmhouse, I expect Thieran to head back to the palace and do whatever he does in his free time. But instead he follows me through the gate and around the back to the barn.

My irritation grows when he leans a shoulder against the stall and watches me. I need some peace from his presence and his scent and everything being so near him makes me think.

"Do you plan on following me around for the rest of my life?" I snap.

A slow grin splits his face. He's amused. The bastard.

"Would you like me to?"

"No," I say through gritted teeth. "I would prefer to never see you again."

He steps closer, wrapping a loose strand of my hair around his finger. "We both know that's not true."

Slapping his hand away, I drill my finger into his chest. "You are the most arrogant, self-absorbed man I've ever met. You think you can—"

He moves so fast I don't have time to anticipate him, backing me up against the rear wall of the barn and caging me in with his hands on either side of my shoulders. He drops his head, tracing the tip of his nose across the edge of my jaw, inhaling slowly.

His voice is a low warning in my ear when he says, "I am not a man. I'm a god. Maybe I should remind you of the difference."

His words, the tone of the them, the threat and the promise, have desire sparking low in my belly and spreading, the embers catching until I'm on fire from it. I hate what he does to me and how easily he seems to do it. And still I can't stop myself from threading my fingers through his hair and bringing his mouth to mine.

His kiss is crushing, demanding, possessive, and it only fans the flames. When his fingers reach for the tie on my breeches, I don't stop him. Instead I encourage him by rocking my hips, gasping when he loosens them enough to slide his hand inside and graze a finger against my clit.

"See," he says, a note of triumph in his voice, "you're already wet for me."

"Shut up and do something about it."

He sinks a finger inside me without hesitating, grinning against my mouth when I buck my hips, forcing him deeper. When he adds a second finger, working my breeches down my thighs with his other hand, I groan low in my throat.

He pumps them in and out, his teeth exploring the skin of my neck until I'm buzzing with the feeling of his body against mine, moving with me, in me, against me. Shoving his fingers deep, he curls them up against the sensitive spot inside me that makes my knees go weak.

I tighten my hands in his hair, fingernails digging into his scalp, which only seems to encourage him. His fingers move faster, his teeth scraping against sensitive skin.

He presses his thumb to my clit, and I couldn't stop it if I wanted to, the blinding, white-hot orgasm racing through me until every nerve ending tingles and sparks. But he doesn't relent. He merely shifts against me, the hard length of his cock pressed against my hip as he plunges his fingers in and out, forcing me back up before I even have the chance to come down from the high.

Wanting to torture him just as much, I reach for him, massaging his cock through the leather. He jerks against me with a groan, his fingers moving faster and more urgently inside me. I fumble to undo the ties with shaky fingers, finally freeing his cock and wrapping my hand around it.

He throbs in my grip, thrusting into my fist when I give him a rough stroke. I want him inside me. I need it. And he must read my mind because he slips his fingers from my pussy and spins me to face the wall, shoving me up against it and gripping my ass to spread me apart for him.

I feel the head of his cock at my entrance seconds before he sheaths himself inside me. Arching my back to take him deeper, I drop my forehead against the wall with a groan.

He fucks me, and he's not gentle about it, driving into me with long, deep strokes. But I don't want gentle from him. I need the hard, fast, rough way he uses my body to remind me I'm using him too. I don't want a lover's caress from Thieran. This frantic, needy fucking is bad enough as it is.

He slams into me with a particularly brutal thrust, his hand snaking around my hip and dropping between my thighs to rub my clit in fast, vicious circles. Everything about the way he touches me is pain translated into pleasure, and I've never needed anything this much.

Holding my hip in his punishing grip, his pace never slowing inside me, Thieran leans forward to whisper in my ear, his voice hoarse.

"You're going to come for me, little one. I want you to scream my name so this entire realm knows who's fucking you."

I don't want to obey him, but my pussy ripples around him in response, and I can feel my orgasm building and racing down my spine.

"Now."

The command is low, urgent, but I'm powerless against it, against him, and his name is on my lips as I explode around him, body shuddering with the force of my release.

"Good girl," he whispers against my neck as he shoves deep and empties himself inside me.

It takes me a minute to stop seeing stars and a few minutes more to get my breath back, my hands braced on the wall as he steps away and rights himself. He reaches forward to squeeze my bare thigh before tugging my breeches back into place and palming my ass.

"Next time, you'll have to scream louder."

"Who says there'll be a next time?"

He chuckles, pressing against me from behind and winding my braid around his hand before giving it a firm tug. "With you, little one, there will always be a next time."

His hold on me loosens and he disappears, leaving me to slump against the wall of the barn and try to piece together what the fuck I just let happen. What I encouraged. Again.

Meera sticks her head out of the stall and pins me with a disapproving stare.

"Don't look at me like that." I sniff, hooking her saddle over my arm and moving to the mouth of her stall on shaky legs. "Maybe my plan is to get him to think I actually want him so he'll let his guard down."

She snorts in disbelief. As I settle the saddle on her back and quickly adjust the straps, I know we both see it for the lie it is. If there's nothing I can do about wanting the God of Death, I'll have to outrun him instead.

CHAPTER TWENTY-FOUR

❖

Elora

My heart beats a frantic rhythm as Meera bunches under me and takes a flying leap over a shallow ditch. We come down smoothly on the other side, her mane tickling my cheek as I lean low over her neck, encouraging her on.

I've been testing the waters with how far I can take her without drawing suspicion. I know Thieran watches me. I feel his heavy gaze all the time, raising goosebumps over my skin.

Usually the watching ends with my clothes half off and his cock inside me. And I've started to mind it less and less, but it's a distraction. Time away from the work I should be doing to move my escape plan further along.

I managed to collect all the ingredients I needed for the shielding ritual, and it's been curing in the back of my wardrobe for about a week now. With only one left to go, I've been desperate to find a way to test my theory about the wards. An impossible task with Thieran's eyes on me all the time.

Testing the wards around the palace isn't an option, anyway. So I started taking Meera further than I normally would on our daily rides. First just a little ways beyond the field behind the farmhouse. Then a little further, pushing the boundary of what Thieran expects of me.

Until one day we went far enough that I felt the first prickling of energy raise the hair on my arms. Thieran's wards, meant to keep me from riding Meera too far. Either he gave me a generous area to start with, or he's widened it in the weeks since bringing Meera here.

Whatever the answer, I'm in luck, because the first edges of the wards in this part of the realm are buried in a grove of trees, out of sight of the farmhouse and other prying eyes.

Thieran can sense my location across the realm. It's how he found me in Videva, trading a shawl from my wardrobe for the last of the ingredients I needed for what I'm attempting today. But he admitted he can't physically see me or what I'm doing. A relief, considering he would absolutely put a stop to it if he had even the slightest idea.

Slowing Meera to a walk, I guide her a few more paces inside the protection of the trees and stop. Dropping to the ground, I loop her reins loosely around a low-hanging branch and flip open the saddlebag.

Under the apples I've brought as a bribe in case this takes longer than I'm anticipating and an extra blanket are the ingredients I've been painstakingly collecting since I found the last piece of the puzzle. Hiding away in a little book tucked at the end of the top shelf of a bookcase in the library's northwest corner.

This book was older than all the others, written in a faded looping script that reminded me of decades long past. It looked more like a private journal than a book written by one of Acaria's historians. The words inside were a treasure trove of information, combining all my theories into a single ritual meant to temporarily dissolve a god's power.

The pages spoke of dissolving bindings in the event a god

was holding the wearer prisoner. The wards aren't ropes around my wrists, but they're no less real a binding.

Glancing around to make doubly sure I'm alone, I pull out my prizes. Salt to protect, vervain to purify, lavender to blind those who would try to see, mugwort to open, and mint to bind. Setting the bundles gently on the ground near the barrier, I go back for the candles—one black and one white, to represent the light and the dark—and some twine. And last, the pretty copper bowl.

I carry it all to the edge of the ward and drop to my knees. Meera paws the ground behind me when I reach up and press my palm flat to the invisible wall preventing my escape.

Ignoring her, I dig the instructions I've scribbled down out of my pocket and smooth them over my thigh. Then I sprinkle a ring of salt around the candles and the bowl, followed by a ring of vervain. I add equal amounts of each ingredient to the copper bowl and stir clockwise nine times. Three times three.

A shiver races down my spine, chilling me to the bone. I glance over my shoulder, but all I see is Meera standing there watching me. Her ears are flat against her head like they were the day I ventured into the forest and set this whole thing in motion.

But I have to try. I haven't come this far only to give up when I'm so close.

Turning back to my work, I light first the black candle and then the white one, dripping wax from each into the bowl. When the waxes collide, shallow sparks fly into the air and spiral around each other before disappearing. I blink, unsure if that's a good sign or not.

Setting the white candle on the ground directly across from the black one, I tie a bit of rough twine around them and tear off the slip of parchment with my intentions on it. Freedom, the life I desire, the ability to make my own choices.

The flames dance as the candles burn down, and I hold my

breath. I have to wait until the twine catches fire and burns into the bowl. Once it does, I'll toss the parchment with my intentions into the fire and repeat them over and over until the flames extinguish.

Then I'm to throw the ashes at the barrier. According to the book I found, it should cleave through the barrier and leave a hole. I don't know how big the hole will be; if it's not big enough to fit Meera through, then I'll need a whole lot more herbs. But before I get ahead of myself, I have to make sure it actually works first.

The twine catches, the flames eating up the thin rope until it disentangles from them and drops into the bowl. The dried herbs ignite with a pop and a hiss, and I toss the parchment in, adding fuel to the fire and sending the flames leaping into the air.

I watch, mesmerized, lips moving rapidly as I recite my intentions. *Freedom, the life I desire, the ability to make my own choices.* It feels like hours, but I'm certain it's only minutes before the fire finally burns itself out.

I reach for the bowl, realizing a moment too late that I should be cautious, only to discover the bowl is cool to the touch where it should be warm. Another chill wends through me. As I rise and make my way to the barrier, I can't help but feel like I'm dealing with something I can't possibly understand.

The wind picks up, singing through the leaves and teasing the end of my braid. I lift the bowl to toss the mixture against the ward, but my fingers tighten on the copper, and I freeze.

An unexpected stab of guilt makes my stomach clench and my heart pound.

Life in the Shadow Realm has been the easiest I've ever known. I've never lived so well as I have these last few weeks. It would be easy to stay. To continue to enjoy the comforts I've become accustomed to in so short a time.

But none of it's real. Not really. It's all an illusion meant to draw me in and keep me compliant. I might give Thieran my body when it suits me, but the rest of me is mine. And I deserve to make my own choices.

Taking a deep breath, I toss the burned herbs at the barrier. At first it appears only to make contact and slide down to the earth. But in the span of a breath, the barrier begins to flicker and ripple. And where nothing stood before, it's now like I'm looking at the grass and trees beyond through smoke, hazy and unclear.

I reach out, fingertips dancing along the edge of the barrier where it's still invisible to the eye, but when I hit the smoky, unfocused air, my hand dips through. Just like it did the night I escaped. But unlike Thieran's tricks, this was my doing.

I have the sudden urge to run through, but I stop myself. I don't want Thieran to sense I've crossed the wards. I'm not even sure if he can tell I've manipulated them or not. Best to gauge his reaction at dinner tonight and see if he suspects anything.

Taking a step back, I watch the smoke slowly blow away and the barrier heal itself until it looks as it did before, clear and unblemished. This time when I touch it, it doesn't yield under my fingers.

The effects don't appear to last long, but it works. And if I arrive ready to leave, I'll have plenty of time to slip through. With Meera, I can cover ground much faster than I did before. And this time Thieran won't know to follow me because he'll have no idea I'm gone.

An uneasy feeling settles in my chest as I collect the remnants of the candles from the ground, toeing dirt and leaves over the bits of wax and ash left behind. I pack everything carefully back into my saddlebag and shove the feeling away. I have nothing to feel guilty about. What's transpired between Thieran and me doesn't change things. Why should it?

Stuffing the blanket back on top of my supplies, I carve a slice of apple off and hold it out to Meera. She doesn't take it, turning her head away from me and staring at the ward's barrier as if she can see it plain as day.

"What? You're disappointed in me now?" She snorts and shakes her head. "I don't know what you want from me. Did you expect me to stay here? And do what? Rot in the Shadow Realm until I die and end up in Meren or Síra for all eternity when Railan and Hayle and Nevon are forced to judge me? There's life out there."

I gesture in front of us and hold up the apple for her again, but she still refuses to take it. Shoving the bite in my mouth, I stuff the rest of the apple back in the bag and sheath my dagger.

"Pout about it all you want." I swing up into the saddle and let her dance and sidestep her frustration before taking charge and turning her toward the barn. "But I'm doing this for both of us."

She nickers her disagreement, and when we step through the trees, the palace looming in the distance, that prickly feeling of guilt returns and settles heavily on my shoulders. I shrug it off.

It's a useless emotion and an irritating one. Why should I feel guilty for taking the one thing that should never have been denied me in the first place?

When the potion for the shielding ritual is ready, I'll test it to be sure it works. And if it does, Meera and I will be on our way back to Acaria not long after. Whether she likes it or not.

CHAPTER TWENTY-FIVE

Thieran

G rass on the verge of death, dried and stiff, crunches underfoot as I patrol the far edges of the eastern border. Garrick walks beside me, silent and stoic as always. It's the first time I've had to visit this part of the Shadow Realm since Elora arrived. And what I see concerns me.

No matter which side of the veil you find yourself, the view is the same. Nothing but miles and miles of forest. Mortals on the Acarian side cannot pass through—usually. Instead they wander and wander in the forest until they eventually find their way back to whatever border town they came from or succumb to the elements or beasts.

From the inside looking out, the souls are actively repelled by the barrier. Residents of Meren are never given tasks that would bring them close enough to the veil for it to be a problem, but in general, they shouldn't even know which direction it lies, let alone be able to get close to it.

And they haven't been. Not for decades. Until this morning. When Garrick rushed into my study to inform me that a group of newer souls had wandered away from their assigned tasks and nearly reached the barrier before one of his men discovered them and pushed them back.

Now I can see why. Where nothing but an unimpeded view of the forest should be is instead a thin haze. As I move closer, it writhes, almost in recognition, and Garrick clears his throat behind me.

"Stay here," I command before shifting to the other side of the veil.

The effect is the same on this side. A mortal might mistake the haze for mist if they wandered in this far and weren't paying attention. They also have less incentive to try and cross than a soul from Meren or Síra might. Most mortals never wander into the forest this far unless they have a death wish already.

I turn away from the veil and survey the forest around me. Unlike on my side of the veil, here you can make out the distinct sound of animals. Birdsong, faint rustling from rabbits and other small game.

Forest guardians roam this stretch of land. They're tethered to the veil and to me. They're not meant to be able to wander far. A deterrent for a mortal who does manage to get too close.

The one that escaped and made its way into Aeris's territory did so when the veil thinned too much and its tether to it stretched until it snapped. Once Aeris drove it back into the woods, it took it upon itself to wander from her territory to Kaia's, where it attacked and then chased Elora. All told, a distance of more than half the length of Acaria's southern border.

I shudder to think of the damage and hysteria it might have caused if Elora had found her way back to Rhagana with the beast on her heels. No doubt word of the incident would have reached Fontoss and my brother's ears.

When it did, he would have paid me a visit, glee sparkling in his eyes at seeing me fail. It has always been one of his favorite ways to amuse himself. That and bedding as many women as possible under his wife's nose to remind them both he married her out of greed and a desperate grasp for power and nothing more.

A small cluster of trees to my left rustles, the tree's limbs shaking violently, followed by a series of grunts and inhuman squeals. A young fawn darts from the brush, followed by the bent figure of a beast meant to terrify. Half man, half wild animal, and covered in fur from head to toe.

It stops when it sees me, falling to all fours and giving its own version of a bow. I flick my wrist in its direction, and it immediately turns and lopes back the way it came, disappearing from view, the sound of its ambling steps slowly fading. The fawn lives to see another day.

I hurl a bit of power at the veil, which trembles but holds. The beast's tether is still attached, but not for much longer if I don't shore up this weak spot and then figure out what the fuck is happening.

Appearing back on the other side of the veil, Garrick still waiting patiently where I left him, I hold out my hand for his dagger. He draws it from the sheath at his waist and presents it to me handle first.

I move closer to the veil and lay the blade in my palm. I'm tired of bleeding for a realm that shouldn't need it. Not with Elora here. Not when her presence has been such a balm to the problem I haven't known how to fix for so long.

Drawing the blade across my flesh, I press my bloody palm to the hazy air and watch rivers of red run down the invisible barrier between the dead and the living. As my blood drips, the air sizzles and the wind picks up. And slowly, much slower than it used to, the haze sharpens to nothing again. As if it's blown away in the wind.

By the time I hand the dagger back to Garrick, the cut on my hand is healed and the veil is whole again. Garrick cleans the blade on the edge of his cloak and slides it back into the sheath.

"What do you think's causing it, my lord?"

I sigh. It's not the first time he's asked me that question since this whole thing began. But I tire of never having an answer for him, for myself.

"I don't know."

"Things have seemed better in recent weeks. Stronger."

"Yes," I agree, taking a step back, eyes still fixed on the veil. "They have been."

"Can you account for the change?"

I can. Or I thought I could. But now I'm not so sure. The timing of Elora's arrival fit perfectly with the realm seeming to heal itself. Not only has the veil held in all the time she's been here, but the power thrumming through the land itself has felt stronger than it has in years.

There's been a change in the Shadow Realm since she came to us, and I might have believed I was imagining it or seeing only what I wanted to see if others hadn't been experiencing it too.

I know I'm not alone in sensing these changes. Kaia found me after breakfast to ask if I'd noticed any oddities with the realm in recent days. And Railan mentioned it over a glass of liquor in my sitting room last night.

If Elora's mere presence in the realm no longer explains the effects we've all noticed, then how did she cross the veil in the first place if she wasn't meant to? And what else could account for the unmistakable improvement these last weeks?

"Have you noticed any weaknesses to the west?" I gesture in front of us. "To the veil or maybe the ferry on the Loret?"

Garrick's brows draw together, and he tilts his head. "No, my lord. The western border is the strongest it's ever been."

I look to my left. I found Elora kneeling by the River Axan, her hand hovering over the surface. I sensed her arrival in the realm immediately. It was a heavy hum on the air and the insistent beat of her heart in my chest.

I tap two fingers over my heart center where the dull but steady beat of hers still thrums. It has never left me in all this time. A feeling so normal to me now I hardly question it anymore.

Whatever it is, there's something about the western border that allowed her to cross unimpeded. And if I can find out what it is, perhaps I can use it to repair the realm permanently. No more patching over the cracks and waiting until another leak springs.

"Thank you, Garrick. I'll look forward to your evening report."

Garrick inclines his head and disappears in a fog. Restoring his demi powers after death was a feat in and of itself, but worth it for all the help he's been over the centuries.

Shifting to the west, I arrive on the Axan's bank, not far from where Elora tried to cross when she attempted to escape. And now that I see it in the clear light of day, it's not altogether far from where I found her either. The veil runs maybe twenty paces from the river's edge, and I cross to it, pressing my hand against the shield.

As Garrick said, it's at full strength. The power of it sighs up my arm and warms me through. I sense the thread of my power as clearly as I feel the breath leaving my lungs. But there's something else too. Something that feels familiar yet foreign all at once.

I coax it forward with my power, attempting to draw it out, but it slips from my grasp and fades into the background. Over and over, a dance of energy, a whisper of power I don't recognize. A power that might be nothing but definitely feels like something.

Leaving the veil, I pace back to the river bank. There was a boulder where I found Elora. Nearly as tall as she is and large enough for her to lie on if she'd had a mind to. It would have been safer than touching the black water.

Around the subtle bend in the river, the boulder comes into view, but something is different about it now. Where before it was nothing but a craggy piece of rock jutting out of the earth, now it's covered on one side by vines. Thin tendrils of them crisscrossing up one side and down the other.

The vines snake across the ground toward the riverbank, stopping at the edge. Crouching down, I run my finger along the length of one, and it warms at my touch, curling toward me.

I stroke it again, and again it moves closer, stretching up to make contact with my skin. These vines weren't here before. When I scooped Elora up from this spot, bloody and barely conscious, there was nothing but grass and rock.

Pushing to my feet, I look past the boulder and see more of the same. Following the trail of vines away from the river and through the trees, I reach a single tree with a thick trunk. Vines climb the bark like greedy fingers but stop abruptly a few feet from the ground. Right where someone stumbling might brace themselves with a hand.

My heartbeat quickens, and I continue following the weaving, winding path of the vines. The closer I come to the veil, the harder my heart pounds. I'm drawing conclusions I don't like. But I have to be sure. I want to be wrong about this. I'm not sure what I'll do if I'm not.

I feel it before I see it. The warm simmering of power on the air. The veil used to feel this way all the time. Warm, magnetic. Alive.

When I break through the last thick copse of trees, I stop short, blood pounding in my ears.

The vines travel up to the veil, reaching for it but not touching it. The veil isn't just stronger here, it pulses. With energy, with light, with power. It's been so long since I've seen it like this I'd forgotten it could.

This must be where she crossed. But it's more than that too. It's the answer to everything. And the one I was dreading. The vines follow the path Elora stumbled through the forest until she reached the River Axan. And now I know what the Shadow Realm has taken from Elora. What it needs.

It's not her presence that's sustained the realm these many weeks. It's her blood.

CHAPTER TWENTY-SIX

Elora

Giving Meera one last pat, I close the door of her stall and make my way up the aisle of the barn. The draft horse is gone from the paddock, hooked up to the wagon when I was saddling Meera for our ride earlier.

Jerund doesn't speak to me much. Our interactions consist mostly of polite waves and nods. But today he told me all about how he trades the soaps and cheeses his wife makes from their goats' milk with the people of Videva for beautiful hand-dyed yarn, fresh vegetables, and handmade trinkets.

When Kaia first told me of the souls in Videva pursuing mortal work even in the afterlife, I didn't understand it. But after weeks with nothing to do but wait, I can see the appeal.

They don't work because they have to. I know Thieran sees to their needs and provides for whatever they don't have. They work because they want to, and they focus only on what they love. Or perhaps, for some, what they know best.

An elderly woman makes the most exquisite jewelry, delicate and intricate. It must take her days, if not weeks, to craft each piece. And in the end, she trades it not for coin but for some of the soap Corinne's family makes, fabric for new dresses, or a basket of freshly baked sweets.

When I asked her where she got all the materials to make the things she trades, she said she found them outside her cottage. And I know that's Thieran's doing too. However much he wants to pretend he cares only about maintaining a balance, it's obvious he governs his people with care.

Corinne waves at me from the shallow front stoop where she's snapping the ends off long yellow beans, and I return the gesture. She looks so young, sixteen if she's a day, and I wonder if souls can really live here as mortals do or if Corinne will forever be sixteen and living with her parents. Frozen in time and unable to move forward for all the centuries she might be here.

Turning away from Videva, I trudge up the path connecting the village to the palace and tuck a hair come loose from my braid behind my ear. The edges of my cloak flutter in the Shadow Realm's ever-present breeze and swirl around my legs.

The constant chill might be bearable if the sun would shine. I never imagined the thing I'd miss most about Acaria would be the weather. At this point, I'd settle for a snowstorm. Something, anything, to offer a change of scenery.

But the thing I'd truly love is to feel the sun on my face. Even in the southern territories' coldest months, the sun will occasionally peek out from behind the clouds and set the snow to sparkling like diamonds.

And with the solstice come and gone, the days will slowly begin to lengthen and warm until the snow melts and green buds signal the first signs of spring. On the other side of the veil, anyway.

I sigh. With any luck, I'll actually be out of here in plenty of time to enjoy both the last of winter's icy chill and the first welcoming notes of spring. But I still have a few days to wait until my shielding potion has fully cured and is ready for testing. And I'm growing impatient with it.

Thieran showed no signs of knowing I'd breached his wards. At least I don't think he has. He's been acting odd these last few days. He still studies me intently from across the room, but now his eyes dart away when I look in his direction.

It's entirely unlike him. Typically he would hold my gaze, a slow grin painting itself across his mouth and sending shivers through me. He hasn't touched me in days either. No more of that frantic coupling wherever we happen to find ourselves, poking and prodding at each other until irritation boils over into frenzied need.

I hate that I miss it. His touch, his warmth, his cock. It's pathetic. I should be glad he's bored playing whatever game he's been playing with me. It will make leaving that much easier once my potion is ready for the ritual. Which shouldn't be long now.

Rounding the last bend, the palace comes into view, stark black against the plain gray of the sky. If it were sunny here, the light would glint off the windows and the smooth obsidian stone, and the palace would glitter.

A lone figure, silhouetted in a tower window, catches my eye. Before I'm able to make out who it is, the figure vanishes, and Thieran appears on the bottom step leading up to the first-floor balcony.

"Coming back from a ride?"

I make a show of looking back over my shoulder at the way I came. His brow is raised when I turn to face him again.

"Obviously. I doubt I could veer very far off the path between here and Videva without running into one of your wards."

Something flashes in his eyes, but it's gone again so fast I don't have time to decipher it.

"The wards are for your own protection."

I snort. "A lie that insults us both. The wards are here so you can keep me right where you want me. To use me for whatever gain you mean to use me for. I only wish you'd get it over with."

He opens his mouth, then closes it again. Thieran's silence is as unsettling and foreign to me as the lack of sunlight. I much prefer when we spend our time arguing or picking at each other.

"Cat got your tongue, my lord? Or have you just become as dreary as the Shadow Realm?"

His brows draw together. "What?"

I gesture all around us with a sweep of my arms. "Day in and day out, everything is the same. No rain, no snow, no storms. There isn't even any fucking sunshine!" I throw my hands up to the sky. "It seems you've finally become as dull as this place is."

It's a barb meant to goad a reaction, meant to poke and prod so he will do anything besides stare directly into my soul with his imploring gaze. I can tell by the shift in his stance and the sweep of his eyes over the waving grass that he won't give me what I want. And I'm suddenly on edge, worried about what he might say next.

"You've lived all over Acaria, haven't you?"

"I...yes."

He could have asked me any question, and likely none of them would have surprised me as much as this one.

"Why?"

"Where was your favorite?"

Those blue eyes abandon the horizon and fix on me. He's sincere in his question. And I'm thrown off just enough to answer him honestly.

"There's a small town in the far north called Tura."

He nods. "In Yorrai's territory."

"Yes," I say of the God of Sea and Storms. "A little coastal town where almost everyone makes their living on the water. I'd never seen the sea before. But the first time I sat on the beach and dipped my toes in the lapping waves, I realized it was its own kind of magick."

Thieran holds a hand out to me, but I only stare at it.

"After all this time, don't you trust me?"

There's a note to his voice I can't quite place, but his gaze on mine doesn't falter. Even though I shouldn't, even though he is the one keeping me here, a part of me trusts him.

"I suppose if you were going to kill me, you'd have done it already," I say, laying my fingers in his.

He draws me close enough that I can't see his face and wraps his arms around my torso. I know I don't need to stand so close, but as the air warms and spins around us, I press my cheek to his chest and listen to the steady beat of his heart as we shift.

When we arrive, he runs his hand up my back to my neck, and the first dull edges of a headache and nausea instantly recede. I expect the air to chill again, but it doesn't, the breeze washing warm over my skin. Stepping away from Thieran, I suck in a sharp breath.

Gone is the usual landscape of the Shadow Realm. Instead we're standing on a stretch of beach with the sand bleached nearly white by the sun—the beautiful, bright, beating sun—and shaped like a crescent. Tall trees sway in the breeze, and waves crash against the shore.

A gull calls, winging out over the water, and I turn my head toward the sound. It's been so long since I've heard the call of a bird. It dazzles me. I watch the gull nose dive toward the sea, disappearing beneath the surface and reemerging a moment later with a fish clutched between its beak.

"Is it real?" I breathe, closing my eyes and turning my face up to the sky. "Or is this an illusion in the Shadow Realm?"

"It's real," Thieran assures me. "An island off the coast of Yorrai's territory."

I look back at him over my shoulder, one eyebrow raised. "Not worried I'll try to escape?"

He does grin now. "It would take you two or three days to swim to shore. But you're welcome to try."

It's just another cage. Something I should be angry about. But with the sun shining down on my face and the smell of sea air in my nose, I don't have it in me.

Dropping to the ground, I tug off my boots and plunge my feet into the sand with a sigh. Wiggling my toes, I glance up at Thieran when he comes to stand beside me.

He looks so out of place in his black robes, his hair whipping about his face as he studies the water. Before I can stop myself, I reach up to caress his calf, and he sinks into the sand beside me.

"Why?" I ask, voice barely audible over the wind coming in off the water and the steady beat of the waves against the shore.

He's silent for a long moment, eyes tracking another gull as it dives from the sky for its prey. But I think he understood my question.

"Because I can."

It's not really an answer, but I'm not ready to push him too far and risk him ending this little trip too quickly. Whatever possessed him, I'll gladly benefit from it as long as I can.

Unhooking the clasp on my cloak, I spread it out behind me and recline against it, letting the warm wind glide over my skin and tease the tendrils of hair around my face and neck. I feel Thieran watching me, but I keep my eyes closed and soak up every bit of the island flooding my senses.

"How old were you when your parents died?"

My eyes shoot open, but I keep them focused on the clear, cloudless blue sky.

"Can't you look through my parent's memories and find that answer?"

Unless they're already reincarnated and my version of them no longer exists in the Shadow Realm. The idea sends an unexpected pang of grief and longing through me.

"I could," he says, my heart thudding at the implication my

parents' souls still reside on the other side of the veil. "But I'm asking you."

I could refuse to answer him. But some unnamed force again has me answering his question with honesty.

"I was four. I don't remember much about them," I admit. "Mostly my mother's smile and my father's laugh."

Sweet and kind and big and rich. The only things I remember clearly after spending so many years trying to forget them in order to survive.

"And who raised you after they died?"

I sit up at that, grateful he hasn't asked me how my parents met their end but just as uninterested in talking to him about life with my aunt and uncle. What does it matter now, anyway? It was so long ago, and I'd rather leave it where it belongs.

Pushing to my feet, I reach for the laces of my corset and begin to undo it. I turn to face Thieran as I let it fall to the sand. I am at his mercy, but I can make him at mine just as easily.

Backing toward the water, I shimmy out of my breeches, kicking them off my feet and reaching for the hem of my tunic. His eyes travel over me from head to toe, locking on the edge of my tunic as I lift it higher up my thighs and over my hips.

The warm water laps at my calves as I back into the sea, and I strip my tunic off, balling it up and tossing it toward the shore. Untangling my braid, I let the wind carry it around my face and shoulders.

With a grin and Thieran's eyes on me, I dive beneath the surface.

CHAPTER TWENTY-SEVEN

Thieran

She's avoiding my questions, and I can't blame her. I wouldn't want to answer questions about my past either. But I'm doing my best to clean up this mess I've found myself in. And finding out more about Elora and why her blood might be the only way to fix my realm seems like the best place to start.

She's right; I could seek out her parents. They live somewhere on Videva's southern edge in a little cabin tending the fruit trees that supply the palace. The apples Elora loves to bring to Meera are picked by her mother's hand.

I'm not sure why I've kept it from her. Perhaps because of that far away, soul-deep look of grief she gets in her eyes whenever I bring up her parents or she sees Corinne with her family.

I don't know what it is to miss a parent or even grieve the idea of one. But Elora does. However much she tries not to remember them. If I could leave her past where she wants it, I would. But the realm is asking too much of her, and I'm trying everything I can to avoid it.

This whole thing was much easier when it was merely a

matter of keeping her tucked away in the Shadow Realm. The longer she stays, the more comfortable she becomes. The more comfortable I become with seeing her there, as if she has never really belonged anywhere else.

Wishful thinking, maybe, but one that crosses my mind far more often than I want it to. The realm needs Elora's blood, her sacrifice. It's a twist I didn't see coming.

Using her blood to fortify the realm would only work for a time before it would require more. As it does with mine. But I don't know if the realm would continue to weaken over the years as I've witnessed.

My blood has only done so much, its effects lessening over time until it seems barely able to patch the holes these days. I can feed the veil and the realm my blood forever, but I fear I'm fighting a losing battle. And as much as I want to save my realm and Acaria from the fate that awaits it should my realm fall, I'm not sure I can bring myself to sacrifice Elora to do it.

And that's what it would take. A sacrifice. Not just drops of her blood. All of it. Better if it's freely given. As mine was so long ago to create the realm from nothing and bind it all together. But not required.

The idea of it turns my stomach. She should be nothing to me. I should have kept my distance from her. This would be an easy decision if I had. It would likely be done already. But I didn't, and it isn't, and thus my insistent questions about her past.

If I can learn more about who Elora was before she came here, perhaps I can find out why she is the one who can heal the veil. And if I can find out why, maybe I can find another mortal to replace her.

It's a theory only, and one I'm keeping to myself for now. I know what Railan would expect me to do were he to find out. What Kaia would reluctantly agree was necessary. So I'm choosing not to tell them for the time being. Until I can learn more, find answers, and figure out a solution.

Elora emerges from the water, shooting me another teasing grin before bobbing up to float on her back. The waves roll under and around her, water sparkling on her bare skin in the bright sunlight.

Rising, I discard my robes and step out of my breeches. Dropping my tunic on the pile, I cross the short stretch of beach and join her in the water. She keeps her eyes closed against the sun, but her mouth ticks up at one corner when I swim out to her.

Despite the heat, goosebumps pebble her stomach, and I like the thought that my presence makes her shiver in anticipation. I paddle closer, reaching up to trace the underside of her breast with my fingertips.

Her nipple hardens in response, and I swipe my thumb over it, making the breath catch in the back of her throat. I do it again just to watch her throat constrict with the effort of swallowing and then lean in and press a kiss to it.

She jerks on the water's surface but continues floating, her eyes still closed, hands moving gently back and forth to keep her in place. A wasted effort since I never want to let her go.

Another gull calls, and she opens her eyes, watching the bird wing out from the shore and back in, riding the breeze. When she finally looks at me, her gaze is full of want and need. A thousand things she wants to say but can't. Or won't.

Dropping her legs, she mirrors my pose, floating in the water with nothing but her head and shoulders exposed. Droplets run down over her temple and cheeks, dripping off her jaw, and I give in to the urge to capture them with my lips.

As soon as my mouth makes contact with her skin, her arms are around me, her fingernails drawing long scratches down my neck and across my shoulders. Usually when she pushes, I give her whatever she wants. Hard, rough, fast. A quick fuck wherever we happen to find ourselves across the palace.

But I want something different from her today. Snaking my arm around her middle, I draw her in close and hook her legs around my waist, lifting her out of the water enough that I can wrap my lips around her nipple.

She groans, dropping her head back when I drag the flat of my tongue against it, and I grin. I trace around it in slow, teasing circles until she's panting with need, desperate for me to make contact again. Instead, I pull back and blow a cool breath across it, her fingernails digging into my shoulders when I do.

Kissing across the valley of her breasts, I show the other nipple the same attention. I never get her with all her clothes off, and I enjoy how her body responds to this new way of touching her.

"Thieran," she groans when I blow another cool breath against her nipple, arching her back and rocking her hips.

I like how she says my name, throaty and full of desire. Finally, I give in to what she wants, what she's begging for, without saying a word, and latch onto her nipple. Dragging my tongue against it, then flicking it roughly back and forth.

"Fuck," she gasps, arching into my mouth, her fingers tightening in my hair.

"More?" I ask, teeth hovering around her nipple.

She looks down at me, pausing a beat before nodding. "More."

The second I bite down, her jaw clenches, and she slowly begins to vibrate in my arms as I increase the pressure until she's writhing against me.

She tries to adjust herself down my body, rocking her hips against my abs, and I give her what she wants, slipping a hand between us and finding her clit with the tip of my fingers.

"Yes," she hisses through clenched teeth.

I tease her clit the way I did her nipple, circling around it without applying too much pressure. Her whimpers are music to my ears as she squirms and twitches in my grip.

Elora's mouth opens, but whatever she's about to say is swallowed by a moan as I plunge my fingers inside her, shoving them deep and grinding my palm against her clit.

Her nails bite into my shoulders, the salt water stinging as she breaks the skin. I like the pain and pleasure I get from Elora in equal measure, and I speed up the movement of my fingers. She grinds and rocks against them, her pussy clenching as I increase the pressure against her clit.

I love to watch her face when she comes for me, love to hear her scream my name.

"Are you going to come for me, Elora?"

"Yes." She shudders when I press harder against her clit. "Don't stop."

I grin. Not a damn thing on this earth could stop me from pushing her closer and closer to her release, from watching her tumble over the edge.

"Good girl," I whisper. "You're so close. Come for me, little one."

I shove my fingers deep when I feel her body go taut, and she throws her head back, my name a scream on her lips as her pussy flutters and spasms.

Leaning in, I kiss across the column of her throat to her jaw, nipping it with my teeth before capturing her lips. Her tongue instantly darts out to battle with mine, her hips subtly rocking against me, each graze of my finger over her clit making her shudder.

"I've never had sex in the sea before," she whispers against my lips.

"Neither have I."

She chuckles, sighing as I latch onto her bottom lip and pull back, slowly letting it slip through my teeth.

"I think you'd like the hot springs."

"We'll have to try those next time."

"Finished already?" I give her hair a tug, and she looks down at me, eyebrow raised.

"Are you?"

"I'll never be finished with you."

I can tell my words surprise her as much as they surprise me, but I realize them for the truth. Just another complicated layer to add to everything I'm already dealing with.

"Thieran," she says, drawing my attention to her mouth and the way her lips are swollen from my kiss.

"Hmm?" I murmur, pressing my lips to her nipple and making her twitch.

"Stop teasing me."

I look at her then, the lust and desperation written on her face. She wants more, and I want to give it to her.

"What do you need from me, little one?"

I shift her down in anticipation of her answer, my cock brushing against her slit, and she bites her lip.

"I need." She sighs, rocking her hips more urgently now. "You know what I need."

I do. But I want her to say it.

"Tell me," I say, voice low and thick with the same desperate want. "Tell me what you need."

"I need…"

Her words trail off as I graze against her clit, still sensitive from her first orgasm,

"Thieran." Her words are rough, demanding. "Please."

I've never heard Elora beg before. I like it, and I reward her by notching my cock at her entrance and tugging her forward by her hips, burying myself to the hilt in a single thrust.

"Fuck," she mutters, groaning when I hook my arms under her thighs and slide out, then back in.

"You're going to come for me again."

"Yes," she agrees, nails scoring my back as I pick up the pace, slamming into her over and over, eager to feel her pulse around me a second time.

"You feel so good when you squeeze my cock."

Her only response is a breathy moan as I thrust into her harder, more urgently. The water swirls around our bodies, my feet digging into the soft sand beneath us.

At the first fluttering signs of her orgasm, I increase my pace, my pelvis grinding against her clit with each brutal thrust of my hips. When her back arches, I dip my head for a taste of her nipple, salty and warm, caressing it with my tongue and nipping it with my teeth.

Closing my teeth around it, I tug it away from her body until it slips free and her breast bounces back against her chest. And with my cock moving relentlessly inside her, her back bowing, her hips jerking under my fingers, she comes undone around me, and I follow her over the edge.

She clings to me, the waves buffeting our bodies, her breaths cool and fast on my neck. I have the sudden urge to stay like this forever. But we have to leave sometime. And Elora seems to sense it too, with the way her body shifts against mine, her arms tightening around my neck and then releasing.

I carry her to the beach and set her down beside her clothes. After running my hands over her from head to waist, she's instantly dry, and she gives a wry laugh.

"That's very handy. I don't suppose you could..." She gestures to her clothes strewn about the beach.

With a grin and a snap of my fingers, she's dressed again, her hair blowing in the breeze, and already I'm missing the gentle curves of her body hidden beneath the fabric.

She laughs, twisting her hair into its usual braid and securing it with a thin leather tie while I dress.

"Ready?" I hold my hand out to her, and she lays her fingers in my palm, lacing them together.

"Let's go home."

She doesn't realize what she's said, but I do. And the words warm me through to my bones. Whatever I have to do, whoever I have to sacrifice, I will find a way to heal the Shadow Realm without Elora's blood.

Because there's not a force in existence that could convince me to give her up.

CHAPTER TWENTY-EIGHT

Elora

"Elora."

I focus on Kaia, seated across from me at the table, and the look on her face tells me she's called my name more than once. I don't mean to be rude, but I'm distracted today. I checked the shielding potion before coming down to eat, and it's ready.

Just as the instructions said, the yellow concoction has changed to a vibrant green. And when I gave the jar a rough shake after digging it out of the back of my wardrobe, streaks of blue and white appeared. All that's left now is to test it. As soon as I figure out how.

I don't really know how or when Thieran searches for me. And I can hardly ask him to do it after going through the steps of the ritual. Which means I'll probably need to do something that would naturally draw him to my side. Like hurt myself.

I don't relish the idea of intentionally injuring myself, but it's the surest and fastest way to test my theory without raising Thieran's suspicions. If it works, I'm free.

And if that thought fills me with a sense of dread instead of hope, it's only because I'm afraid of getting caught and dragged back here again. Nothing more.

Kaia clears her throat, and I fix her with an apologetic look.

"I'm sorry," I say. "I didn't sleep well last night, and I'm having trouble focusing today."

It's not entirely a lie. I did toss and turn last night, eyeing the wardrobe in the dark and unable to sleep for knowing what the potion being fully cured actually means.

Things have been different with Thieran since we returned from the island, and I don't really know what to make of them. We seem to be in an entirely different place than we were before. And I'm not sure I dislike it either. Both of those things leave me unsettled more than anything else.

"Perhaps you should have a rest before going for a ride today." Kaia's brow furrows with concern. "Unless you think you're coming down with something. I could fetch a healer from the village."

"No, no. I'm fine," I assure her. "Just a night full of bad dreams. I'll be all right after a good night's rest. What were you saying earlier? About the ball?"

Kaia waves a hand in the air as the servants come to clear the main course and lay down a tray of delicate pastries, including my favorite lemon tarts.

"It's not important. I don't want to bore you."

"You aren't. Honestly. I want to hear about it."

And I'm surprised by how much I do. How easy a friendship with Kaia has been, even though I am woefully unskilled at it. I haven't stayed in one place this long since my time in Tura.

"You've heard of the winter ball in Fontoss?"

I nod. I'd picked pockets there once on the day of the ball. Lots of demis and gods and favored mortals decked out in their finest silks and furs and jewels. The mortals never missed a bit extra gone from their pockets.

But after nearly getting caught by a demigod—a son of the

God of Fire—I'd moved on to other pursuits, continuing north and settling on the border between high court lands and the Goddess of the Harvest's territory. By the time I'd reached Tura, I was tired of stealing to keep food in my belly and turned to honest work instead.

It ended up being both a blessing and a curse.

"Thieran used to hold a grand ball every year for the dark court," Kaia says, pulling the corner off a chocolate-stuffed bread and popping it into her mouth. "Soon after the realm was created."

"Did he?"

I try to picture the God of Death dressed in all his finery, celebrating with his court. It's impossible to conjure the image of him dancing, laughing, enjoying the company of others.

"Yes." Kaia nods, then sighs. "They were lavish, beautiful. I miss them."

"Why did he stop?" I ask, forking up a bite of lemon tart and relishing in the bright burst of citrus on my tongue.

She pauses with her glass halfway to her mouth before recovering and taking a sip. "His brother, the king, began hosting the winter ball and made it a mandatory event for all the gods."

The way Kaia talks about the King of the Gods gives me the distinct impression she doesn't like him much. I can't say it really surprises me. The gods are known for their infighting and petty squabbles. Ones that seem to always spill over onto mortals in one way or another.

But Kaia strikes me as the kind of person who is good and kind to everyone. Somehow it makes me like her more to know I might be wrong.

"Why doesn't Thieran just choose another time to host a ball?"

Sitting back in her chair, Kaia sighs. "The mandatory high court functions have put him off balls for the last few centuries.

Celebrations entirely, really. He doesn't even attend his own feast days."

"He has feast days?"

"Of course he does." Kaia flicks her wrist in dismissal. "Every god has feast days. But the living don't exactly worship the God of Death. They're celebrated here. In Videva."

"When are they?" I ask, leaning back so the servants can clear the last of the dishes.

"They start tonight with a bonfire in Videva's village proper." She sits up straight in her chair, and a small smile flutters the corners of her mouth. "We should go."

"What?"

I shake my head, but Kaia leans forward, intent on the idea now she's had it.

"It would be fun. You could use a bit of fun. And so could I."

I drum my fingers on the tabletop and stare out the window. I really should stay in and test my shielding ritual, but Kaia looks so eager. And she's seemed a bit out of sorts these last few days.

Surely a few hours' delay couldn't hurt. Everything will be right where I left it tomorrow morning. And a bit of celebration and dancing, good food and wine, will be a nice ending to my time in the Shadow Realm.

I rub at the sudden ache in the center of my chest but give Kaia a wide smile. "All right. Why not? It does sound fun."

Kaia claps her hands under her chin and laughs. Then her eyes drop to my corset and linger long enough to have me glancing down to make sure I didn't make a mess of myself.

"You should let me dress you before we go."

"Before you go where?" Thieran asks from the doorway.

He's leaning his shoulder against the frame, arms crossed, and my mouth waters at the sight of him, my heart beating a little faster. A curious and unnerving reaction I've had to him since returning to the Shadow Realm after our little excursion into Acaria.

He's fucked me every day since. Just this morning when he found me reading in the library. But none of it compares to the way he touched me in the sea, the way my body pulsed with need for him.

I wish I didn't have the memory of that day seared into my memory. I'm not sure I'll ever be able to purge it. No matter how far I go from the Shadow Realm. What's worse, I'm not sure I want to.

"To your feast day bonfire." Kaia rises from the table, and I follow her. "It's tonight."

"I know when it is," Thieran replies, eyes on me over Kaia's shoulder but not budging from his spot in the doorway. "Why are you two going?"

"We could all use a good celebration," Kaia says, a pointed look passing between them with a meaning I am not privy to.

"You could come with us," I add, pulling Thieran's gaze to mine.

"I haven't attended my feast day in a very long time."

"A shame," Kaia says.

"And maybe a little rude."

Thieran eyes me, eyebrows raised. "Rude?"

"Yes. They're celebrating you," I remind him. "The least you could do is attend."

"They merely enjoy a good feast, drinking too much, dancing in the square. That's all."

I tilt my head to study him. "If that were true, they wouldn't wait until your feast day to do it."

Kaia ducks her head to hide a smile, and Thieran straightens. He gives me one last long look before turning on his heel and striding down the hall.

"Well done," Kaia says, looping her arm through mine and leading me from the room. "Every year, I try to get him to attend. The souls don't want me or anyone else there in his place. Whatever Thieran wants to think."

"Does anyone else go?" I wonder, climbing the stairs to our rooms.

"Railan usually makes an appearance, and Nevon, of course. I don't think anything could keep him from a good celebration. And now you."

We stop outside my rooms and Kaia looks at me expectantly, her hands gripping my upper arms gently.

"You'll let me dress you, won't you?"

I look down at my standard outfit. It's not exactly fancy or fit for a feast day celebration. But it's what I'm most comfortable in.

"What's wrong with what I'm wearing?"

"Well, nothing. But…" She bites the inside of her cheek, and I imagine she's trying to find a polite way of saying the way I dress is boring or unladylike. "A celebration is a special occasion."

"I…" Kaia's look is imploring, and I give in. "All right. What did you have in mind?"

She grins, taking my hand and pushing into my suite of rooms. We cross the sitting room into my bedroom, and my heart skips a beat when she goes right for my wardrobe.

Opening the doors wide and shoving my clothes back and forth, she doesn't seem to notice the jar pushed to the recesses. It would be a difficult thing to explain if she did.

She pulls out a bright yellow gown with frills down the length of the skirt, and I wrinkle my nose.

"Yes," she says, holding the dress out in front of her. "I see what you mean. Maybe something a little less…bold."

The next dress she pulls out is a soft lavender, and she holds it up to my shoulders, shuffling with me to the long mirror hidden behind a tapestry in the corner. Adjusting the sleeves to lay over my arms and give the appearance I've tried it on, she cocks her head, studying my reflection. There's something about it that doesn't look quite right, and I meet her appraising gaze in the mirror.

"It's not the right color for your skin tone."

I nod in agreement, and she goes for a different one. Blue this time, and the color reminds me of the sea and Thieran. I shake the idea from my head, and Kaia takes that as dislike.

"All right, if you insist."

I watch her replace the dress in the wardrobe and breathe a small sigh of relief. I hardly need to wear a dress that will remind me of Thieran all night. Going to his feast day will be bad enough.

What I really need is distance from him so I can do what needs to be done with this ritual. And I will. First thing tomorrow, I'll test it. Go through the ritual and cut myself in a way that would make Thieran seek me out.

If he does, the ritual hasn't worked. If he doesn't, then all that's left is to choose the right time for my escape. But that's for tomorrow. Tonight, I'll celebrate the end of my time in the Shadow Realm. Because I don't have much of it left.

"Oh, what about this one?" Kaia calls, voice muffled, with her head in the wardrobe on the other side of the room.

She emerges with a beautiful velvet gown and a wide grin. Crossing to me, she holds it under my chin, arranging it until she's satisfied.

"What do you think?"

I think my first thought shouldn't be how much Thieran would love to see me in this dress. Or how much I'd love to have him take it off me.

I finger the edge of the sleeve and smooth a hand down the skirt. "It's perfect."

CHAPTER TWENTY-NINE

Thieran

Against my better judgment, I find myself making my way to Elora's rooms as the day fades to night. Her door is closed, the light shining out from underneath the only indication she's still inside. Occasionally her shadow passes in front of it, and I wonder if she's second-guessing her decision to go as much as I am second-guessing standing here.

I wasn't going to attend my feast day celebrations. I never do. Or at least not anymore. I've left the souls in Videva to create their own celebrations. A habit of tradition more than anything else.

They continued to celebrate without me after I stopped throwing the ball on the third night of my feast days and then after I stopped making any appearance at all. They don't need me to throw a party. My feast days are a convenient excuse.

I should be in the library, poring over the scrolls Kaia brought back from her most recent trip to Acaria. The ones that will hopefully confirm my theory that a blood relative might be a good substitute for Elora. Assuming I can find one she wouldn't mind parting with.

So why am I standing outside Elora's rooms dressed in my ceremonial robes edged with glittering silver thread?

As I consider leaving, I hear a door open down the hall. I don't turn to watch Kaia approach, but she stops beside me, and there's a smile in her voice when she speaks.

"Change your mind, then?"

"Apparently," I mutter, adjusting the collar of my robes. "I'm going to regret this."

"Oh, I wouldn't say that."

"And why not?"

Her grin has a teasing edge to it. "Because I know what she's wearing."

Kaia steps forward and knocks twice on Elora's door. It takes only a moment before a shadow appears at the crack and the door swings open. The sight of her steals my breath from my lungs.

I've seen her in a gown before. The night I followed her and Nevon into the forest. But that creation was nothing compared to this. She's bewitching and uncomfortable with it if the way she's tugging at the sleeves and fidgeting with the skirt is any indication.

The deep green velvet highlights the flecks of gold in her eyes, and the bodice shows off every sumptuous curve. The cut of the dress is lower than anything I'd ever expect her to wear, and the rounded tops of her breasts rise and fall with each breath. Her chest is flushed, whether from nerves or desire, I'm not sure, but the result makes me want to press my lips to her skin until she begs me to stop.

Elora looks between us, hesitation on her face, before her gaze finally lands on mine.

"Is it really that bad?"

"Bad?" How could she possibly think such a thing?

She runs her hands over her stomach and around to her hips, where the material clings, and then combs her fingers through her hair. Her usual braid is replaced by long, elegant waves that fall softly over her shoulders and down her back.

My fingers twitch at the urge to touch them, run my fingers through them. An urge I won't give into until later. I imagine I'll be giving in to a lot of urges before the night is out.

"You look stunning," Kaia assures her. "Did you want to wear the overcoat? You could catch a chill if you're not close to the fire."

"I'll keep you warm," I say on impulse.

There's not a chance I'll let her to cover up any part of that dress with something else. As it is, it takes everything I have to extend my hand to her so we can go and not push her back into the room and have my way with her on every fucking surface.

Forgoing the overcoat, she takes a fortifying breath and places her hand in mine. We shift to the edge of Videva, the distant sound of voices carrying over the air as soon as we arrive.

I run my hand up her back to her neck, giving it a gentle squeeze as I send power through her. Both to help with the effects of shifting and to keep her warm against the cold. I don't have to touch her to do it, but I can't help myself.

"I haven't been to a feast day since I was a child," Elora admits as we walk the last few steps to the square.

"You'll love it," Kaia assures her. "Bonfire night is my favorite. My people do something similar."

"Do the celebrations still last three days here? Now that there's no ball?"

"They do," I supply. "Although it's really just three nights of the same."

"Would you ever consider hosting the ball again?"

Her question is quiet, but something about it has me itching to touch her, so I lay my hand on the small of her back, sliding it around her side and giving her a squeeze.

"Balls are better with proper hostesses."

Her gaze drifts beyond me to Kaia, but she doesn't respond, instead turning at the first stirrings of a lively song. The buzz of voices becomes louder, punctuated by the occasional laugh or shout.

The party is well underway by the time we step into the square, and the jovial conversation of the people closest to us soon fades to stunned silence. Their eyes dart from Kaia to Elora to me, and then they slowly drop into deep curtsies or bows.

The more people take note, the more they follow suit until all talking and music has stopped. The only sound left is the crackle and pop of the bonfire as it ignites the large tower of tree limbs laid out in the middle of the square.

"Elora!"

Corinne's happy greeting seems to jerk the crowd out of their trance, and the conversation resumes as Corinne weaves her way toward us. She stops in front of me and bobs a quick curtsy before turning to Elora.

"What a lovely surprise it is to see you here." She takes a step back, smiling at Elora's gown. "And you look so beautiful!"

Elora smooths nervous fingers down her skirt. "Thank you. I hope it's all right we've come." She glances up at me. "We don't want to make things uncomfortable."

"Don't be silly. You're more than welcome." Corinne turns her bright smile on me. "All of you. Of course, my lord. Can I bring you anything to drink?"

"Oh, I—"

"Yes. Thank you."

Elora looks up at me as Corinne races off, disappearing around the edge of the fire. Her gaze catches on the musicians sitting just beyond the flames, testing their instruments and calling songs to each other.

"I haven't danced in ages," she admits, watching the handful of people make space as the next tune begins.

"Neither have I."

She smiles softly, the frown smoothing from her brow for the first time since we arrived. I want to pull her close, ask her to dance with me, but Corinne returns with ale in simple wooden cups and passes one to each of us.

"To life after death," Corinne toasts, lifting her cup and taking a sip.

"To the promise of rebirth. And to the god who rules both."

Elora surprises me by finishing my tribute and takes a deep drink, watching me over the rim of her cup. The fact that she even knows it warms something inside me.

"Could I steal you, my lady?"

Elora glances up at me.

"I'll be watching," I say, and her eyes drop to my mouth before darting back up to meet my gaze. "Behave yourself."

Corinne reaches for Elora's hand and leads her off into the crowd, Elora peeking back at me over her shoulder until I lose her among the revelers. I can sense her, but I don't like not being able to see her. I'm just about to go in search of her when she reappears next to an old woman and a man probably somewhere around her own age.

They exchange a few words, and jealousy flares in my chest when his hand moves to her elbow. He leans close to her ear, and whatever he says has her looking away from him. Her eyes scan the crowd, and I'm not sure what she's searching for. Until she finds me.

We share a long look before she turns to the man and nods. He leads her to the edge of the group of dancers and lays his hand about her waist, taking her other in his own.

I grit my teeth as she nervously follows his lead, faltering in the steps until finally finding her footing. The music speeds up, and she grins wide as they twirl and weave among the other dancers.

She's perfect. Her long, dark hair flies around her face and shoulders while her skirts swirl around her legs. When the song ends, the man gives her a dramatic twirl, and she laughs, clapping for the musicians even as another song begins.

Another man steps up to ask for a dance, and just like the first time, her eyes find me in the crowd before she agrees.

"You should ask her to dance," Kaia says at my elbow.

"I haven't danced in years."

"I hardly see what that has to do with anything. It isn't as if you've forgotten the steps." She nudges my elbow. "Go before you make a scene over all these men asking her instead."

Moving into the crowd, Kaia greets a couple seated near the fire as if they're old friends. Then again, Kaia greets most people that way, whether she knows them or not. I don't know how she has the stomach for it.

The song ends, and I watch Elora throw her head back with laughter, offering another round of applause for the music. The urge to be near her, to touch her, overrides anything else, and I move along the edge of the crowd toward where she stands, accepting a fresh cup of ale.

I barely acknowledge the murmured words of greeting as I pass people, too intent on my goal. When I finally reach her, she finds me immediately in the crowd. As if she's as drawn to me as I am to her. She throws back the rest of her ale and sets her cup on a nearby table laden with food.

"Do you plan on hiding in the shadows all evening?"

"I'm not hiding. I'm watching."

She looks around us, standing just beyond the light of the fire, the dancing flames casting long shadows, and raises a brow.

"Could have fooled me. Why did you come if you were just going to skulk about and make everyone uncomfortable?"

I dart a look at the people standing closest to us, talking and teasing until they realize they've caught my eye and scurry away.

"I told you they don't want me here."

"You could try being a little more personable." She holds out a hand to me. "Dance with me, Thieran."

The words are softly spoken, and they have all the more impact for it. I reach for her hand and lead her into the square as the song changes again. I know this one. It's an ancient tune. And I remember the steps to it well enough.

Slipping my arm around Elora's waist, I draw her close, much closer than the song requires, and feel her warm breath against my neck. She grips my shoulder, her fingers curling into the fabric of my robes.

"Do you know this one?" I ask as the other dancers begin to swirl and dip around us.

"Of course."

I grin before spinning us into the first steps. She follows my lead perfectly, her movements fluid and sure. She steps closer to avoid another couple, and her scent is intoxicating, spiced ale and the honeysuckle soap she prefers.

When the song finishes, I'm reluctant to let her go, but she moves away to catch her breath, eyes shining as she laughs.

"You're a better dancer than I thought."

There's a teasing note to her voice, and I can't help but chuckle. "I've been alive long enough to practice here and there."

Another song begins, and she takes my hand, but rather than dance, she leads me back to the edge of the crowd. She releases me but doesn't move away, her body brushing mine.

"You're just full of surprises, aren't you?"

"Am I?"

I catch a wayward piece of hair as it blows across her face and tuck it behind her ear, tracing my fingertip down the edge of her jaw to her chin and tilting her face up.

"You are," she says softly. "I never know what you might do next."

I lean down to kiss her, but someone calls her name and she leaps away from me, making me frown. An elderly woman draped in a shawl that looks vaguely familiar approaches us, and I bid her remain standing when she tries to curtsy.

"You look beautiful, my lady," the woman says, and Elora squirms under the title.

"Thank you, Dania. And please, I've asked you to call me Elora."

"I'm sorry, my lady. Old habits are hard to break. But I am glad to see you. And you, my lord. You honor us with your presence."

"The honor is mine."

Dania beams at that. She's been in the Shadow Realm a long time, attending feast days longer than Elora's been alive. She's never wanted to reincarnate, and I sense she's waiting for her family to arrive before making such a decision.

"I made the boiled sweets you like so much," Dania says to Elora.

"Raspberry?"

Dania smiles and inclines her head. "And blackberry, my lady."

The woman moves away, and more people come to take her place, greeting Elora with a familiarity that surprises me. I didn't realize she'd spent enough time in Videva for people to know her so well or for her to know them.

There's something about it that tugs at me. Even though I've kept my distance these many years, I like that she has taken the time to get to know my people. That they seem to like her as much as they do.

When the last person leaves, she sags back against me, sighing when I trail my fingers down her arm and capture her hand in mine.

"I didn't realize you were so friendly with the souls in Videva."

"I ride Meera into the village sometimes. She likes the attention, and it's a nice change of scenery. They've been very kind to me."

I bend down to whisper in her ear. "As they should be."

She smiles, leaning into me even more. Someone adds taller tree limbs to the bonfire, and the flames dance higher, sending off a wave of heat and a rush of sparks.

Slipping my hand around her waist, I flatten my palm against her stomach and pull her body flush with mine. She tilts her head to look up at me, the firelight shimmering in her eyes.

"Careful, my lord. There's quite the crowd."

"There doesn't have to be. We can be anywhere in the blink of an eye."

She captures her bottom lip between her teeth, glancing at the people dancing and laughing, chatting and wandering. When she looks back at me, desire is written clearly on her face.

"It would be rude to leave so early."

I lean down until our lips are barely touching. "I don't care."

She closes the distance between us, her lips on mine in an urgent kiss. And before she can protest, I shift us away from the festivities.

CHAPTER THIRTY

─────── ❦ ───────

Elora

When the air stops swirling, it takes me a moment to realize we've landed somewhere other than the palace. Thieran tilts his head and drags his teeth over my jaw, his breath hot on my neck.

I can't see him in the pitch black that is night in the Shadow Realm, but I feel him acutely. Every brush of his lips over my skin, the warm, heavy weight of his hand on my stomach, the press of his body against mine.

It's disorienting and enthralling all at once.

His fingers tug at the laces of my gown, and I spin in his arms, sliding my hands up his chest and linking my fingers around his neck.

"Where are we?"

"Just wait," he murmurs, his breath moving the hair at my temple.

His hands skim around my waist to my lower back, and he makes quick work of my laces, deftly undoing them until my dress loosens enough for him to pull it down my arms.

I feel his lips press against my shoulder, and I wonder if he can see in the dark in a way I cannot. If he's brought me here—wherever here is—to give himself the upper hand. Or perhaps he's keeping the promise he made to me in the library. That the next time he had me, he wanted me screaming when I came on his cock.

I shudder at the memory, my pussy clenching at the thought, and feel his lips curve against my skin. He's thinking the same. I know he is.

"Thieran," I whisper, breath snagging on a soft sigh when his tongue traces along the curved line of my corset.

"Any minute now," he assures me, quickly dragging my dress down until it pools at my waist and loosening my corset.

The moment I'm free of it, his mouth finds my nipple, his teeth closing around it and tightening until I'm gasping from the pain and pleasure of it. There's something exhilarating about not being able to see him, anticipating his touch. I'm at his mercy in the dark, and heat pools in my core at the realization.

He reaches up to cup my breast, drawing circles around my nipple without touching it. I've discovered I like when Thieran teases me, even though I'd rather cut out my own tongue than admit it to him.

The frustration of waiting for him to move his fingers or teeth or tongue right where I want them never fails to pile up into a needy pain, a desperate wanting only he can ease. It's a pain that blooms bright with pleasure when he finally, blissfully, drags his thumb over my nipple, making me gasp.

He dips his head for a taste, swirling his tongue over the bud he's made swollen and sensitive. The first contact makes me groan. The second has my hands fisting in his hair, holding him against me.

"Desperate for me, are you, little one?"

I don't speak. I can't. And even if I could, my voice would betray me. How right he is. How much I crave him. I try never to give Thieran the upper hand if I can help it. I'm sure I'm failing miserably.

When his teeth close around my nipple again, I squeeze my eyes shut tight enough that light blooms across my vision. The pain and pleasure race to my core. But the light flashes again, and I open my eyes just as Thieran drops to his knees and reaches for my hand, lacing our fingers together.

Above us, the sky is open. We're not in the forest, as I suspected, but in an open field blanketed with snow. My breath leaves my lips in little white puffs. I should be freezing, but my body is on fire, either from need or Thieran's power or both.

"What is this place?" I wonder, sighing when Thieran tugs me to my knees and eases me onto my back, covering my body with his.

"The southernmost point of the Shadow Realm."

He leans down to capture my mouth, teeth digging into the flesh of my lower lip until I squirm against him. Pulling back with a grin, he kisses his way down my chest, flicking each of my nipples with the tip of his tongue just to make me arch and groan.

"Eyes on the sky, little one," he commands as his hand smooths up my inner thigh, taking my dress with it.

I feel his breath against my pussy, but before I can tease him into giving me more, color explodes across the inky black of the sky, and my words are lost to wonder. It dances in ribbons, vibrant greens and pinks and yellows.

Thieran drags the flat of his tongue over my pussy, and my hips jerk, rocking up to seek more. The lights illuminate his face, and the way he looks at me makes my heart pound.

He's beautiful, all sharp angles and eyes so blue they almost glow in the dark. He keeps his gaze on mine as he again extends his tongue and gives my pussy one long, lazy lick.

I can't stop watching him, not as he spreads me open with two fingers and swirls his tongue over my clit, not as he slips one finger, then two, then three inside me and pushes them deep, his tongue still pressing against my clit before he sucks it between his lips.

He holds my gaze through all of it, the bright beams dancing across his face, light and shadows playing over his features.

"Do you remember what you promised me in the library?" he asks, pulling his fingers out and shoving them roughly back in, smiling when a low groan escapes me.

"I do," I pant, writhing as his fingers quicken, roughly fucking me until my thighs quiver and my hands dig into the snow cushioning our bodies. "But I promised to scream on your cock. Not your fingers."

He grins, raising a brow as he shifts his hand to press his thumb against my clit and resumes his brutal pace. Even with his fingers filling me so well, I ache for his cock.

"I want both." He settles his body over my mine, leaning down to trace my bottom lip with his tongue. "And you're going to give it to me."

"And if I don't?"

My voice is breathy, hips arching up to meet a particularly deep thrust as my pussy clenches down around him.

"Then I'll fuck you until you do."

The threat makes my pulse pound and my pussy flutter, and he grins, working me faster, edging me closer to release.

"You'd like that, wouldn't you? For me to use this perfect little pussy until I'm satisfied, until you can't move without thinking about my cock buried inside you."

"Fuck you," I manage to grind out, my hips meeting the thrust of his fingers in frantic jerks.

"I will," he promises. "As soon as you come all over my fingers screaming my name."

I don't want to. Ignoring Thieran's commands is as much a part of the pleasure of fucking him as anything else. But so is giving in to them. Something else I can't reconcile when it comes to this unnamable thing between us.

He must be able to see it on my face. How close I am. How hard I'm fighting to not give him what he wants. His fingers shove deep, and he grinds his palm against my clit until I have no choice but to give over to the very thing he wants to claim from me.

Back bowing, throat tight with the force of the orgasm racing down my spine and pooling in my center, I fist the fabric of his robes and scream just the way he wants me to, the sound of it carrying on the wind.

"That's it," he groans, pulling his fingers free and dancing them over my clit before shedding his robes. "That's what we both need."

The lights illuminate the hard plane of his chest as he strips off his tunic and works open the tie to his breeches. Still catching my breath, I reach up to trace the outline of his abs, making his stomach muscles contract. I think I could look at him every day and not tire of it.

The thought catches me off guard, and I'm instantly grateful I didn't say it out loud. I don't have days with him. I have hours. Because leaving here is the right thing to do. I shouldn't want to stay. I don't want to stay.

I'm just caught up in the moment. In the weight of him as he settles his body over mine and the brush of his cock against my too-sensitive clit and the way the light skipping and twirling above us makes him look as ethereal and powerful as he is.

"Ready to scream for me again?"

He notches his cock at my entrance, and I roll my eyes even as I drag my fingernails down his chest and dig them into his hips, urging him forward as much as holding him in place.

"Your arrogance is really—"

He slams his cock inside me, and my words fade into a gasp and then a needy groan as he grinds deep.

"What was that?"

Wrapping my legs around his waist, I squeeze the length of his cock buried inside me, grinning when he drops his forehead to my breast with a groan.

"Shut up and fuck me, Thieran."

I expect him to hesitate, to remind me he'll use me as he pleases, but he doesn't, rearing his hips back and plunging into me again and again. With each powerful thrust, his pelvis grinds against my clit until I see stars.

He's ruined me. It's all I can think as he takes what he wants from my body, his head turning to capture my nipple between his lips, and gives me what I need. I didn't expect to enjoy it this much. And I want to savor it before leaving it behind forever.

The lights flash from green and blue to pink and purple, and I slide my hands up Thieran's broad back and into his hair, wrapping it around my fingers and bringing his mouth to mine. He groans against my lips when I nip his tongue roughly, his fingers replacing his lips on my nipple, squeezing and twisting.

I want to sear him into my memory as much as I want to forget him when this is all over. Whatever happens, I should have known from the start it would be impossible to forget the God of Death.

He pulls away from me, capturing my bottom lip in his teeth before sitting up and shifting me on his cock, hooking his arms under my thighs to hold me in place as he pounds me relentlessly.

His eyes are locked on where we're joined, his cock driving into me with each urgent thrust of his hips. Another orgasm builds, tingling along my skin until I can barely breathe.

"You take my cock so well," he growls, burying it inside me again. "Every fucking inch."

I whimper, and his gaze snaps to mine, his hand shooting out to cover my clit, strumming it in time with his sharp thrusts.

"That's it, little one. Come all over me. Take what you need. Give me what I want."

I couldn't stop it if I tried. The inevitable crash of my orgasm, the groan my clenching pussy draws from Thieran's throat as he slams into me, his fingers never stilling on my sensitive and swollen clit.

"That was perfect," he praises, covering his body with mine, giving me his weight while his hips resume his brutal pace and push me higher before I've even had time to come down. "I want one more."

"Thieran. I-I can't."

"You will."

His voice is a growl, low and commanding, and every part of me, a part I didn't think existed before Thieran, screams to obey. The things he does to me scare me, but it doesn't stop the wanting.

"Elora."

It's a warning and a promise. And I won't deny him. I can't. My body is too on edge, a bowstring pulled taut by an expert marksman.

"Now," Thieran whispers into my ear, voice hoarse, and I give over to it, to him, wrapping myself around him as my orgasm blinds me and he thrusts deep, finding his own release.

"Good girl," he murmurs, lips brushing the shell of my ear and making me shiver.

Rolling onto his back in the snow beside me, he reaches for my hand, linking our fingers together and bringing my hand to his mouth for a kiss. My stomach clenches at the sweet intimacy of it, and I distract myself by rearranging my skirts around my legs, brushing at the snow clinging to my skin without melting.

"Why aren't we freezing?"

I hear the grin in Thieran's voice when he replies. "Magick. Do you like the lights?" he asks after a beat.

Glancing up at the sky as they continue to weave and wind their way across the vast stretch of black, I sigh.

"They're stunning. What are they?" I give him a sideways glance. "More magick?"

He chuckles, giving my hand another kiss and then sitting up and reaching for his tunic.

"A natural phenomenon, as far as I can tell. But no less magickal in their own right." He stands and hands me my corset, watching me hook it back into place and tighten the laces while he reties his breeches. "I wanted to show you the Shadow Realm holds its own kind of beauty."

There's a weight to his words, a meaning I can't decipher. It's not for me to understand. Not if I'm going to make a clean break from here. A choice I can't stop second-guessing.

Slipping my arms into my gown, I reach around to try and tighten my laces, my fingers grasping the edges of the ribbon but unable to get a good enough purchase to pull them tight.

"Let me—"

Thieran's fingers brush my arm and then grip it, tightening as he spins me so my back is exposed to him. I try to squirm free, but he holds me fast. I know what he's finally seeing for the first time, what I've managed to keep hidden from him until now.

I didn't know how he'd react, but his silence is enough to convince me he finds me as hideous as everyone else always has.

"Who did this to you?"

The venom in his tone surprises me, and I jerk around to look up at him as much as his grip on my arm will allow. The rage and possessiveness on his face are enough to make my blood hum, and it warms and soothes a place deep inside me. A place I thought had died a long time ago.

"It doesn't matter."

"The fuck it doesn't." His hold loosens slightly, but he doesn't release me. "Tell me, Elora."

"Most of them are from my uncle. Some are from other men who thought the easiest way to control a woman was to beat her into submission."

He growls low in his throat, easing my hair off my neck and studying my back. The crisscrossing patchwork of scars left behind from my uncle's leather strap and horse whips and tree branches and whatever else came to hand when he wanted to remind me what a burden I was to him.

"Your uncle is still alive."

It isn't a question, but I answer him anyway. "As far as I'm aware. I haven't seen him since I was eleven."

I close my eyes against the memory of when he abandoned me on the steps of the workhouse. *You can be someone else's mouth to feed now*, he said before dropping a paltry bag full of tattered clothes at my feet, climbing back into his cart, and driving away.

Without a word, Thieran slowly laces up my gown, cinching it tight and tying the ribbons in a bow at the base of my spine. I move to step away, but he wraps his arm around my shoulders and pulls me back against his chest.

His hair tickles my cheek when he leans down to whisper. "I swear to you. By all the gods, I will never let harm come to you ever again."

My heart somersaults into my stomach, and I lean into him when I should lean away. I can't rely on his comfort or his vow, however much I want or believe them. Because as soon as I test my shielding ritual, I'll be leaving the Shadow Realm and the God of Death.

My chest tightens at the thought. And when Thieran buries his nose in my hair, inhaling deeply as he shifts us back to the palace, I try to remind myself of all the perfectly good reasons I have for leaving. Only I can't remember any of them.

CHAPTER THIRTY-ONE

Thieran

The man trudges back and forth across the field, snow clinging to the thick wool of his breeches. His coat, threadbare at the elbows and tattered at the hem, drags behind him.

I watch him stop next to a thin, sickly looking cow and drape a blanket over its back before slapping its rump and urging it toward a lean-to barn. The barn looks as pitiful as the cow, with wide gaps between the boards and wood rotting around the edges.

He gives the animal a rough shove under the shelter and mutters a stream of complaints as he grabs a pitchfork from the corner and sticks it into a meager pile of hay. The cow huffs when her breakfast flutters to the ground in front of her but leans down to take a bite, her shoulder bones poking out from her skin.

He's already milked her, cleaned out the barn, and collected fresh eggs from a tiny troop of squawking hens. I've been standing here long enough to watch him toil away since sunrise, grumbling to himself nearly the entire time.

The dark brown hair on his head is streaked with gray, and

his scraggly beard is also shot through with silvery strands. He looks older than his years, his face weathered and tired, his body bent from hard labor on a farm that's seen better days.

With the cow munching dutifully on her breakfast, he picks up the pail of milk and carries it around the side of the house, letting himself in. Smoke puffs out from a faded chimney, and I shift to peer in through a window.

A woman stands in front of the fireplace, an old shawl draped around her shoulders while she pokes at something in a pot with a long spoon. She looks up when the man sets the pail on the counter, and they exchange terse words about how little the cow seems to be producing these days, barely worth its keep.

It's been the same every morning since I began watching them three days ago. The woman makes a modest breakfast while the man does all the morning chores. They argue about the cow, and then the man complains about the breakfast she's made while shoveling it into his mouth.

They have five children, but none of them remain, not even a dutiful daughter to take care of them in their old age. Perhaps they beat them the way they did Elora. And now they've been left to fend for themselves.

I haven't been able to coax any more information from Elora about her mistreatment at the hands of her uncle, but the scars on her back were all the motivation I needed to seek him out. The idea to make him pay was formed the moment I saw the marks on her skin. Only now, he might be useful to me. In more ways than one.

Their small property backs up to the forest on the edge of the Goddess of Nightmare's territory. Elora was born in the capital city of Dremen, which isn't far from here but far less remote than this parcel of land. Although it's perfectly placed for my purpose here today.

No one will hear the screams.

Stepping away from the forest's edge, I cross the snowy stretch of ground. They're still arguing about the fucking cow when I pause at the door hanging crooked on its hinges. Rolling my eyes, I open the door with a flick of my wrist, mouth quirking up into a wry grin when the old woman shrieks. I'm going to enjoy this more than I anticipated.

"Who in the fuck do you—"

The man's words die on his tongue when he realizes who I am, and he drops the knife he'd reached for on the table.

"Beg pardon, m'lord. I didn't know we had the honor," he mumbles, the bluster leaving him.

"Sit."

A chair jerks out from the table at my command, making him flinch, but he ambles over to take a seat, tensing when his wife lays her hand on his arm for comfort.

"Can I get you anything, m'lord?" The woman asks. "We don't have much, but there's ale and some fresh bread."

"You had a brother," I say to the man, ignoring the woman's offer.

"I did. He died a long time ago."

"But he left behind a little girl."

He glances up at the ice in my tone, shifting in his chair and gripping his hands in his lap.

"My brother and his wife, they had a daughter. Yes. But I..." He casts a sideways glance at his wife, whose hands are clutched so tight in her lap her knuckles are white. "I don't know where she is. She ran away a long time ago."

Even if I wasn't a god, something about the way he says it signals it's a lie. Or maybe it's the dart of his eyes around the room, landing anywhere but on me.

"We both know that isn't true."

He sucks his teeth and pulls at his thinning beard. "She was a handful, that girl. We did what we could for her, and when we couldn't, we let her go."

"After you were finished beating her, you mean."

"Every child needs discipline," he snaps.

His wife sucks in a sharp breath when I step closer, the knife disappearing from the table and materializing in my hand. I crouch in front of him, the firelight glinting off the blade when I hold it up to his face. His eyes are cold, unfeeling, and I imagine Elora staring into them each time he took a strap to her and left his scars behind.

"You marked her," I growl, trailing the tip of the knife over the pounding pulse in his throat. "With scars and pain she still carries today. There's a price to pay for that."

"Please, m'lord," his wife begs, leaning forward in her chair. "We're sorry. He's sorry," she assures me even as her husband snorts his disagreement. "We didn't know any better."

"Did you watch him beat her?" I tilt my head when she purses her lips. "Tend her wounds when he'd worked out all his rage on a little girl? Answer me," I snap when she remains silent.

"A wife must support her husband in all things. Even when she disagrees."

Unsatisfied with her answer, I draw back the blade and plunge it into her husband's thigh. He screams and thrashes against my hold on the handle, blood soaking through the wool and coating the steel when I pull it free.

"Elora deserved better than the two of you."

"She got exactly what she deserved," her uncle replies, pinning me with a hard stare. "And if you want to kill me for raising her as I saw fit, then go right ahead. I'm not afraid of you or any god."

Pushing to my feet, I grin, reaching down to grip his collar and haul him up.

"Then you're as much of a fool as I think you are. And killing you is exactly what I'll do." I turn to his wife when she whimpers and then slaps a hand over her mouth. "If you breathe a word of this to anyone, I'll be back for you next. Understand?"

She nods frantically. I'd expect her eyes to be filled with tears, but they're dry and wide. Even now, she can't think about anyone but herself. Shaking my head, I shift away to the veil with Elora's uncle in my grasp.

He stumbles when we arrive, bending over to retch his breakfast into the grass. When he rights himself, swiping a hand over his mouth to clear away the sick, his eyes narrow at our surroundings.

"Why not just kill me in my own house? At least then my wife could bury me."

"You don't deserve a proper burial." I twist the knife in my fingers, grinning as he eyes it. "You deserve nothing except to find your place among others like you in Síra. And here you'll be useful. For once."

His hands clench into fists, and I chuckle at the gesture. I want to take my time and carve every mark I've mapped on Elora into his body. His screams would bring me such pleasure, but I promised her we'd spend some time in the training yard today.

When his muscles bunch and his body jerks, I reach out and grip him by the throat before he can lunge for me, lifting him off the ground until his feet dangle and kick.

"Did you think you'd take me by surprise?"

"I'm not afraid of you—"

"Or any god. Yes, I know. You can lie to yourself if you want. The end result is the same."

"Since when do gods care so much about mortals and their pain?" he sputters, his lips beginning to turn blue.

"Since you marked what is mine."

He opens his mouth to speak, but I'm faster, dropping him to his feet and drawing the blade across his throat before the words can pass his lips. He attempts to suck in a ragged breath, his hands going to his throat and coming away wet and dripping.

I grab him by the back of the neck before he can stumble away and shove him against the invisible barrier of the veil. He's Elora's blood relative on her father's side. I'm hoping whatever healing power she has in her blood passes through her father's line because her mother was an only child and has no living relatives.

He twitches against my hold, his blood seeming to float in mid-air as it slides down the veil and pools on the ground. There is no sudden sprouting of vines, no change to the veil or the surrounding landscape. He is as useless in death as he was in life.

Releasing him, I watch his lifeless body slump to the forest floor and huff out an annoyed breath. Killing him for touching Elora was satisfying, but he hardly solved my problem.

Either Elora's power comes through her mother's line, or my theory about being able to substitute a blood relative to heal the realm has been disproven. Either way, the Shadow Realm will continue to worsen until I can find another solution.

Because sacrificing Elora is not an option. And I will shed the blood of as many mortals as it takes to keep her by my side.

Leaving her uncle as a feast for the forest guardians, I shift back to my rooms and change my blood-spattered robes for fresh ones, cleaning the muck from my face and hands. As I reach up to adjust my collar, searing pain shoots down my arm from elbow to wrist, and I feel Elora's heartbeat flutter in my chest.

In an instant, I'm by her side in the training yard. Her tunic is split down her forearm and stained red. Nevon is standing next to her, her arm cradled in his hands while he inspects the cut.

"What the fuck did you do?" I snarl, shoving him back a step and inspecting the wound.

It's long and thin, a clean cut from a sharp blade. It likely won't even scar, but I don't like the fact that someone else has hurt her, marred her skin, even for a moment.

"Get out of my sight, Nevon."

He takes another step back when I pin him with a dark look and quickly disappears.

"It's not that serious," Elora assures me, trying to tug her arm free. "No need to overreact."

"He cut you."

"You say that like he attacked me." She again tries to draw her arm from my grasp. "It was an accident."

"They were only sparring," Railan says, appearing at my elbow. "She feinted left, and Nevon was faster."

"I imagine he would be. Given he's immortal and she's just..."

"Oh, no," Elora says when I don't continue. "Please do finish that sentence. Just what? A weak little mortal?"

I frown. "I didn't say that. Will you stop squirming?" I add through gritted teeth.

"Thieran, you're being dramatic." She prods at my fingertips and sighs. "Are you going to let me go so I can get a bandage, or are you going to wait for me to bleed out right here?"

"Apply pressure to that," I say, dropping her arm. "I'll send a healer to your room."

She rolls her eyes even as her mouth ticks up at one corner, cradling her arm as she stomps away from me. When I turn back to Railan, prepared to admonish him for letting their sparring match get so out of hand, his eyes are trained on the ground.

I follow the path of his gaze, and my chest tightens. There, where Elora's blood has dripped onto the grass at the edge of the training ring, are a series of vines twisting in on themselves and crawling along the ground until they slowly come to a stop.

Railan looks up at me, but before he can say anything, before I can come up with an excuse for why that isn't what it looks like, a wave of power announces the arrival of new souls in the Shadow Realm.

He wants to stay and ask me every question I see cascading across his face, but the pull to his duty is stronger than his curiosity.

"I'll come find you," he says simply before disappearing.

I crouch down and rip the vines from the earth, but they hold fast, driving their branches deep into the soil as soon as I pluck them. As if they were meant to thrive here.

Shoving to my feet, I stalk toward the palace. Railan's judgments will only take so long. And then I'll be forced to explain something I hardly understand myself. And why I currently have no plan to do a fucking thing about it.

CHAPTER THIRTY-TWO

Elora

"I promise it won't scar, my lady."

The healer wraps a soft linen bandage around my forearm, securing it at my elbow, and I sigh at the title I haven't been able to get her to stop using since she stepped foot in my rooms.

"I will come back before you're ready for sleep to change it for you."

"That really isn't necessary. Just leave whatever supplies I need to change the dressing, and I can manage."

Her eyes dart from the bag she brought with her to my arm to the table I've indicated with a wave of my hand.

"I don't think Lord Thieran would approve of that, my lady."

"I'll see to it that he does. I've had worse. I know how to tend to a wound."

She hesitates a moment more before reaching into her bag and pulling out a small jar of the salve she applied to the cut that smelled of juniper berries and mint. Setting it on the table, she produces a fresh roll of bandages and clean cloths.

"You'll want to change the bandage twice a day until it

begins to close, and then keep using the salve until there is no scar."

I smile and nod. She seems particularly worried about whether this shallow wound might leave a mark. But she doesn't need to know that scars are nothing new to me.

"Thank you," I say.

Following her to the door, I close it behind her and lean my forehead against it, grateful for the silence. Piecing together the events of the last hour or so was infinitely more difficult with her fussing over what is really nothing more than a scratch.

Turning for the bedroom, I cross straight to the wardrobe, shoving gowns and tunics out of the way and crouching down to pull the heavy jar full of my shielding potion forward.

All that work. All that waiting. And the damn thing doesn't work.

After a few days of procrastinating, I forced myself to perform the ritual this morning before breakfast. Then I made mention of wanting to spend some time in the sparring ring, both for the exercise and the perfect opportunity to test my theory. Thieran promised to spar with me after an errand, but I managed to talk Nevon into getting a head start.

He took it easy on me. But not that easy. Spinning, feinting, and bringing his blade to my throat or my belly, but never puncturing the skin. Nevon would know better. I was having so much fun hefting a sword in my hand and sparring with a good partner I almost forgot the point of the whole thing.

So I went left when I should have gone right, and Thieran was there before I could even comprehend Nevon's blade had pierced flesh. The look on Thieran's face… I shake my head. I'm likely misremembering the horror, the concern, the anger.

Shoving the jar to the back of the closet, I rearrange my clothes and change my bloody tunic for a fresh one, rolling the sleeve of my injured arm up to my elbow. If the ritual doesn't work, I must have made a mistake. A step or ingredient I missed.

Or it just doesn't work. A bit of old folklore passed down that's more fiction than reality. The idea doesn't have the heaviness I expect it to. Perhaps sex with Thieran really has addled my brain.

Closing the doors to the wardrobe, I make my way to the library. I tucked the book back into its spot to avoid any of the servants happening on it in my room. I'm not sure what I expect to find by looking again at a ritual I copied down and then memorized weeks ago.

Or if I want to find anything at all.

The library is empty, the smell of old parchment and leather wrapping around me as soon as I step through the vaulted doors. My footsteps echo into the ceiling, and torches flicker and pop in the silence.

I hesitate at the base of the shelf where the book belongs. I'll need the wrought iron ladder to reach it because it's tucked between a thick book about wildlife and a tall book about herbs and their properties on the sixth shelf.

Wrapping my fingers around the ladder's railing, I take a deep breath and quickly make the climb before I can talk myself out of it.

The book is right where I left it. I pluck it free and tuck it under my arm, carrying it to a small seating area arranged against a window between two bookcases. I prop my feet up and lay the book against my thighs.

The ritual is close to the end, the pages more worn than the others, as if the previous owner used this one ritual more than the rest. I trace my fingertip over the crescent moon and sprig of lavender burned into the leather cover.

It's a simple thing, opening to the right page. I don't know why I'm hesitating.

A noise from the hall catches my attention, and I look up in time to see the swing of black robes passing by the open door. It's only seconds before Thieran fills the frame, and he's making his way toward me in a blink. I quickly slip the book between the cushions and turn to press my back against it.

He seems angry as he claims the chair across from mine, tension etched between his brows and in the hard set of his mouth. His bright blue eyes are cold and calculating.

Whatever the cause of his mood, I could use a good fight. It might remind me to stop delaying where my escape plans are concerned. And I'll take any motivation I can get at this point. I've become entirely too comfortable here.

"I thought I sent you to your rooms."

I snort, rolling my eyes. "I'm not a child, Thieran."

He pinches the bridge of his nose and sighs before looking at me. "I never said you were."

His tone is full of exasperation, his face expectant. Like I should explain why I'm in the library instead of tucked into bed like an invalid. He'll get no such explanation from me.

I leave him to the silence, head tilted, and a muscle ticks in his jaw while he seemingly recounts what he's just said to me. His mouth opens, and he pauses before huffing out a little breath.

"I see the healer fixed you up," he tries instead.

I follow his gaze to my forearm and the faint pink line drawn down the center of the fabric where the blood has soaked through.

"She did. It feels better now that I'm not writhing in agony."

I don't know why I said it, but Thieran lunges forward, eyes wide, and grips my wrist. Tugging me into his lap, he runs his fingertips up and down the bandage until my arm tingles and warms. The smell of cedar, cinnamon, and woodsmoke surrounds us, and I realize he's using his powers to soothe my wound.

It strikes a chord deep inside me, and my heart flutters in my chest. I can't remember a time since my parents' deaths when someone wanted to take care of me. To make sure I was unhurt, safe, comfortable, wanting nothing in return.

"Thieran."

He doesn't react to the sound of his name, intent on his work. I run my fingertips over his cheek to his jaw and turn his face to mine.

"Thieran. I'm fine. I was only teasing. The cut was shallow. I barely lost any blood. And the healer gave me a salve, so it won't even leave a scar."

Leaning into my hand, he turns his head and presses a kiss to my palm. I'm as surprised by my need to soothe him as I am by his need to be soothed.

I expect him to release me, but when he doesn't, I lean into him instead of extracting myself from his grasp. He settles me back against his chest and buries his nose in the nape of my neck, inhaling deeply.

My gaze tracks to the book hidden in the cushions and the ritual inside that is supposed to be my freedom. Freedom I thought I still wanted. Freedom I should still want.

Missing a step or an ingredient is an easy fix. The most I'd have to wait is a fortnight for another potion to cure.

"How did you know I was injured?"

My heart pounds a furious rhythm in my chest. Because I'm not entirely sure why I asked the question.

"I…" His fingers dance down my arm, and he kisses my shoulder. "I felt it."

I still, fingers tightening on his forearm. A power I didn't know any of the gods possessed, let alone the God of Death.

"You what?"

He clears his throat. "I felt your pain like it was my pain."

"H-how is that possible?" I ask, my voice barely above a whisper.

He pauses, and I hear the click of his throat when he swallows.

"I honestly don't know. There's always been something about you. Since the first moment I saw you kneeling next to the River Axan, hand hovering over the surface."

"Is that how you always know where I am in the Shadow Realm?"

"No. Usually I have to intentionally seek you out."

I want to ask him about the wards, but it seems too dangerous a question. Instead I ask him something I haven't asked in a long time.

"How long are you going to keep me here?"

"Eager to leave?"

His voice is hard but edged with possessiveness, and his arm tightens around my waist when I try to slide off his lap. The truth is, I'm not eager to leave. But that seems a dangerous thing to say too.

"Whether I stay or don't, shouldn't that be my choice?"

His body stiffens beneath me, and he stands up so fast I lose my balance, stumbling forward before he catches me by the elbow and rights me again. A deep crease forms between his brows as he scans my face.

"I have to go," he announces, releasing me and striding to the door.

He takes one last look at me over his shoulder before disappearing, and I stare at the empty space he left behind long after he's gone. I don't really know what to make of the conversation we just had. Or the things he made me feel with his confession.

All of it's a jumble in my head, tangled and looped like knotted string. A few weeks ago, the choice was easy. And now...

The faint scent of Thieran's power still hangs in the air, and I press a hand to my bandage and the lingering warmth from his power. Bending to retrieve the book from its hiding place, I run my fingertips over the cover and down the spine. I only have to flip to the right page and read the passage detailing the ritual again.

If I do that, I'll know for certain whether the ritual didn't work because I missed something or if it would never have worked at all, no matter what I tried.

Instead I carry the book to the shelf where it belongs, climb the ladder, and fit it back into place.

CHAPTER THIRTY-THREE

Thieran

"You're sure this is everything?" I stare at the parchment in my hand, studying Kaia's neat script.

"No." Kaia shrugs when I glance up, brows drawing together. "It's been a very long time since I helped write the ritual, let alone watched it being performed."

She leans over my shoulder and plucks one of the pieces of parchment I've been making notes on off the pile, tilting her head as she studies it.

"Why are you so intent on putting together the pieces of the ritual that formed the Shadow Realm?"

I've still not told Kaia about Elora, and Railan has been sworn to secrecy. Though I imagine he would defy me if he thought he had a reason to. So far he doesn't. But that day may come sooner than I'd like.

The Shadow Realm is weakening at an alarming rate. It's taken everything I have to reinforce the borders between the realm and Acaria. Garrick and his men are on constant patrol around Meren and Síra to make sure souls stay where they should and don't wander.

I won't be able to keep my secret about the condition of the

Shadow Realm from Kaia or the rest of my court for much longer. And once they find out, my brother and his high court will follow.

If Kaia hasn't begun to sense it yet, she likely will soon. And she would say the same thing Railan said when he confronted me after seeing the effects of Elora's blood in the sparring ring. The solution might not be ideal, but it's the right one.

I only wish I could accept that.

"I need a more permanent solution than keeping Elora here indefinitely. I thought performing the ritual again might do it."

At least half of that is true. I hope performing the ritual a second time and rebinding the Shadow Realm will stop whatever is eating away at the power that created it. But I have no intention of letting Elora go.

Even though her question about her right to choose to stay has been sitting heavy at the back of my mind since she asked it. One day I might give her the choice. But not now. Not yet. Not until I know the Shadow Realm will no longer require this of her.

"Are you thinking of letting her go?"

"No. But one day she'll succumb to old age." Another thing I try not to think about. "And then what will happen? Will her soul still affect the realm in the same way?"

Kaia gently sets the piece of parchment back on the table. "I'm not sure. But blood rituals are meant to be permanent. You shouldn't haven't to do the ritual twice."

"So you think it won't work."

Sighing, she grips her hands in front of her and shifts to stare out the window. "I don't know. But it's better to try it than not. We can't let the Shadow Realm fall."

"I'm doing my best," I assure her.

Movement out of the corner of my eye catches my attention, and I glance up to see Elora making her way through the waist-high grass. Her hair is loose today, flying behind her, and her cheeks are pink from the wind.

I don't relish the idea of unleashing the darkness my realm contains on Acaria. I know the destruction and devastation it would cause. But I would for her. I would set fire to Acaria a thousand times over to keep Elora safe. She is more important to me than anything else now.

"Which is why I'm going to Fontoss."

"What? You can't. Winter ball preparations are well underway. It'll be too busy. Someone will recognize you."

I push to my feet and give Elora one last long look before turning to Kaia. Running a hand over my face and through my hair, I grin when she shakes her head.

It's been a long time since I disguised my appearance with a glamour, but the key to successfully getting the information I need will be to move around Fontoss unnoticed. I change my black robes for red, and Kaia snorts.

"Even with someone else's face, I hardly think anyone will believe you to be a priest."

"I'm sure I'll manage."

"Do you even know where the Fontossian temples are?"

"I'm going for the library, not the temples. Don't worry. I won't be gone long."

"Thieran," Kaia says, giving me a pointed look. "Don't do anything stupid."

I raise a brow, shifting to a secluded flower garden outside my brother's palace. The air is warm, too warm, and already I miss the cool breeze from my own realm. My brother's obsession with eternal summer is at least half the reason I love the cold and the dark so much.

Bees buzz around the fat, heavy blooms as I make my way to the stone path and follow its curve around an elaborate fountain and neatly pruned beds bursting with bright colors.

The closer I get to the palace, the busier it becomes. Mortal servants bustle about carrying linens and pushing carts rattling with silver. The queen really is going all out with this year's ball. No doubt she and my brother have something big they're planning to reveal.

Unable to conjure much interest in what that might be, I glide effortlessly through the crowd of servants and curious spectators. Occasionally people pause to bow their heads to me in a sign of respect.

My brother and his wife take the worshipping of themselves very seriously. So much so they grant their priests and priestesses the social rank equivalent to a demigod. Which is why in this disguise, I'll be able to move unrestricted around the capital.

Rounding the side of the palace, I weave through the throng of people entering and leaving the tall gates fashioned from pure gold. The sunlight glinting off them is blinding, and I cannot understand why Elora missed such a garish thing.

Beyond the gates, Fontoss is laid out in a spiral, the winding streets paved with rough cobblestones. Homes closest to the palace are large and ornate, most of them mimicking my brother's flair for white stone and gold accents with pops of bright red.

The further you wander from the ostentatious display of wealth, the smaller the homes become, squeezed together in tight rows. Wander too far and you'll encounter poverty my brother likes to pretend doesn't exist in his city. How could it not when he makes sure far too few have far too much and leaves the rest to fend for themselves?

But my brother and how he treats those who dwell in his territory are not my concern today. I have a singular goal here. To scour the records in the Fontossian library curated and maintained by the Fates and be sure I have everything I need to repeat the ritual that created and bound the Shadow Realm.

I turn left at a large house flying a banner with my brother's lightning symbol on it and shake my head. Zanirah must love glancing out the window from the palace's east wing and being reminded of one of my brother's many bastards. Then again, she's rumored to have more than a few herself. The two of them really were made for each other.

My next turn reveals a sprawling two-story building that dominates the entire street. The triple moon symbol of the Fates flies above the rotunda tipped in gold, and despite the late hour, the marble steps are bustling with people. Some entering or leaving the library, others simply enjoying the last of the sun's rays on the wide, deep steps.

I pace myself up the stairs, barely acknowledging people who call out a greeting or tribute to my brother. The smell of mortals has begun to overwhelm, and I'm eager to get what I came for and leave.

I can't shift in this form without calling unnecessary attention to myself, even though my patience is thinning with all the stairs and the people. Unless they've moved it, the book I need should be in the ancient history room on the second floor in the rare books section.

One of Acaria's oldest history books, penned at the beginning of time by beings far more ancient than I. Beings I helped my brother defeat and exile when we took over Acaria. I wonder if I would make the same choice to help him if he asked me again.

Not likely, knowing what he would become. A monster who hides behind the benevolent mask of a king.

A woman in a red robe with a white stripe down the front, her golden skin enhanced by a halo of dark, tightly coiled curls, lifts her arm in greeting. I nod, hoping to avoid a conversation, but she slows her pace and smiles.

"Brother, it's good to see another servant to their majesties outside of the temple."

"Yes," I say simply, hoping she'll take the hint and move on.

"Most everyone is locked away in preparation for the upcoming holy day. But I think it's good to get out and stretch one's legs and one's mind."

I nod, acutely aware of my brother's penchant for declaring holy days whenever he has a mind to be worshipped by the entire territory. He must have added one for the winter ball to keep the attention on himself. He does so hate to not be the center of everyone's focus.

"I couldn't agree more. If you'll excuse me. I'd like to get a few hours of reading in before the call to dinner."

"You mean devotions."

"Of course. Devotions and then dinner. Thank you for the reminder."

She opens her mouth to reply, but I give her a curt bow and walk away quickly, disappearing around the next corner. This hallway, at least, is empty of people who might stop me and insist on a meaningless conversation.

The ancient history room is likewise empty, and I take the chance to shift to the shelves housing Acaria's rarest history books. They look new despite their age, preserved by power and tethered to the shelves to keep them safe.

As much as I would like to take the one I need back with me to study it as thoroughly as I can, even I could not take it farther than the nearest table. The Fates rule this library with an iron fist.

I move down the rows, scanning each book in turn, frowning when I reach the last of them and still don't see the one I need. I can't imagine why it wouldn't be here. Or who would have the ability to remove it from the library. The Fates' power here is absolute.

It has to be here. I must have missed it. Working my way backward, I trace my fingertip over the spine of every tome lining every shelf in this section until I reach the beginning again.

Pushing down the rising anger, I again check to make sure I'm alone and close my eyes. Pulling the image of the book's brown leather cover, pages filled with ancient, angular script and the occasional drawing or diagram to mind, I attempt to conjure it into my hands. Nothing. Meaning it's likely not anywhere in the library at all.

The fucking book is gone.

I cannot perform the ritual without the proper instructions. And performing it without all the right steps and potions would be at best ineffective and at worst dangerous. The ritual Kaia and I pieced together is only from our memories. It could have holes or wrong steps or wrong ingredients.

I know the ritual was recorded because I watched the court historian add it to the final pages. I watched him sprinkle sand across the ink to dry it. It should be shelved in this section of the library with all the other books on how Acaria was created. And yet...it isn't.

Stalking toward the nearest table, I pick up a chair and hurl it at the wall, satisfied when it splinters apart. Turning from the wreckage, I wave my hand to clear it and shift back to the palace, shedding my glamour and using my power to throw open the doors.

I conjure a dagger in my hand, twisting it through my fingers. A long session in Síra would help work out the frustrations—no, the rage—I feel at having gone all the way to Fontoss only to walk away empty-handed. At knowing I'm no closer to solving this problem I have than I was when I left.

Then the faint scent of honeysuckle reaches my nose, and I suddenly have a much better idea about how to spend my evening. As I close my fist, the dagger disappears, and I eat up the distance between me and the end of the hallway with long strides.

By the time I reach the main corridor, Elora is so close I

nearly run into her. She steps back, looking me up and down, a grin twitching across her lips.

"Did you give up the black for Fontossian red?"

I glance down at the robes I haven't bothered to change, moving toward her until her back hits the wall and the grin falls from her mouth.

"Someone's in a mood," she says, her voice soft and breathy.

I brace my hands on either side of her head, leaning down to trail the tip of my nose across the line of her jaw all the way to her ear, pressing my lips against it and making her shiver.

"You have no idea."

"Is there…"

Her words trail off when I trace the shell of her ear with my tongue, capturing her earlobe between my teeth.

"What was that?"

"Is there anything I can do to help?"

I pull back and look into her eyes, darkened to emeralds. Her cheeks are flushed a soft pink, and I imagine the rest of her is as well. I suddenly have the overwhelming urge to spend the night with her. To have her in my bed naked and begging until we're both satisfied.

The idea consumes me until I can think of nothing else. Until I want to think of nothing else but Elora writhing underneath me, taking my cock and demanding more.

Looping my arm around her waist, I haul her up against my chest and murmur against her lips, "You want to help, little one?"

She nods, her eyes locked on mine, her warm breath fanning my skin.

"Good girl. Let me show you how."

And with that, we disappear.

CHAPTER THIRTY-FOUR

Elora

We arrive in what I assume is Thieran's bedroom, a large four-poster bed looming at his back. It's draped in black silk and piled with a mountain of pillows. It manages to look both inviting and intimidating all at once, and my mouth goes dry.

Thieran's lips are hot on my skin, trailing down my neck and across my shoulder where he's pulled my tunic out of the way. His hands skim up my sides and tug at the laces of my corset, loosening it enough to slide his hands underneath.

A small gasp escapes me when he brushes his thumbs over my nipples, and when I lean into him, I feel his lips curve against my shoulder. But there's something about being here with him. In his personal space. Behind closed doors where we're sure not to be interrupted. Where there's nothing but time to explore each other…

"We don't do beds."

He spins me to face him, urging me to lift my arms over my head so he can pull off my corset, tossing it behind him. My tunic is next, and his eyes are hungry, his touch greedy as he peels it off and cups my breasts, tracing circles around my nipples, already hard and aching for him.

"We haven't done beds. Yet," he corrects.

Dipping his head, he presses a lingering kiss to the top of my breast and then all around my nipple until I'm panting with desperation. He knows what he's doing. I can tell by the teasing curve of his mouth as he continues to kiss me anywhere but where I really want him to, where I need him to.

Threading my hands in his hair, I try to guide him to my nipple. I need him to relieve the ache he's building inside me, but instead he lifts me up and carries me to the edge of the bed. Setting me down gently, he slides off the bright red robe and lets it fall to the floor.

It's an unsightly color, contrasting the shades of black adorning his room. Everything from the candles in shiny silver sconces to the smooth, hand-carved wood of his bed is black. And as night descends in the Shadow Realm, taking all the light with it, I find myself more at home in this room than I would expect to be.

When the last of the light disappears from view, we're left in pitch black. And only then, only when I can't anticipate his movements, does he take my nipple into his mouth, swirling his tongue around it before closing his teeth over it, squeezing until my back arches and my breath catches in my throat.

"Are you going to give me what I want, little one?" he murmurs against my skin.

I open my mouth to respond, barely catching myself before I promise more than I can give. I want to tell him I'll give him anything he wants as long as he keeps touching me.

But I can't tell him that. It's too intimate. My heart is in danger of falling already, and this is hardly helping.

"What do you want?" I ask instead.

"You. I want all of you." He kisses between the valley of my breasts, and my heartbeat quickens. "You belong to me."

The words are so softly spoken I think I must have imagined them. I've never belonged anywhere, to anyone. I didn't think I deserved to. But Thieran makes me believe I could.

I don't know what it means to be his. But I want it more than anything I've ever wanted before. All I have to do is take what he's offering me.

"Yes," I whisper.

As soon as the words leave my lips, he pushes me onto my back, and his fingers make quick work of my breeches, peeling them down my legs and throwing them to the floor in a soft whoosh of fabric.

Then his lips are on my inner thigh, his tongue swirling over my heated skin and raising goosebumps as he inches closer to my pussy. He pushes my legs wider, hooking them over his shoulders before blowing a warm breath against my core.

I jump, and he chuckles low in his throat. His tongue darts out to drag up the length of my slit, and I lift my hips with a groan. The darkness, the removal of one of my senses, only heightens the pleasure of his touch.

But it's more than it was in the forest under the dancing lights. I don't know if it's being in his bedroom surrounded by his scent and his things or the new feelings fluttering behind my ribs, but it's so much more. And I don't want to miss a second of it.

"Thieran," I say, his name fading into a breathy moan when he spreads me open with his fingers and flicks his tongue against my clit. "I want to see you. Let me see you."

I don't even finish my sentence before candles flame around the room, illuminating his beautiful face between my legs. His eyes are dark and hungry, his lips shiny with my arousal.

Holding my gaze, he leans in closer and wraps his lips around my clit, sucking hard as he slides two fingers inside me, tilting them up to tap against that sensitive spot that makes my thighs tremble and my breath ragged.

"Watch me, little one," he says when my eyes slip closed as his teeth tighten on my clit. "Watch me make you come undone for me."

I push onto my elbows at his low command, anticipation and nerves and something unnameable slithering through me when he starts to move his fingers in and out. He watches me as I watch him, eyes never leaving mine as he pumps into me, slowly at first and then faster.

Capturing my lip between my teeth, I can't help but rock my hips against his thrusts, needing more of him inside me. He again flicks his tongue against my clit, his fingers never relenting in their deep, quick pace.

I groan when he scores my clit with his teeth, my hands fisting in the soft silk coverlet beneath me. I'm mesmerized by him. By the candlelight shining in his impossibly blue eyes. By the way he looks at me as if no one else could ever hold his attention the way I do.

It's a heady, terrifying feeling to be the center of his attention. The security and the danger of it are all wrapped up in each other, twining around my heart and taking root. Loving Thieran is dangerous, but I couldn't stop it even if I wanted to.

The Fates were certainly playing a curious game when they sent me stumbling into the Shadow Realm. For the first time in my life, I find myself grateful for their meddling.

When my pussy flutters around Thieran's fingers, he grins, adding a third and pressing them deep while he uses his other hand to stroke my clit in fast, rough circles.

I want this moment with him to last forever, but Thieran is eager to push me over the edge, working his fingers in and out until I can't hold back any longer. My orgasm zips down my spine and pools in my center until my pussy clenches around him, and I cry out with my release.

He pulls his fingers free, leaving me aching and empty. But he's naked and covering my body with his in the center of the bed in a blink. I laugh softly, pressing kisses along the toned plane of his chest and leaning up to nip his chin.

"That's a much better trick when you're taking your clothes off instead of putting them on."

He leans down, capturing my lips as he slides his cock inside me with one languid thrust.

"No. This is better."

"Yes," I agree, wrapping my legs around his waist and pulling him deeper. "Thieran," I groan when he does nothing more than grind his pelvis against my clit and make me shiver.

"Yes, little one?"

"Stop teasing and fuck me."

He pulls his hips back, sliding nearly all the way out, and then slams home again, stealing my breath.

"Is that what you need?"

I nod, unable to speak as he does it again and again, driving his cock into me until I can feel nothing but him as he fills me, the sensation of how deep he's fucking me casting stars across my vision.

Canting his head, he drags his teeth over the underside of my jaw, his hips setting a frantic pace, every part of my body on fire from his touch. An orgasm builds low in my belly, my nails scoring Thieran's back. I arch up to meet his thrusts, teetering on the edge of release until his words push me over.

"Give me what I want. Now, Elora."

My release is all-consuming, blinding, and I squeeze his cock tightly as he shoves deep and empties himself inside me.

Thieran buries his face against the crook of my neck, his breath hot on my skin even as his tongue darts out to taste me, slick with sweat. I comb my fingers through his hair, and he kisses me softly.

Rolling onto his side, he wraps an arm around my waist and pulls my back flush with his chest. He presses his lips to a raised scar on my shoulder, his fingertips gently brushing the underside of my breast.

"Stay with me," he says, and it's the most vulnerable I've ever heard him.

Staying would be vulnerable for me too. Exposing myself to someone else in sleep without a dagger gripped tight in my fist. Allowing Thieran to hold me, his legs tangled with mine, his arm wrapped possessively around my waist. But as much as the wanting of it terrifies me, I don't know if I can give it up.

"All right," I whisper, snuggling closer and tilting my head to kiss the inside of his elbow as he pillows my head with his arm.

And just as I'm slipping into sleep, the cool sheet covering us even as Thieran keeps me warm, I hear him murmur against the back of my neck.

"You are mine to protect. Whatever it takes. Forever."

CHAPTER THIRTY-FIVE

Elora

T he room is dark when I wake, the pillow soft and cool under my cheek. I know without reaching for him that Thieran is not here because each time I woke up last night, he was wrapped around me, his nose buried in my hair and his hand gently cupping my breast.

I've never shared a bed for an entire night with a man before. Or a god. But I liked sleeping in Thieran's arms. I liked being woken up in the early morning hours with his cock too.

My lips curve into a grin, and I find myself disappointed he's up early. I can't imagine he'd object to me sliding down his length and riding him until we're both satisfied.

Pushing myself up against the pillows, I notice my dressing gown and a clean set of clothes folded neatly at the foot of the bed. Slipping out from underneath the covers, I pull on the gown and belt it at the waist. It doesn't smell like Thieran's power, but it seems like something he would do. Or order to be done.

The thought that the servants might know I shared Thieran's bed last night sends a wave of unease through me. But it's not exactly a secret. He's claimed me all over the palace and half the realm. His bed is the most private place we've been since he first fucked me in the forest. And I feel all the different for it.

A basin and pitcher made from black glass sit on a stand beside the window, and I cross to it, tugging the curtains back and allowing the Shadow Realm's misty light to filter in. The water is warm when I pour it into the basin, which is definitely Thieran's doing.

I dip a fresh cloth in and run it over my arms and face. I could do with a proper bath after last night, but I settle for running the cloth between my thighs and down my legs. I'll ask the servants to prepare one for me later. Or see if I can talk Thieran into a trip to the hot springs.

The idea of him running soapy hands over my breasts and against my pussy has me shivering, and I move the springs to the top of my list. Plenty of time for everything else later.

The thought is equal parts comforting and unnerving, and I drop the cloth beside the basin, staring out the window at the ragged line of black trees. Thieran claimed me last night, and I gave myself over to him. Even if I didn't say it out loud.

He hasn't given me the choice of staying of my own free will. Not technically. I still felt the buzz of the wards when I took Meera out for a ride yesterday.

But I've made it all the same. I shift on my feet, catching my faint reflection in the glass, and wrap my arms around myself. The moment I slipped the book back onto the shelf after the shielding ritual didn't work, I chose to stay.

The realization is heavy in the light of day, especially after last night. I haven't spent so much time in one place in years, and the thought of doing it now, of doing it with Thieran, constricts my throat and makes my pulse pound. Running would be easier; staying detached would be easier too.

But if I left now, I'd be leaving a little piece of myself behind. And I'm tired of scattering myself across my past because I'm too intent on escaping it.

The rattle of porcelain against silver draws my attention to the bed where a breakfast tray has appeared. The smell of fresh bread and bacon makes my mouth water, but I need to see Thieran.

To assure myself that every word he whispered against my skin the night before was the truth. I need to tell him that as much as he never wants to let me go, I never want to leave.

Quickly shedding my dressing gown and tugging on my clothes, I snag a piece of bacon off the tray and pop it into my mouth. Doubling back from the door, I grab a piece of toast too. No sense in having this conversation on a completely empty stomach. It'll hardly help with my nerves.

Thieran's sitting room is decorated much the same as his bedroom in blacks and purples so deep it's hard to tell the difference between them. An ornate black and silver chandelier hangs over the seating area in front of the fireplace, and more silver candelabras grace the tables.

But it's empty, and I step out into the hall in search of him. I know he has a study somewhere, but the palace is vast, and even though I've been here for months, I know I've yet to explore every room it has.

Stopping at the top of the grand staircase, I have the option of following it down to the main floor, where the dining room and closest stairs to my rooms are. Or I could take it up where I've been told are mostly rooms for Thieran's dark court gods to use when they're in residence.

Gripping the banister, I decide to go up, pausing with my foot on the first step when I hear raised voices echoing down the hall. I glance to my right. If I remember Kaia's extensive tour from my first weeks here correctly, the other side of this hallway is mostly parlors and entertaining rooms.

I suppose Thieran's study could be in this quieter section of the palace. Not too far from his rooms, but still with plenty of privacy. Abandoning the stairs, I make my way down the hall, stopping short outside of what must be Thieran's study when I hear my name.

"You can't keep putting it off like this. It's not going to get any better just because you're fucking her."

"Watch yourself, Railan," Thieran warns. "My patience has limits."

"You're only making it worse by delaying. If your trip to Fontoss was successful—"

"It wasn't."

Thieran sighs, and I imagine him standing and crossing the room to stare out the window when a chair creaks. He seems to think best staring out the window at the realm. At his realm.

But I don't understand what they're talking about. What has Thieran been putting off? And was a trip to the capital the reason he was wearing the red robes of a royal priest yesterday? And what does any of that have to do with me?

A heavy weight settles into my stomach. I should go. But I'm frozen in place. I want to know what secrets Thieran has been keeping from me. I have to know.

"You said it was the only way." Railan's voice is gentle but firm.

"Sacrificing Elora isn't the only way. It's just the best one."

The rest of Thieran's words are lost to the rush of blood pounding in my ears. I stumble back from the door, slapping a hand over my mouth to keep from screaming in rage.

I'm such an idiot.

I should have known this was all a lie. Every word he's ever spoken to me. Everything he's ever done. None of it was true. From the moment I found my way into the Shadow Realm, I have been nothing but a pawn in Thieran's game.

Willing my heartbeat to slow so Thieran doesn't sense my distress, I turn and head back for the main staircase, taking them down two at a time. I should have known better than to lose my heart to someone again—especially to the God of Death.

I have no one but myself to blame for this seething, penetrating, all-consuming feeling of betrayal winding itself around my heart and squeezing until I can hardly breathe from it.

Letting my guard down, letting myself be vulnerable with someone like Thieran, was a mistake. Mortals and gods alike only know how to use someone up for their own gain and spit them back out again.

My uncle did. When he beat me bloody for the smallest offense, no matter how many times I begged him to stop. Then again when he sold me to a workhouse so he could wash his hands of me. And five years later, when the owner of the workhouse sent me to a brothel in exchange for a forgiven debt.

It wasn't until I escaped from the brothel that I felt I was finally free of men who would treat me carelessly. Until I met a boy who reminded me that people cannot be trusted. That I can never trust anyone but myself.

A fire smolders in the hearth of my sitting room. No. Nothing in this place is mine except my dagger. I need only it and the herbs to get past the wards.

Crossing to the bedroom, I yank open the wardrobe doors and feel around on the floor for the small bag with the supplies. My fingertips brush the jar containing the failed shielding ritual, and I recoil.

I should never have lost my focus. Something else I can add to the long list of mistakes I've made in my life.

Plunging my hand back into the wardrobe, I close my fingers around the bag and pull it free, slipping the strings over my wrist and wrapping them once to secure it. My dagger sits on the bedside table, and I quickly fasten it to my thigh.

The cloak I usually wear is draped over a chair in the corner. It'll be cold without it, but I want nothing to remind me of this place when I'm gone. Tears prick my eyes and I blink them away, drawing in a ragged breath. I will not cry over this, over him.

And I don't have time for tears anyway. I need to get to Meera and through the wards while Thieran is occupied with Railan. If he's busy planning my demise, he won't think to look for me. And I might not have much time.

I take the same side stairs I used during my first escape attempt. In the dark, with Thieran toying with me at every step. Only this time, I mean to make a clean break. I don't know if Thieran will be able to track me beyond the Shadow Realm, if this entire thing is a fruitless endeavor. But I do know I'll hate myself if I don't try.

I set off toward Videva at a fast pace, caught somewhere between getting away from here as quickly as possible and doing my best to remain calm so Thieran doesn't come in search of me.

I quicken my steps when I see the first puff of smoke from the little farmhouse's chimney but stop short when Kaia crests the small rise on her way back from Videva. For a god, she certainly chooses to walk everywhere far more than I would if I could shift from place to place.

She waves, a smile breaking out across her face, and I barely manage to force mine to match. Does Kaia know of Thieran's plan? Has she been pretending to be my friend this entire time? Another layer to Thieran's lie meant to keep me distracted.

Whatever the answer, I can't let her know I'm upset. If I do, she may not let me go.

"Did you run all the way here?" she asks, stopping in front of me.

"What?"

"Your cheeks. They're flushed."

"Oh." I reach up to rub my fingers across them. "No. I'm fine. I just got a little overheated reading by the fire. Thought I'd take Meera out for a ride."

"I'm sure she'll be happy to see you." Kaia tilts her head and studies me for a moment. "Are you all right?"

It takes everything I have to retain my composure and offer her a small smile.

"Of course. Just feeling a little restless today."

She nods slowly, as if she doesn't quite believe me but is too polite to say.

"Well, I should get going."

I move to step around her and pause. I should just go. But I can't stop myself from asking the question.

"We're friends, right?"

A small crease forms between her eyebrows. "Of course we are. Why do you ask?"

"I've never really had friends before." I fix her with a pointed stare. "People are all too often eager to betray you."

She crosses her arms over her middle, gripping her elbows, and nods. I get the sense my words struck closer to home than I want them to, but I'm not entirely sure she's talking about me when she replies.

"Yes. They can be. Which is why true friends are hard to come by. And I have always tried to be a true friend to you."

I swallow hard. I don't want to believe her. But her words ring true to me. Whatever Thieran has been plotting, I don't think Kaia knows about it. And that, at least, eases some small part of the hurt inside me.

"Go," she says, pulling me from my thoughts. "Enjoy your ride. I'm here to talk later if you need to."

I smile again, but I can tell by the look on her face it's not as bright and eager as I tried to make it. Before she can ask me anything more, I skirt around her and head for the barn behind the farmhouse.

Meera nickers in greeting, but even she can sense my mood, her ears flattening as I cover her back with a soft blanket and fit her saddle. She dances and snorts when I seat myself, resisting me when I guide her out to the stretch of field behind the barn.

"Enough," I snap, kicking her into a fast trot. "We're leaving."

She snorts again but obeys my command until we're galloping toward the cropping of trees hiding part of Thieran's wards from view of the palace. I force myself not to look back at the stretch of black and glass towering over the landscape as Meera eats up the ground beneath us.

It would do me no good anyway. I'm resolved to leave now, and I can't afford any more distractions. Especially not the tug of my traitorous heart.

CHAPTER THIRTY-SIX

Thieran

Now that our shouting match has devolved into stony silence, Railan sits across from me, hands clenched into fists on his thighs, eyes hard. I know what he wants from me. And I know I can't give it to him.

But he isn't wrong when he says the situation is dire. I feel the Shadow Realm weakening more by the day. Kaia asked me about it at dinner last night. I deflected, but I know she'll figure it out soon enough if she hasn't already. And then I'll have both of them whispering in my ear about using the only solution I've managed to find. The only one I cannot go through with.

Sacrificing Elora hasn't been an option for weeks, and it's even less of one after last night. I intend to keep the promise I made to her in the dark. To protect her—for as long as there is breath in my lungs. Because if I have to choose between my existence and Elora's, I will choose hers every time.

Which is why I slipped out of bed early this morning, intent on doing more research into finding this missing book. The ritual it contains is my only hope, my best lead, and I will search for it until I find it or the Shadow Realm fractures into nothingness. Whichever comes first.

Something Railan didn't like when I informed him of my intentions. He doesn't have to like it. He only needs to obey. No one knows better than I do what's at stake if the Shadow Realm were to fall. I'm going to do my best to make sure that doesn't happen. But not at Elora's expense.

I'm feeding the realm my blood multiple times a day, allowing me to maintain control of it all for now. Garrick's reports grow more fraught, focused especially on the eastern border.

Whatever is infecting the realm is doing so from that distant point. But I don't have the time to devote to figuring out what might be causing this, only to how to stop it.

"You're not thinking clearly," Railan says, and I can tell he's forcing his tone to remain even.

"My thinking is fine. Your problem is I'm not doing what you want me to."

"You're not doing what you know you should. The realm will not last much longer. You and I both know it. And what happens when you can't hold it?"

"I know very well what will happen. I was here long before it existed."

Railan bristles. Apparently he doesn't like to be reminded that he knows barely a fraction of what life was like before the Shadow Realm. But I don't have time to coddle his feelings. What he knows of Acaria when death roamed the land is nothing compared to my knowledge.

Acaria will survive. My brother will make sure of it. He'd never let a little thing like death best him. He was perfectly content to let it wreak havoc before. And in this case, with Elora's life at stake, I'm content with the outcome as well.

As long as she is safe and far away from here, Acaria can burn for all I care.

"So you're just going to waste time while the realm falls? I thought it was your top priority."

My reply is silenced by a knock on the door, and I am grateful for the interruption. I've been awake far too long this morning, and my patience where Railan is concerned is waning.

"Come."

Kaia pokes her head around the door, eyebrows winging up when she sees Railan seated in one of the chairs flanking my desk. Then they drop into a frown at the look on his face.

"What's going on here?" she asks, taking the empty chair and smoothing her skirts.

"Nothing."

"It's not nothing."

I wave a dismissive hand at Railan, but I can tell by the look on Kaia's face I'm not going to get out of this one so easily. Railan merely lifts a shoulder in a casual shrug when I glare at him.

"Why is everyone acting so odd today? First Elora, now you. What happened, Thieran?"

"What's wrong with Elora?"

"Later. Don't change the subject. Tell me what's going on."

She glances at Railan, who gestures at me with a broad sweep of his arm.

"The Shadow Realm is weakening again."

"I know that."

"You do?"

She huffs out a breath. "I can feel it as you can. And then you went to Fontoss yesterday looking for the ritual. I assumed it was more serious than even I understood."

Kaia looks between us, her frown deepening.

"There's more you're not saying. What happened in Fontoss?"

I shove out of my chair and cross to the window, clasping my hands behind my back. There's no avoiding it now.

"Nothing. The book with the ritual was missing."

"Missing? How can it be missing? You can't take rare books from the capital library."

"Well," I say, clenching and unclenching my jaw, "someone did."

"All right." I hear the rustle of fabric as Kaia shifts in her chair. "That's not the end of the world. We just need to consider some other options. Surely there's a solution here."

"Tell her all of it," Railan says, his tone flat.

"All of what?"

I open my mouth to reply, but I can't bring myself to say it. Not again. I don't like even thinking the words, let alone giving voice to them.

"The realm is weakening again because Elora's simple presence is no longer enough," Railan supplies.

"Which is why you needed the ritual from Fontoss."

I turn from the window, my entire body tensing as Railan delivers the next blow.

"What he needs is Elora's blood."

"Her blood."

Kaia stares at Railan, turning the words over in her mind. Then her body jerks as understanding sinks in, and she pivots her gaze to mine.

"A sacrifice. You mean to kill her?"

"I don't mean to do anything to her," I snarl, stalking back toward my desk and dropping into the chair. "I intend to find that fucking book and perform the ritual again, no matter who I have to threaten or maim or kill to get it."

"And what if the realm doesn't have that kind of time?" Railan wonders.

"That's a problem for tomorrow."

Railan pounds his fist on the edge of the desk, making Kaia jump. "You're putting everything at risk. Everyone from the lowliest of mortals to the gods. Acaria has lived free from the shadow of death for centuries. They are not equipped to deal with it again."

"I'm not going to let it get that far. I'll find the book, perform the ritual, and it will be done."

"And if you can't find the book?"

Kaia's question is soft, but it carries no less impact. I feel the weight of it settle around my shoulders until they droop with it.

"I will. End of discussion."

"But if you can't," she says again. "Will you give her up? Or will you let the Shadow Realm fall?"

She won't like the truth—neither of them will—so I dance around it instead.

"I'll cross that bridge when I get to it. Right now, my time is better spent finding the book so I can recreate the ritual. If someone were going to remove it from the library, they'd have to do it with the permission of the Fates, wouldn't they? I can start there."

I don't relish the idea of going to the Fates. What they don't already know, they're nosy about, and I hardly want the other gods to know there might be something wrong with my realm. At best, I'll look weak. At worst, someone may try to take advantage of that weakness. Neither of which would have a good outcome.

"I'm not sure that's the best idea," Kaia says gently.

"Do I have any other options?"

"Yes," Railan snaps, shoving out of his chair and storming to stand in front of the fireplace. "I like her. You know I do. But this is bigger than her. It's bigger than all of us. And sometimes we have to make sacrifices."

"I've sacrificed plenty to hold this realm, to rule it well. And I will not be lectured on the merits of sacrifice by someone who has never known it."

He snorts, eyes trained on the flames. "There is only one way this will end. The question is, how bad will you let it get before you do something about it?"

Before I can hurl back a retort, he crosses to the door and slams it behind him. Kaia stares after him for a long moment, the silence hanging heavily between us. When she finally drags her gaze to mine, her eyes are sad.

"Don't say it," I warn her. "I can't take it from both of you."

"You should have told me."

I tap my fingers on the edge of my desk. Maybe I should have, but it isn't as if it would have made this situation any easier. The only thing it would have done is bring us to this inevitable conversation much sooner. And what good would that have done?

Rubbing my temple in rough circles, I pivot to stare out the window as lightning lances down from the sky and strikes a tall tree, instantly setting the dry wood to flame.

It was, all of it, easier to manage before Elora arrived. Before she filled up an empty place inside me I hadn't known existed. I have waited centuries for someone like her. And now the Fates have decided I should give her up? I won't do it. I cannot.

"I should have told you," I agree. "But what good would it have done?"

She doesn't answer. She knows as well as I do there was never a good outcome here.

"Does Elora know of this?"

"No, of course not. I can't imagine she would take knowing such a thing very well."

Sucking her bottom lip between her teeth, Kaia nods thoughtfully.

"What is it?"

She sucks in a breath, then releases it. "Something she said to me earlier. I thought it odd then. And now..." She spreads her hands out in front of her. "Even odder."

I sit forward in my chair, elbows braced on the edge of the desk, body tense. "Why? What did she say?"

"She asked if we were friends. When I asked why she would ever doubt such a thing to be true, she said something about betrayal. *People are all too often eager to betray you.*"

No. I shove up from my desk, rocking a little on my feet as my heart plummets into my stomach. She can't know. How would she have found out?

I shift to my rooms but find them empty. I left her sleeping there this morning, curled up against the pillows, her dark hair fanned out behind her, pale skin stark against the black silk sheets. I liked the look of her in my bed so much I almost woke her up with my cock again, but I left her in favor of doing more research on finding the missing book.

But the dressing gown is discarded at the foot of the bed, the clothes I conjured for her gone. She simply dressed and went to read in her rooms or for a ride. That's all.

I shift to her room and find the wardrobe door hanging open, her clothes shoved to one side. At the bottom of the wardrobe is a large jar filled with herbs and a bright green liquid. Some kind of potion. For what?

The barn, then. I'm sure of it. But when I arrive, I find Meera gone. Panic clawing at my throat, I do what I should have done from the first moment and scan the palace and inside the wards, looking for her. But there's nothing.

Nothing except a break in my wards just beyond the pasture where she likes to ride. Shifting there, I instantly see why I haven't been able to locate her inside the usual boundaries. She's breached the wards with simple magick.

And if I don't find her, I might lose her forever.

CHAPTER THIRTY-SEVEN

Elora

I t took more than a little convincing to get Meera through the hole I created in the wards. But once I did, and once she stopped shying away from me and let me mount her, we were able to cover ground much faster than I did during my first escape attempt.

I don't know this path as well, but at least I'm not navigating it in the dark or on foot. Once we reach the veil, I hope it's as easy as stepping through it to the other side. If it isn't, I'll have to think of something else. But it can't be that complicated.

I wandered in without doing anything special. And if Thieran wasn't worried about me being able to cross the veil into Acaria should I ever reach it, he wouldn't have put up wards keeping me close to the palace in the first place. I should be able to get back out again.

I sit up straighter when I hear rushing water, and Meera slows to a walk. I didn't expect to reach the River Axan so quickly. Unless the map in my head is too fuzzy to be accurate and we've been going in the wrong direction.

How many rivers are in the Shadow Realm? Three, if the stories are true. I came in by the River Axan, said to contain all the sorrow of the realm. Any souls who touch its surface become trapped inside with their heartache and misery. I shake my head at the vague memory of kneeling over the black water, a hand pressing to the surface from the other side as if trapped beneath.

Urging Meera through the brush, we clear it to find a river bubbling softly over brown rocks and lapping at the shallow banks. Its waters are a pale golden yellow that reminds me of the sun, and since the River Loret is rumored to be green, I know this must be the River Grense.

I pause for a fraction of a heartbeat. I would give anything to forget. To have my mind wiped clear of my time in the Shadow Realm. I don't want to remember the God of Death and his impossibly blue eyes, the deep tone of his voice, the feel of his hands on my body.

I want to rid myself of this soul-deep ache over his betrayal. It would be easy. I could slide off Meera's back and drop to my knees, cup the water in my hands, and bring it to my lips. It would be cool and crisp, sliding down my throat as everything fades, my mind clears, and my body goes numb.

I would rather forget, but not at the expense of being stuck here and again at Thieran's mercy. I'd rather be alive and in pain than numb and the God of Death's unwitting sacrifice. I need to be free. Then I'll figure out how to put all of this behind me.

Turning Meera from the river's edge, we pick our way over rocky ground. I'm impatient with the slow pace. Any minute now, Thieran could realize I'm not where he wants me to be, that the caged bird has flown free. And when he does, he'll come after me. I need to be as far into Acaria as possible before that happens.

I don't know where I'll go or if it's even possible to outrun him. But even if he does haul me back here and kill me, at least I will know I did everything in my power to escape him first.

The rocky ground smoothes into tall grass, and again I take

Meera into a gallop. We can't waste any more time. I have to focus if I'm going to get us both out of here alive.

The breeze whips my hair around my face, and I clench my teeth to keep them from chattering in the cold. I should have taken the damn cloak. But it's too late to turn back now. Once I get to Acaria, I'll trade labor for a warm place to stay and some food.

I've been on the run before without coin or shelter and starting out with far less than I have right now. A sure horse under me, a means to protect myself, and instincts honed to razor sharpness. If only I hadn't ignored them when it came to Thieran. I'd be in a much different place right now.

But I can berate myself for being so stupid later. Right now I need to concentrate on where we're going so we don't end up wandering the Shadow Realm until we're caught.

I see the forest up ahead and crouch low over Meera's neck, pushing her faster. We're so close. The forest hides the veil. I don't know what it looks like, if it looks like anything at all. But as long as we keep going, we should run into it. And if we can't get through it, then I'll figure that out when we get there.

The further we get into the forest, though, the more wrong it feels. I wouldn't say the Shadow Realm is known for its beauty, though Irios is lovely and serene and Videva is fun and lively. But there's something about the earth here, the trees. Something isn't right about them.

Black dust swirls up from the ground with each pounding step Meera takes. The trees spearing out of the soil are dry and cracked and splintered. Like a barren field in desperate need of rain. The land looks as if it is decaying.

Roots poke above the ground, gnarled and twisted, but with one touch of Meera's hoof, they crumble into dust and are carried away by the wind. The Shadow Realm is...disintegrating.

Can the Shadow Realm fall? And if it does, what happens to

all who rest here? To Dania and Jerund and sweet Corinne? Will they cease to exist? Will Thieran?

My heart squeezes at that thought, but I shove it down. Whatever is infecting the Shadow Realm is none of my concern. And it's likely the very reason Thieran is so intent on sacrificing me in the first place. But he can't have me. My blood or my flesh or whatever he needs to restore the realm. He can find another victim.

Something shimmers in the distance, beyond the dense line of trees. I push Meera harder, trailing my fingertips over the side of her neck and giving her a reassuring pat. We're so close, the hair rising on the backs of my arms and neck. The veil must be just up ahead.

Breaking through the thickest part of the tree line, Meera stops short, and I nearly lose my seat, gripping her mane to stay in the saddle. The veil is a writhing, glistening thing, and something about it feels wrong, though I don't know what.

I've never seen the veil before. I have no real memory of how I crossed it the first time, let alone what it looked like. And I've never asked Thieran or anyone else in the Shadow Realm about it so as not to raise suspicions.

But the way it dances like a living, breathing beast doesn't seem right. None of Thieran's other wards look like this. And what is the veil but the strongest ward between Acaria and Thieran's realm?

I give Meera a gentle nudge forward, but she doesn't move, her ears flat against her head.

"Come on," I say, trying again to get her to step through the undulating air with a squeeze of my knees. "The only way out is forward."

She snorts in disagreement and takes two steps back. I don't have time for this. I've been gone long enough that if Thieran isn't looking for me now, he will be soon. And I don't want to be in the Shadow Realm when he comes searching.

Sliding off Meera's back, I loop the reins over her head and give them a gentle tug. She still refuses to move, staring over my shoulder at the veil.

I understand her hesitation. I feel the veil at my back as if it were a tangible thing. But it isn't. It's nothing but air and power, and we should be able to step through it without getting hurt. I hope.

"Meera. We're running out of time."

She takes another step back, dragging me with her, and I huff out an irritated breath. If I'd brought the damn cloak, I could toss it over her head, take her mind off the scary thing keeping her from doing the one thing I need her to do.

Keeping the reins wrapped around one hand so she doesn't bolt, I step closer to the veil and stretch my arm out toward it. Maybe if I can show her the veil won't hurt me, she'll be less apprehensive about going through it.

But my fingertips hover a hair's breadth from the swirling air that creates no breeze, and I can't bring myself to touch it. I'm stuck between my desire to go and my fear that I might not survive the crossing a second time.

Except staying isn't an option. Steeling myself, I force my hand forward and watch as it's swallowed up by the writhing mass until it disappears. Nothing happens. The life doesn't drain from my body. I'm not jolted by power. I'm not shoved back into the realm.

When I pull my hand back through, cradling it against my chest, my fingers are cold, and I watch a single snowflake slowly melt on my skin. It must be snowing in Acaria.

"Meera," I plead. "We have to try. I cannot stay and let Thieran kill me."

"I would never do that."

Thieran's voice is low and soft behind me, and the ache in the center of my chest swells. I'm too late. And when his attempts to get me to go with him willingly fail, he'll surely take me by force.

I turn slowly to face him, keeping Meera between us and taking a step back until I feel the power singing through the veil brush against my back. His robes are hanging open, his hair disheveled, and there's worry etched into the lines of his face.

Of course there is. He almost lost his prize.

"Forgive me if I don't believe you," I say. "Not after I heard you telling Railan you mean to sacrifice me."

His brows knit together and his hands ball into fists. "You weren't supposed to hear that."

I scoff, and pain twists in my stomach. "Clearly. Is that how I ended up here? You needed a mortal to sacrifice, so you sent an unnatural beast to chase one to the right side of the veil?"

"No." He takes a step forward, pausing when I shift away from him. "Of course not. Elora, I—"

"Don't lie to me," I tell him, hoping he doesn't hear the catch in my voice. Swallowing around the tightness in my throat, I meet his pleading gaze with my defiant one. "The least you can do is tell me why. I deserve that much."

"No, Elora," he says, and my heart sinks.

He's more of a monster than I thought he was. How did I not see it before? I should have known not to expect any kindness or compassion or mercy from the God of Death.

Thieran takes a deep breath, blowing it out slowly. "You deserve so much more."

His words catch me off guard, but I clench my hands into fists, digging my fingernails into my palms. I will not allow Thieran to charm me to my death.

I want to toss insults at him. To hurt him the way he has hurt me. But of all the things I should say to him, my mind snags on only one thought. And it crosses my lips before I can stop it.

"If you wanted to kill me, you didn't have to make me fall in love with you first."

CHAPTER THIRTY-EIGHT

Thieran

Her words knife into me, spreading warmth and pain in equal measure. She doesn't realize what she's said, the gravity of it. But I do. And it strengthens my resolve to fix this, to save her. To keep her by my side.

"I have never wanted to kill you."

She crosses her arms over her chest, and every emotion drains from her face. She's cutting herself off from me, and I hate it more than I hate her anger and the sadness that lies just beneath it.

"I deserve the truth, Thieran. All of it."

I hardly know where to begin, and I don't understand half of it myself. I don't know what is happening to my realm or why she is seemingly the only one who might be able to fix it. But she's right. She deserves to know whatever bits of information I can give her. I owe her that much.

Lifting my arms, I gesture all around us at the diseased trees and earth gone to dust.

"The Shadow Realm is dying."

Nearly the whole of the border looks like this, the veil thin and throbbing. When I bleed myself, it's fine for mere hours before it fades to this again. As much as I hate to admit it, Railan's right. The realm likely doesn't have much time left. And still that is not enough motivation to use Elora as the solution to my problem.

"What's wrong with it?"

"I don't know," I admit. "I've been more concerned with stopping it than finding out why it's happening."

"And stopping it means killing me."

"No." I take a deep breath when her eyes narrow. I've committed to telling her the truth. I might as well give her all of it. "It needs your blood."

"Why?"

"I don't know that either."

"Then how do you know this will even work?" She thumps her fist against her chest. "You're just going to plunge a knife into my heart and hope for the best?"

The visual makes me uneasy. The thought of spilling her blood sparks rage deep in my bones.

"I would rather watch the Shadow Realm splinter into a thousand pieces than spill a single drop of your blood to hold it together."

Her eyes widen, her mouth dropping open at my words. But they aren't a lie. It's the truest thing I could say to her.

"Then why, Thieran?"

Her voice is soft, measured, but I hear the pain in it, and I want nothing more than to erase that for her. I want nothing more than to shift time back to yesterday so she never had to know about any of this. So I could fix it before she found out.

She swallows hard, her throat contracting, and I sigh, raking a hand through my hair.

"I don't know why the realm is asking this of you. But the day you came here, you were wounded."

She nods. "I know that."

"You fed the Shadow Realm your blood, and for weeks, it was stronger than it's been in decades."

Her fingertips dance over her side, where the faint scar from the beast's wound stretches across her abdomen.

"I didn't understand it at first," I continue. "I thought your mere presence was keeping everything together."

"So you put up the wards to keep me here."

I nod, jaw clenching when she hugs herself tightly. She's waiting for me to continue, so I oblige her.

"But the realm began to weaken again. As it had before. So I went out to the spot where I found you. Trying to make sense of it, of you and your arrival here."

"And what did you find?" she asks when I don't continue.

"You brought life to the Shadow Realm. Wherever your blood touched the ground, vines sprouted and grew. I traced them back to the veil where you must have crossed over from Acaria."

She shakes her head, unconvinced. "There is life in the Shadow Realm already. The people of Videva grow plants, tend animals."

"That is sustained by my power. This was something else entirely. This pulsed with something outside of me all on its own."

"It's not possible." Her eyes meet mine, full of questions and uncertainty. "How is it possible?"

I take another step closer, grateful when she doesn't retreat from me further. Meera's ears flatten when I advance again, and I stop. I won't hurt the horse just to get to Elora, but I don't like how closely she's standing to the veil. She could easily slip through to the other side. And then I would be forced to follow her.

"I don't know. But Railan saw it. When you were injured in the sparring ring. A drop of blood bloomed on the ground, and vines took root."

She shakes her head in disbelief, her fingers reaching for the hilt of the dagger strapped to her thigh. Unsheathing it, she holds the tip against her forefinger, pausing for a heartbeat before pressing it in and breaking the skin.

Squeezing her finger until a drop of blood wells, she turns it upside down and watches it fall to the ground. Almost instantly, the black dust of the forest floor where it makes contact turns into spongy earth, and a single, thin vine sprouts, curling at the tip.

Her head jerks up to look at me, eyes wide and breath sawing in and out of her lungs.

"I don't understand."

"Neither do I. But I am not asking this of you. I will not sacrifice you to the realm. I would sooner sacrifice myself."

"What happens if it falls?" she asks, gaze dropping to the tiny vine.

She squeezes another drop of blood next to the second, watching in awe as the process repeats. The vines curl toward each other as if seeking comfort, their stems twining.

When I don't answer, she looks up at me and draws a deep breath. "Thieran. What happens if the Shadow Realm falls?"

"It doesn't matter. I'm not going to let it fall."

As Railan's was, Elora's face is full of disbelief.

"It doesn't matter. Because you will be somewhere safe, somewhere far away from here, if it does."

"What happens?" she whispers.

"If it falls, all the souls on this side of the veil will be free to roam through Acaria."

"Even the ones in Síra and Meren?"

I nod, and the grim reality dawns on her. Acaria would most likely not survive the onslaught of unredeemable souls caged up for centuries wreaking havoc on the land and its people. The gods might be able to battle them back, but without a Shadow

Realm to battle them back to, what could they really do besides protect themselves?

And that's to say nothing of the ancient beings hidden away in the bowels of the realm, locked in their caves, their powers bound and chained. Those beings are eager for vengeance on the very gods who put them there.

The problem is, I no longer care about any of it as long as I can keep Elora safe. If the book is lost to me, if there's no way to fix the realm, I need to get her far enough away from here that no harm will come to her. And I think I can. If only she would let me get close enough to do it.

"Let me ensure your safety." I take one step closer and another, emboldened by the fact that she is no longer shrinking away from me. "I can get you far away from Acaria. You'll live a happy life without me."

"My life would never be happy without you."

Closing the distance between us with long strides, I wrap her in my arms and claim her mouth. Her hands fist in the fabric of my tunic at the small of my back, and her tongue darts out to drag along my lower lip before she bites it hard, tugging it away from my teeth and letting it slip through.

"I hate you," she says, voice low, breaths ragged. "I hate you for making me feel things I thought I was content to never feel again. I hate you for making me want."

She draws in a shaky breath. "I love you. And I hate that too."

Cupping her face in my hands, I run my thumb over her lips. "Why?"

"Because love has never been kind to me." I press my forehead to hers, and she squeezes me tight. "Come with me," she says.

"I can't." She tries to pull back, but I tighten my arms around her. "I have to stay and try to hold the realm."

"But what if you can't? Will you come to me?"

"No."

She wriggles out of my grasp and looks up at me, eyes searching mine. "What happens to you if the realm falls?"

"It doesn't matter, as long as you're safe."

"It matters to me."

I reach for her, but she shakes her head, and I drop my arm to my side, staring over her shoulder at the veil. It's a stark reminder that I've failed not only Elora in this, but my duty to the Shadow Realm as well.

"Years ago, at the first sign of weakness, I bound my power to the realm. I thought the blood ritual we used to create it was weakening, so I used my power to fortify it."

"What does that mean?" Her voice is thin, as if she already knows the answer to her question.

"It means I am as much a part of the Shadow Realm as it is a part of me. If it falls, I fall with it."

Elora leaps forward, grabbing the edges of my robes and tugging until our bodies are pressed together. I feel the impossibly fast beat of her heart against mine.

"You're a god. Gods can't die."

"I wouldn't die." I cover her hands with mine and give them a gentle squeeze. "I would cease to exist."

"You have to unbind them, then. Release yourself from the Shadow Realm."

"I can't."

Tears well in her eyes until one slips down her cheek, carving a path through the fine dust coating her skin from her ride across the realm. She squeezes them shut, and I catch the next tear with the pad of my thumb.

"I'm sorry, Thieran."

I don't understand her apology; I'm the one who should be apologizing, but she shoves onto her toes and fuses her mouth to mine before I can speak. I drink from her in greedy gulps, eager to get as much of her as I can before I send her away to keep her safe.

When I nip her bottom lip in a rough bite, she pulls away from me with a gasp. Then she shoves at my chest with enough force that I stumble back a few steps. Her eyes meet mine and the smile she gives me is sad, and I'm so mesmerized by her gaze that I don't realize what she's doing until it's too late.

Within the span of a breath, she draws the blade of her dagger across her hand, vines instantly springing up around her feet where the blood drips and revives the earth.

"No!"

I leap toward her, but I'm too late. She presses her bloody palm to the veil, and I'm swept back by the force of the gale that whips around her body. Rearing onto her hind legs, Meera paws at the air and then bolts.

I stumble forward, bracing myself against the worst of it, but just as I get close enough to touch her, I'm forced back. I try again and again, but the result is the same.

Elora screams, and the agony of it rips through me. I shove my power against the wind keeping us apart. If I can stop her in time, it might not take her. I have to stop her.

Smoke swirls around my legs, winding up to my waist and over my arms, but it's useless. Nothing can penetrate whatever force is holding her to the veil while it drains her.

Her face has gone pale, and she wobbles before falling to her knees. I rush forward, but I'm still unable to get close enough to grasp her and tug her free.

"Why?" I demand over the roar of the wind.

She reaches out to me, and I press my fingertips to hers. "Because Acaria needs you more than it needs me. And I've lost enough already."

Her eyelids flutter, and when the wind shears to dead silence, I catch her before her body hits the ground. Cradling her in my arms, I shift us back to the palace, frantically searching for a heartbeat.

CHAPTER THIRTY-NINE

Thieran

I sit in a chair in the corner of Elora's room, watching the subtle rise and fall of her chest. I haven't let anyone else touch her since I brought her back from the veil and tucked her into bed. But I've upended every potion Kaia has left outside the door down her throat.

None of them have worked. Her heart still beats, but she will not wake. And I have sat vigilantly by her bedside for three days and three nights, only to be treated to the same view.

Elora, as pale and still as she was when I scooped her up and carried her back with me. Nothing has changed in all that time. Not with her, anyway.

The Shadow Realm is revived, stronger than it's been in decades. I feel a renewed sense of power thrumming through not just the realm, but myself. Like her sacrifice has woken some long-buried power in me as much as the realm.

I'm not sure if it's my connection to the realm or to Elora that's sent this surge of power through my veins, but I would give up every drop if it meant she would open her eyes.

Someone knocks softly on the bedroom door, and I glance away from Elora's sleeping form to see Kaia step through. She moves to the side of the bed and reaches out a hand to brush Elora's hair back from her forehead.

"Don't touch her," I snap, and she instantly drops her hand, gripping the skirt of her gown.

"No change?"

I don't answer her. I don't need to. We can both plainly see Elora is no better than she was when I first brought her here. No worse, but that's hardly a consolation when she's stuck in this state. As unreachable to me as if she were dead and her soul lost.

"Railan would like—"

"I don't care what Railan would fucking like," I say through gritted teeth.

As far as I'm concerned, Elora wouldn't be in this condition if not for him. If he hadn't insisted on arguing with me about it, insisted on trying to change my mind, she wouldn't have overheard us.

And then she would still be blissfully unaware while I searched for the book and the ritual. She would still be awake, alert, alive. She might not be dead now, but I feel as if I've lost her all the same.

"She'll wake, Thieran," Kaia assures me, but I hear the doubt in her voice.

There's no guarantee Elora will ever open her eyes again. And what do I care if the Shadow Realm remains intact if it means I have to rule it alone?

Any more words from Kaia now would be empty, so she doesn't try, simply laying a hand on my shoulder and giving it a light squeeze before crossing the room and slipping out. The following silence is heavier than it was before.

I feel the tug of Garrick requesting to meet with me, but I ignore it. I left Elora alone once today already. I won't be doing it again. Seconds later, a roll of parchment secured with a wax seal appears on the table beside me.

Tearing my gaze away from Elora, I break the seal with my thumb and unfurl the sheet of parchment. Another report. This one more upbeat than the last, if that's possible.

Not only has the veil been fortified to the point of glimmering with a golden light, but the borders of Meren and Síra have been strengthened as well. The entire realm looks and feels the way it did when it was first created. Pulsing with power and possibility.

But the price that was paid to restore it was too high. No matter how much Railan wants to assure me it had to be this way or Kaia wants to pretend Elora may some day return to me. It should never have come to this.

I wave my hand over the parchment, and it disappears from my lap. Rubbing my temple, I close my eyes against the pain blooming behind my right eye. I haven't slept in days, and while I can push my body to do many things, operating without sleep will only take me so far.

A noise from the bed startles me, and my eyes shoot open. Elora hasn't moved, but I could swear her breathing is faster, deeper. My eyes narrow on her chest. Is it rising and falling quicker than it was before?

I rub a hand over my heart. I haven't been able to feel her heartbeat next to mine since she gave herself to the veil. I find I miss it desperately.

She sucks in a sudden deep breath, and I shove out of my chair, crossing to the bed and perching on the edge of it. Reaching up to brush a stray hair off her forehead, I tuck it behind her ear.

She feels warmer; her cheeks look pinker. But I can't decide if that's a trick of my imagination. Is she better? Or am I seeing what I want to see?

Her eyes flit behind her lids, her lashes dancing against her cheeks. Tracing my fingertip down the edge of her jaw to her chin, I sigh. But all the air is ripped out of my lungs when her eyes slowly open.

She blinks up at me, and my heart squeezes painfully in my chest.

"Thieran?"

I've never heard a sweeter sound than my name on her lips.

"Elora."

Her gaze darts beyond me, and I see recognition there. She knows who I am and where she is. That seems like a good sign.

"Am I dead?"

I drop my lips to her forehead and press a long, lingering kiss there, centering myself before speaking.

"It would appear you are not."

She opens her mouth, but no words come out. Clearing her throat, she tries again.

"Am I supposed to be?"

I chuckle in spite of myself. "I'm not entirely sure. How do you feel?"

"Like the Shadow Realm swallowed me whole and spit me out again. What happened?"

"You did something incredibly stupid and reckless. That's what happened."

Fire flashes in her eyes, and the wall I've been building around my heart while she lay sleeping fractures and crumbles. She's back with me. I don't know how or why, but my Elora is here, and I will never let her go again.

"I seem to recall I saved your life." She tries to reposition herself, shrugging me off to rearrange the pillows on her own. "And the souls in the Shadow Realm. And all of Acaria, for that matter."

"Fine, then," I concede. "You're a hero. Feel better?"

She gives me a wry grin. "I've never wanted to be a hero. Heroes are boring."

I lean down to capture her lips with mine, sinking into the

kiss by degrees when she immediately responds. She's soft and giving, and when her hand finds mine on top of the coverlet, she laces our fingers together.

"I love you too," I whisper against her lips.

She smiles softly, leaning her forehead against mine. "Did it work, at least?"

"It did. The realm is the strongest it's been since its inception."

"Then how am I not dead?"

"I have no idea." I give her fingers a squeeze. "But I thought I'd lost you just the same. You've been asleep for three days," I add in response to her questioning frown.

She lifts her bandaged hand from the bed and holds it in front of her face. "Another scar to add to the rest, I suppose. You think magickal scars are different from mortal ones?"

"They can be. Though the gods tend to leave bodies behind, not scars."

Elora shivers at that, disentangling her fingers from mine and reaching up to play with my hair. When her stomach growls, she blushes, color rising to her chest and face. I laugh and kiss each of her pink cheeks in turn.

"I'll bathe you and then feed you."

"You will not," she says indignantly, wriggling back against the pillows as I slide off the bed. "I'm perfectly capable of bathing and feeding myself."

Ignoring her, I conjure a copper tub in the center of her room, moving it close to the fireplace so she'll be warm enough. I wave my hand and the tub fills with steaming water, the surface sprinkled with lavender and eucalyptus leaves.

"What would you like to eat?"

When she doesn't answer, I turn back to her, frowning when I see her staring down at her unbandaged hand in disbelief.

"What's wrong?"

"There's nothing." She holds her hand out to me, and I cup it in my own, palm up. "No wound, no scar. Nothing."

It's odd for it to heal so quickly, but it's not as alarming as her tone suggests. And all the better for her not to have a reminder of yet another time she almost died for the sake of someone else.

"I've been applying that healing salve three times a day. I'll have to let the healer know it works better than she thought."

"Is it possible for a simple healer's ointment to completely heal a magickal wound?"

"I've never had a mortal attempt to sacrifice themselves to save the realm before. Anything is possible."

I dislike speaking the words even now, even with her clear green eyes looking up at me, knowing she's all right. That I get to keep her.

She nods, not altogether convinced by my assessment, but not willing to argue with me either.

I sit beside her again, cupping her face in my hands.

"I'm never going to let anything happen to you ever again. You are mine to protect."

"Whatever it takes," she replies, echoing my words from the last night she shared my bed. "Forever."

"You heard me?"

She nods, leaning up to kiss me again. I ease her back against the pillows, sliding my hand up her side. She wiggles beneath me, but I stop just short of her breast, grinning against her lips when she groans in disappointment.

"Not yet, little one. I want to make sure you're as well as you can be before I take you again."

"I feel perfectly well," she says, gripping the front of my robes with her healed hand and pulling me in for another kiss. "Let me show you."

Her fingers glide down my chest to the tie of my breeches, and I'm hard in an instant. I should stop her when she works open the thin leather tie, when she slides her hand against my skin, when she gently grips and strokes me. But I don't.

Because I thought she'd never touch me again, and if this is what she needs to feel like herself after what happened, I'll gladly give it to her.

Peeling the coverlet back, I pluck her from the bed and set her on her feet, smiling when she makes contact with the cold floor and squeaks.

"What are you doing? I thought—"

I undo the tie on her own breeches, hooking my thumbs into the top and dragging them down her legs.

"I'm going to fuck you in that tub until you scream for me. You know how much I love to hear you scream my name."

She looks over my shoulder at the tub, lips curling into an enticing grin.

"I like that plan. I overheard you in your study because I was coming to ask you to take me to the hot springs and fuck me there."

"Were you?"

I shed my robes as she reaches for the hem of her tunic. Shoving down my breeches and stepping out of them, I stalk toward her, smiling as she retreats from me until the backs of her thighs hit the edge of the tub.

"We've fucked next to them," she reminds me. "But not in them."

"I remember."

I loosen her hair from its braid, threading my fingers through it before stripping off my tunic as she does the same. But when I turn from discarding both on the floor beside us, her eyes are trained on her hand again instead of on me.

"You marked me?"

My brows draw together. "Marked you? What are you talking about?"

She shoves her wrist into my face, and I have to catch her

forearm before she punches me in the nose. When it comes into focus, I freeze.

"I can appreciate that I saved the realm, that you love me as I love you, but I am not a piece of property. You can't just carve your symbol on me and expect me to be fine with it."

"I... This isn't..."

It doesn't make any sense. I don't even understand how such a thing could be possible.

"This isn't my symbol."

"They're the same," she insists, wrenching her arm from my grasp and reaching for my opposite hand.

She holds her wrist next to mine. They are similar. Similar enough to make me wonder what kind of game the Fates are playing now.

The outline of a skull that adorns my wrist is an exact match to hers. The only difference is the skull on her wrist is wound through with vines. And the vines look identical to the ones that now grow like a wall along the entire length of the veil.

"This isn't my symbol," I repeat, and she scoffs.

Brushing my thumb over the outline on her wrist, I feel it for the first time. That hum of power. Familiar and comforting. It's what I sensed the day I found the vines where she crossed the veil.

Foreign but familiar. A thread of Elora's power.

"If it isn't your symbol, then what is it?" she demands, brows drawn together in anger.

"This...is a godmark." I look up at her, and her eyes slowly widen. "Elora. You are a goddess."

A NOTE FOR THE READER

Dear Reader,

In the iconic words of Elle Woods, "We did it!"

I am so appreciative of you. Thank you, from the tips of my toes for reading. I hope you enjoyed Elora and Thieran's story in the first book in the Shadow King Trilogy.

Don't miss the next installment, *Queen of Souls and Sorrow*! You can purchase it by visiting https://pipereaston.com/qosas/.

If you enjoyed this book, I would really appreciate a little more of your time in the form of a review on Goodreads or Amazon or wherever you purchased it.

For exclusive bonus content, early chapters, behind the scenes sneak peeks, early cover reveals, and more, subscribe on Patreon.

With love and gratitude,

Piper

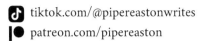

tiktok.com/@pipereastonwrites

patreon.com/pipereaston

ACKNOWLEDGMENTS

Paula. I thought I knew what a ride or die was, but you are redefining that for me in the best way. I am so grateful for your love, support, honest feedback, endless questions, and cheerleading. I don't say it enough, but I am grateful for you.

Bunny, we became fast friends in a way I did not anticipate but would not change. Thank you so much for listening to me ramble about this world and its characters, making my ugly ass maps beautiful, and encouraging me to keep writing when I felt like giving up. Your support means more to me than I could say.

TGC. Your continued friendship is everything to me. You never fail to make me laugh when I need it most, pick me up when I feel like I can't stand, and tell me what I need to hear. Getting to be friends with all of you is one of the coolest things I've done to date.